P9-CMY-312

DISCARD

JA - - '78

EMPIRE
of
RACHANA

JOPU

PRAVIT

PUURVA

MAHYAA

Volcanic Wasteland

KHUMA

VEDANTHA

The Sacred Lands

Samraat's Fortress

THOMH

RUMJAH

SAANDHI

BHAVINI

Praise for

REBEL GENIUS,

the first book in the **Rebel Geniuses** trilogy

"**Action and adventure galore**, including narrow escapes, surprising twists, and stunning turns." —*Booklist*

"DiMartino keeps it **fresh with a richly imagined setting**, a fast-paced story line, and numerous deftly sketched illustrations." —*Publishers Weekly*

"Giacomo's lush and intricate world **does not disappoint** . . . Give this one to fans of Lisa McMann's *The Unwanteds*." —*School Library Journal*

"DiMartino masterfully weaves a thrilling action-adventure epic into an imaginative and terrifying world." —**BRYAN KONIETZKO**, co-creator of *Avatar: The Last Airbender* and *The Legend of Korra*

"Charming young heroes, magical creatures, an innovative magic system, and mysteries galore. There is so much to love about this book!" —**GENE LUEN YANG**, National Ambassador for Young People's Literature and author of *American Born Chinese*

"DiMartino delivers a magical take on the power of art. With a cast that will charm you and an innovative new world to get lost in, *Rebel Genius* is a gift for fantasy lovers and a treasure for anyone who has ever tried to pick up a brush or a pen and make something new. **A lively, thrilling spin on the struggle to create.**" —**LEIGH BARDUGO**, author of the **Grisha** trilogy and the **Six of Crows** series

"*Rebel Genius* contains all of Mike DiMartino's hallmarks: an exquisite world dripping with magic and color, a cast of incredible, diverse characters, and artwork that will take your breath away. **Get ready to fall in love.**" —**MARIE LU**, author of the **Legend** trilogy and the **Young Elites** trilogy

"*Rebel Genius* is **a mind-blowing new series**, a passionate blend of adventure, mystery, and puzzle-solving that has no end to its imagination." —**SOMAN CHAINANI**, author of **The School for Good and Evil** trilogy

WARRIOR·GENIUS

Also by MICHAEL DANTE DIMARTINO

Rebel Genius

PROPERTY OF CLPL

MICHAEL DANTE DIMARTINO

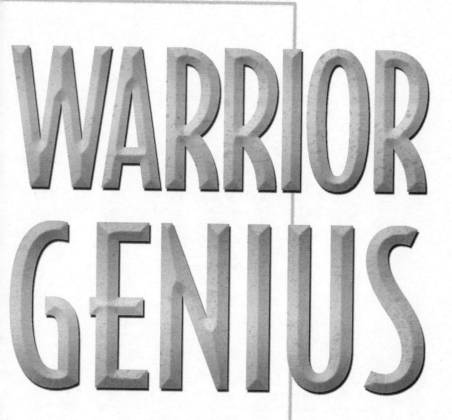

WARRIOR GENIUS

Roaring Brook Press
New York

Copyright © 2018 by Michael Dante DiMartino
Published by Roaring Brook Press
Roaring Brook Press is a division of Holtzbrinck Publishing Holdings
Limited Partnership
175 Fifth Avenue, New York, NY 10010

mackids.com

All rights reserved

Library of Congress Control Number: 2017944680

ISBN: 978-1-62672-337-5

Our books may be purchased in bulk for promotional, educational, or
business use. Please contact your local bookseller or the Macmillan Corporate
and Premium Sales Department at (800) 221-7945 ext. 5442 or by e-mail at
MacmillanSpecialMarkets@macmillan.com.

First edition, 2018
Book design by Andrew Arnold
Printed in the United States of America by LSC Communications,
Harrisonburg, Virginia
1 3 5 7 9 10 8 6 4 2

For Hawk and Opal

Though the physical demands of this journey have pushed my body to the limit, it is my soul that has endured the worst suffering. For I have discovered a world that is fraught with all manner of bizarre creatures, once thought only to be myth. They stalk this physical plane, spreading fear and terror wherever they roam.

I admit, there is part of me that is desperate to turn back and return to the comforts of my former life. Yet having glimpsed the world beyond Virenzia's walls, my other half yearns to press on and confront the monsters that await me. Am I mad? Or simply impelled by a greater force to see this quest to its end?

Tonight, I lie under the glimmering heavens and pray to the Creator once again to watch over me, so that I may see another dawn.

—Poggio Garrulous
(975, age of the pentad)

CONTENTS

WARRIOR◆GENIUS

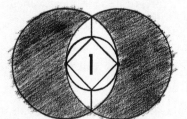

THE COUNCIL OF TEN

Giacomo Ghiberti was not long for this world.

From her throne's perch in the Salon dei Guerra, Supreme Creator Nerezza gazed down at the cloaked figures of the Council of Ten and demanded that one of her ministers explain how a twelve-year-old Tulpa, a man-made being, could have been living in Virenzia all these years without her knowing it. None of them could provide an adequate answer.

The young Tulpa had brought chaos to her city, brazenly defied her, and fled. Soon, Nerezza would make him pay for his rebelliousness. But for now, she needed to create the perception in the minds of her citizens that last night's violence had been quelled.

"Minister Monti, do you have the statement prepared?"

The Minister of Information, a woman half Nerezza's age with a frog-like face, nodded and began to read from a piece of parchment. "'Loyal subjects of Supreme Creator Nerezza, let it be known that the treasonous artist Ugalino Vigano and his Tulpa,

Zanobius, returned from exile and attempted to assassinate your beloved leader. They were aided by a new Tulpa, but—'"

"Stop," Nerezza interrupted. "Make no mention of the second Tulpa. We need to calm the masses, not send them into a panic."

The minister nodded and went back to her parchment. "'But with the power of her Genius, the Supreme Creator repelled the attack.'"

Nerezza's Genius was curled up on the dais, her massive body safeguarding the throne. Nerezza reached a bony hand from under her robe to run her fingers along Victoria's long, gnarled beak, then scratched behind one of her large, pointed ears. The Genius raised her head and acknowledged her master with a groggy grumble.

"'Once again, our great city is safe thanks to the leadership of Her Eminence,'" Monti continued. "'The traitor Ugalino is dead.'"

And plans are already in place to deal with Zanobius, Nerezza thought.

"'But make no mistake, it is a time of great strife in the Zizzolan Empire, and enemies both foreign and domestic seek our annihilation . . .'"

As Minister Monti laid out the present-day dangers facing the Zizzolan people, Nerezza turned her attention to past threats, immortalized in the frescoes lining the Salon dei Guerra.

The paintings portrayed Zizzolan forces triumphing over Rachanan warriors through the ages. Some depicted ground battles with swords and spears crisscrossing amid thrashing bodies. Others showed clashes in the sky between bird-Geniuses and winged horse-Geniuses. Artists wielding brushes and pencils soared on the backs of giant bejeweled crows, eagles, and falcons, launching patterns of light from the gems in their Geniuses' crowns. Mounted warriors wielding large daggers countered with their own sacred geometry attacks, which radiated from gems on the horse-Geniuses' faceplates. The frescoes served as a reminder that Zizzola was—and needed to remain—the dominant force in the world. Nerezza wasn't about to let Giacomo and his friends threaten her supremacy.

"'. . . And in trying times like these, we must remain strong, vigilant, and fearless.'" Minister Monti looked up from her parchment.

"Good," Nerezza said. "Now go deliver the message to the people."

The minister hesitated. "But we must also address the matter of the Geniuses, Your Eminence. There may have been witnesses to the battle. What if word spreads that there is a new generation of children with Geniuses?" Monti cleared her throat, then added, "Not to mention the reemergence of Pietro Vasari and his Genius."

Nerezza's face twisted with annoyance at the mention of Pietro. She had stuffed her memories of him into a mental coffer that she kept locked, even to herself. *Especially* to herself.

"It's your job to make sure word *doesn't* spread," Nerezza ordered.

Monti bowed her head. "Yes, Your Eminence."

On one side of the vast hall, a door opened, and two armed guards entered, pulling a shackled man behind them. The rattling chains echoed through the chamber. "Here's the mercenary who was detained last night, as you requested," one of the guards said.

Ozo Mori's feet shuffled along the shiny marble and his head hung forward. Long black hair, matted with blood, covered half his face. On the other half, a scar ran from temple to jowl. As the mercenary passed the Minister of Culture, Baldassare Barrolo, the two men scowled, casting blame upon each other. Both had failed miserably in their mission to help Nerezza obtain the first Sacred Tool. But Barrolo had always been a loyal, if disagreeable, servant. The brunt of Nerezza's punishment would fall on Ozo.

"For allowing the Tulpas to escape with the Creator's Compass, it is the decision of this Council that you shall be executed," Nerezza declared. "Perhaps I shall feed you to Victoria." With a long metal hook, Nerezza stabbed a piece of raw meat that had been laid out on a platter near her feet. Blood spattered across the dais as she flung the slab to her Genius. With a snap of her fangs, Victoria devoured the meal, then let out a satisfied snort.

Nerezza expected the mercenary to plead for his life, but instead, Ozo met her with an icy stare.

Barrolo strode over to Ozo and leaned in close. "You had better pray the Creator takes mercy on your soul."

Ozo let out a wolfish growl, exposing some missing teeth. Barrolo flinched.

"That's enough, Minister Barrolo," Nerezza commanded. "I'll decide who gets mercy. The Creator has no say in the matter."

Barrolo stepped back in line with the other ministers. "My apologies, Your Eminence."

"If you kill me, what I know about Giacomo dies too," Ozo remarked.

"And what is that?" Nerezza asked.

Ozo glanced at Victoria. "I'll tell you, but only if you promise I won't become your Genius's next meal."

"Very well," Nerezza said. "I don't think she has a taste for Rachanans anyway."

"Ugalino's Tulpa isn't the one you want," Ozo said. "Zanobius tried to take the Creator's Compass and failed, but Giacomo alone was able to remove it from the site."

Impossible, Nerezza thought. *How could this new Tulpa possess powers even greater than Zanobius's?*

Her Minister of War, Carlo Strozzi, stepped forward. He carried his burly frame with the confidence of a man who had survived many harrowing battles. "Don't believe a word he says, Your Eminence. He's only trying to stave off his execution. My soldiers witnessed Ugalino and Zanobius in the piazza with the Creator's Compass."

"Because they took it from Giacomo," Ozo rebutted.

Nerezza stared into Ozo's eyes, trying to discern if the mercenary was lying, then turned to her Minister of the Occult. "What do you make of this, Minister Xiomar?"

As the hunchbacked man lurched forward, his fellow Council members eyed him with long-standing distrust. At 140, he had become the oldest man in Zizzola's history. Though his bizarre regimen of imbibing foul-smelling elixirs had caused an enormous fleshy hump to grow on his back, the fact that he was still alive proved his methods were effective.

"While much has been written about the creation of Tulpas," Xiomar began, speaking between labored breaths, "very little is known about how their power manifests, or why one Tulpa differs from another. It is believed that the intention of the Tulpa's creator is somehow infused into its being."

"But is it possible Giacomo could have obtained the Compass alone?" Nerezza said, growing impatient.

"Certainly," Xiomar replied.

Nerezza clacked her red-tipped nails on the throne's golden arm. Giacomo did have a Genius, she reminded herself—impossible for a Tulpa, or so she had thought. And according to Barrolo, the young Tulpa also had been able to access the Wellspring. Clearly, Giacomo possessed great abilities. Maybe it wasn't so far-fetched to believe he was the only soul capable of acquiring the Sacred Tools. Together, the Compass, the Straightedge, and the Pencil held untold power—power that rightfully belonged to her.

Nerezza turned to her Minister of War. "Ready one of the new ships, Minister Strozzi. And assemble a crew. I want Giacomo captured—unharmed."

"As you wish," Strozzi replied. "And the prisoner? What do you want to do with him?"

"Free me and I'll help you track down Giacomo," the mercenary offered. There was a flicker of desperation in his eyes.

"The Supreme Creator already let you live; don't get greedy," Strozzi said, puffing out his chest. "My soldiers are more than capable of capturing a few children on the run."

"They'll be hard to capture with a vicious Tulpa protecting them," Ozo countered. "And from what I saw, your soldiers didn't fare very well against Zanobius. At least I was able to take one of his arms. I know his weaknesses better than anyone." Ozo turned to Nerezza. "I'm offering you my services, free of charge this time."

"What assurances do I have that you won't abandon the mission and flee to Rachana?" Nerezza asked.

"Rachana hasn't been my home since I was a boy," Ozo said. "The last thing I want is to go back there."

Nerezza considered Ozo's offer. He had provided her with vital information about Giacomo, and the reason she and Barrolo had hired him to escort the children to find the Compass in the first place was because of his reputation as a tracker. As a mercenary, he had worked for dukes and merchants throughout the empire, so he knew the lay of the land even better than Strozzi did.

"Remove his shackles," Nerezza ordered the guards.

Ozo's chains clattered on the marble, and he rubbed his wrists. "You won't regret this, Supreme Creator."

"I'd better not," Nerezza grumbled.

Barrolo stepped forward. "Your Eminence, I'd also like to join the mission. I want to bring my son, Enzio, back home."

"Very well," Nerezza said.

Ozo and Barrolo nodded begrudgingly at each other.

"We do have one problem," Ozo said. "I've never tracked anyone who had a magic Compass that can take him anywhere he wants to go."

"Not anywhere," Barrolo corrected. "The Creator's Compass will allow the user to travel only to places they've been before."

"Perfect," Ozo said. "We'll search the route I took the children on."

Barrolo shook his head. "Pietro is with them and can call upon his own memories. He's too smart to tread recent ground."

"Then where do you suggest we look?" Ozo challenged.

The Minister of Intelligence, a tall, slender man with an arrogant look about him, stepped forward. "I will send word to my spies. If anyone has seen Giacomo or his friends, we'll soon know."

"In the meantime, I'm going to contact some of my dealers in the black market," Barrolo said. "Pietro may try to seek refuge with one of them."

"Wherever Giacomo is hiding, let's find him quickly," Nerezza urged. Her heart, which usually beat weakly, began to thump. The hunt was on.

REFUGE

Zanobius stepped into the portal and surrendered to the streaming light. As his body sped through space, his mind drifted toward a brighter future, one full of possibility. Warmth enveloped him, relieving his tense muscles. Knowing the serenity would be short-lived, Zanobius allowed himself to enjoy the peace.

Recently, his life had been the opposite. His master had died, a vengeful mercenary had severed one of his four arms, and he had nearly been ripped apart by Supreme Creator Nerezza's Genius. He'd helped Giacomo and his friends flee Virenzia, and since then, the group had been searching for food, supplies, and somewhere to hide that was out of sight of Nerezza and her minions. On top of that, Ugalino's most recent mind wipe had left Zanobius's memory still full of holes.

Pietro Vasari, the children's teacher, was the best traveled, so he had used the Creator's Compass to take them to places he had once visited. Though he was blind, the old master's powers of recall were still sharp. But Pietro was dismayed to learn that Zizzola had changed much in the decades since he had last journeyed through it. Villages stood where once there were empty fields; soldiers on horseback patrolled even the empire's farthest borders.

Zanobius had offered to take everyone to an uninhabited island where he and Ugalino had lived for a few months during their exile, but Pietro had informed him that to wield the Compass, you need a Genius. They had forged onward.

It wasn't the relentless travel that wore on Zanobius, but his mental struggle. Ugalino's death had freed Zanobius's mind, causing agonizing memories to return. Long-forgotten victims surfaced from the past, shouting at Zanobius that he was a killer. Ugalino might have given the violent orders, but Zanobius was far from blameless. He could never erase the deaths of so many people at his hands.

Zanobius was jettisoned back to reality. He flew from the portal and slammed into a stone wall. He went down on one knee, recovering as he waited for the others.

Savino appeared out of the light first, followed a moment later by his falcon Genius, Nero. Though he was only fourteen, Savino had become the group's de facto leader throughout its journey, a role that seemed to fit his brash personality. "Any signs of trouble?" he asked.

Zanobius scanned their surroundings. He realized he hadn't hit a wall, but a massive rock jutting out of the earth. Dozens more stood all around. His eyes tracked the monoliths up a slope to the top of the hill, where they ringed a crumbling stone villa. In the distance, a ribbon of mountains glowed pink in the morning sun. Wind gusted up from a wide valley.

"The coast looks clear," Zanobius answered, and Savino sent Nero back into the portal to signal to everyone that it was safe to come through.

One by one, the rest of the group emerged. Next came Pietro, riding his owl Genius, Tito. Pietro eased himself off his Genius's neck and pulled the large Creator's Compass down after him. With a dissatisfied hoot, Tito shook, jangling his earrings and sloughing off gray feathers.

"I don't think Tito is ever going to get used to portal travel," Pietro said, catching his breath. "I'm not sure I will, either." He felt the ground with a walking stick until it tapped the side of a rock. With a groan, he eased himself down.

"Let me help you." Zanobius reached for Pietro, but the old man waved him off and took a seat on the rock.

"I'm . . . I'm fine. Leave me be."

Zanobius backed away, not wanting to test Pietro's tolerance or seem the least bit threatening. He was still the outsider, tied to the group by only the tenuous thread of Giacomo's kindness. Pietro had the power to cut that thread at any moment.

Milena jumped nimbly from the light, accompanied by her crane Genius, Gaia, who cut a graceful curve through the air and landed on her shoulder. As soon as Milena noticed her teacher sitting hunched on the rock, she went to check on him. "Master Pietro, are you all right?" she said, her face full of concern.

"I'm used to spending my days in a cellar, not traveling the empire," Pietro complained. "But really, it's nothing to worry about."

Aaminah—the youngest of the group, and the only musician—sprang out next, joined by her robin Genius, Luna, who chirped excitedly. Milena called them over and asked Aaminah to help ease their teacher's aches. Aaminah pulled out a small flute and played a bright tune. Circles of yellow light leaped from her Genius's gem and danced over Pietro, whose grumpy expression started to soften.

The portal spat out Enzio, the only one of the children without a Genius. Even though Ugalino had taken him from his home and nearly killed him, Enzio and Zanobius had forged a friendship.

Last, Giacomo appeared, along with his hummingbird Genius, Mico. Since learning that Giacomo was a Tulpa, Zanobius had felt a deep connection with the boy.

With everyone accounted for, Giacomo took the Compass from Pietro and held it up to the portal, then spun its legs. The circle of light shrank, and with a *pop*, it vanished. Giacomo slid the Compass into the leather holster that Savino had fashioned from an old sword scabbard and slung it across his back. He took in their new location, his shaggy brown hair blowing in the wind. "Pietro, where are we?"

"Northern Rapallicci," Pietro said, sounding more energetic. He pushed himself up with his walking stick.

Milena gazed up the hill. "There's a villa covered in ivy and moss that looks centuries old. Pietro, whose house is that?"

"It belonged to one of my former students . . ." Pietro hung his head. "Before Nerezza killed him."

Everyone fell silent, and Zanobius felt a pang of guilt. It wasn't a coincidence that Nerezza had begun wiping out artists and their Geniuses shortly after Ugalino had created Zanobius.

With Zanobius leading, the group crested the hill and approached the villa. To everyone's shock, a man's voice shouted from inside. "You better get lost, Tulpa, before I make you get lost!"

Zanobius clenched his three
fists. He had a feeling the man
wasn't referring to Giacomo.

"I thought this place was supposed
to be abandoned," Savino complained.

"Me too," Pietro said.

Zanobius looked up at a broken window on the second floor
where the sunlight glinted off a long, tubular barrel. He ushered
the children back. "Get away, he has a gun!"

BLAM!

13

Smoke billowed from the window. The bullet hit Zanobius in the shoulder. He recoiled but held his ground. The children screamed, and their Geniuses squawked and scattered.

Zanobius dug his fingers into his wound, which oozed gray liquid. He pulled out a round metal ball and tossed it into the grass. His skin began to grow back almost immediately.

The man with the gun poked his head out the window, his eyes wide with fury. He had long, stringy hair and a scraggly beard. "I warned you, Tulpa! I don't want any trouble. Now, turn around and leave." He packed the gun barrel with powder, preparing his next shot.

"Time to go!" Giacomo said, holding the Compass at the ready.

"Wait! Not yet." Pietro strode past Giacomo and Zanobius and approached the villa.

The bearded man raised his gun again. "Hold it right there, old man!"

"Niccolo? I thought I recognized your voice," Pietro said. "Is that really you?"

"Depends who's asking," the man hollered back.

"It's Pietro Vasari."

The man slowly lowered his weapon and scrutinized Pietro. "Impossible . . ."

"I thought you were dead!" Pietro said, sounding elated.

"I thought you were dead too!" Niccolo erupted.

"Now, stop being a fool and put that gun away!" Pietro ordered.

"Yes, of course! Hold on, I'll be right down!" Niccolo disappeared from the window.

"Uh . . . what's going on?" Giacomo said. "Who is that guy?"

Pietro turned to face the group. "Niccolo is the former student

I was telling you about. He and his Genius must have escaped Nerezza somehow."

Zanobius looked to the rooftop, but didn't see any sign of Niccolo's Genius. He probably kept it inside for its safety, Zanobius reasoned at first. But if that were the case, why had Niccolo fired at him with a gun and not sacred geometry?

The front door burst open, and Niccolo rushed to Pietro, embracing him. "Where have you been hiding all these years?" Niccolo said, holding Pietro at arm's length. Some of his teeth were missing, and those remaining were rotting. Dark rings hung under his eyes.

"Long story," Pietro said.

"Your irises are cloudy . . ." Niccolo said in a hushed voice, then looked over at Pietro's Genius, who had two holes in place of eyes. "You and your Genius are both blind?"

"For many years now," Pietro said. "But our connection is stronger than ever."

"Are you able to perform sacred geometry anymore?" Niccolo asked.

"Oh yes, and Tito still loves to fly when he gets the chance."

Zanobius had witnessed the old master and his Genius in action and had been astounded by how well they functioned together. Pietro explained to Niccolo that Tito's gem emitted a vibrational signal that helped him navigate the world. It was also what allowed him to sense other bird-Geniuses nearby.

"But enough about that," Pietro said. "We need your help. We're on the run from Nerezza, and we've been trying to find somewhere to hide out."

Niccolo's friendly demeanor turned sour and his bloodshot eyes locked on Zanobius. One pupil was a large black orb, the other a speck. The man's unbalanced stare put Zanobius on edge. "I'm sorry, Pietro, but you can't stay if you're keeping company with this abomination."

Zanobius tensed. He'd been called that before. And worse. But the names still pricked.

"Zanobius isn't dangerous," Giacomo insisted, stepping forward. "He helped us get away from Nerezza."

"And he helped save my life," Enzio added.

Niccolo cocked an eyebrow, looking dubious. He studied the pattern emblazoned on Zanobius's chest, then pointed at his amputated arm. "What happened there?"

Zanobius crossed his arms, covering his injury. "A mercenary cut it off."

Niccolo scratched his cheek, shedding flakes of gray skin. "And why hasn't your loathsome master fixed it yet?"

"Because Ugalino is dead," Zanobius said. "He doesn't control me anymore. I'm no threat to you."

"I doubt that," Niccolo snarled. "You need to go."

"Go where?" Zanobius said sharply. "I'm a walking target, as you well know. I made a promise to help Giacomo. I'm not going to abandon him and his friends now."

Niccolo's gaze darted to Giacomo. "And what's so special about you?"

Giacomo looked up at Zanobius and gave him a committed nod that said, *We're in this together*. He turned back to Niccolo. "I'm also a Tulpa."

Niccolo scrutinized Giacomo. "You look pretty human to me. Did Ugalino create you too?"

"No, my parents did," Giacomo replied.

Niccolo looked surprised. "What were their names?"

"Orsino and Amera Ghiberti," Giacomo said proudly. Then his voice lowered. "But they're gone now . . ."

Niccolo seemed like he was about to say something, but he stopped himself and let out a frustrated groan instead. He scratched the back of his neck and looked off toward the horizon. "You know how risky it is if I let you stay here?"

"Please, Niccolo. We need your help," Pietro said.

"If Nerezza finds us, she'll kill our Geniuses and turn us all into Lost Souls," Giacomo said.

As he pondered Giacomo's request, Niccolo reached up and touched the chain of a necklace he wore, running his fingers down its links.

"And we have something that might be of great interest to you," Pietro added.

Niccolo looked intrigued. "What's that?"

Pietro nudged Giacomo. "Go ahead, show him. We can trust him."

Giacomo pulled the Compass from its sheath; it glimmered in the sunlight.

Niccolo's eyes widened in awe. "The Creator's Compass . . . Then it's true, the Sacred Tools *are* real."

"After all these years, we finally have the means of removing Nerezza from power," Pietro said.

From his time with Ugalino, Zanobius understood that an artist who controlled the Sacred Tools held the power to shape the course of history, for good or ill. In the hands of a tyrant, their combined energy had the potential to destroy an empire, so it was crucial to find them before Nerezza could.

Niccolo looked around the group. "Do you have the Straight-edge and the Pencil as well?"

"Not yet, but I think I can find them," Giacomo said. "That's why we need somewhere to lie low for a while. Please, signor. If you and your Genius were able to escape Nerezza, then you must understand what we're going through."

"You're right, I don't have any love for the so-called Supreme Creator," Niccolo said.

"Does that mean you'll let all of us stay?" Giacomo asked hopefully.

Niccolo swung open the door to his villa and waved everyone in. "Come on."

Once everyone was inside, Niccolo slammed the door and latched it. His hand reached down the front of his stained tunic and rubbed what appeared to be his necklace's pendant. To Zanobius's surprise, a faint purple glow appeared.

A STRANGE HOST

Giacomo crossed the threshold into the dank villa and eyed Niccolo's gun leaning against the wall. Its vented metal barrel was attached to a long wooden handle, similar to the gun that one of Ozo's mercenaries had carried.

Niccolo slung the weapon over his shoulder, then reached for the Compass Giacomo carried under his arm. "If you want, I can lock that in a cabinet where it'll be nice and safe."

"Uh . . . that's all right, I'll keep it with me," Giacomo said, clutching the Compass close. He had nearly died finding it, and he wasn't about to turn it over to a man he'd just met.

The villa was packed with antiques, floor to rafters, and the only way to move through the house was to navigate the narrow passages that Niccolo had kept clear. Giacomo followed his friends through a labyrinth of tables, chairs, mirrors, chandeliers, vases, and armoires. Mixed in with the furnishings were countless decorative items: sculptures, bowls, carvings, stuffed animal heads, and piles and piles of books. There were enough suits of armor, shields, swords, and spears to equip a small army.

"Why do you have all this stuff?" Giacomo asked.

"Several of my family members were enthusiastic collectors," Niccolo said brusquely, then disappeared behind a dark cherry cabinet and into another room.

Giacomo thought he noticed a strange expression cross Pietro's face, but he wasn't sure. Right now, he was more concerned about Mico. His hummingbird and the other Geniuses were circling overhead, letting out a chorus of distressed squawks.

"Think they're trying to tell us something?" Giacomo whispered to Savino, who looked around warily.

"Maybe coming here was a mistake," Savino said. "Do you think we can really trust this guy?"

"I'm not sure yet," Giacomo admitted, dread creeping over him. "But it's not like we have anywhere else to go."

"Just keep your guard up."

Niccolo reappeared, dragging an old trunk. He dropped it with a *thud* and opened the top, revealing dozens of pencils, brushes, inks, and sketchbooks. "You're welcome to whatever's in here. It's not doing me any good."

Giacomo snatched up a leather-bound sketchbook and a pencil. After two weeks without any art supplies, he was eager to draw again and resume his sacred geometry lessons.

"I don't suppose you have any clean clothes we could wear?" Savino asked. "I'm getting pretty tired of my own stench."

"One of those should have some garments that might fit you all," Niccolo said, gesturing to a row of armoires at the back of the room.

"Where's your Genius?" Aaminah called out to Niccolo. "I'm sure our Geniuses would love to meet it."

"Yes, how is Furio?" Pietro said. "He must be nearly as big as Tito by now."

Niccolo turned away and busied himself opening and closing some drawers. "Oh, Furio is probably outside hiding in a tree."

"Come on, Luna. Let's go find him!" Aaminah exclaimed. Her purple-and-orange-plumed robin Genius swooped to her shoulder, and they headed for the door. "Luna's still learning to track other Geniuses, but she found Giacomo's Genius and—"

"No, stay in here!" Niccolo snapped.

Luna let out a startled squeak. Aaminah froze. "I'm sorry . . . Did I say something wrong?"

"Furio doesn't like to be bothered, is all," Niccolo said, then quickly changed the subject. "Anyone care for some roasted-barley tea?" He kicked aside some wooden crates to reveal a hearth, then wound his way toward what appeared to be a kitchen. "I know I have some cups around here somewhere . . ."

"I'll look for some kindling," Zanobius offered. Then he added, "I'll be sure not to disturb Furio."

Enzio followed Zanobius. "Let me help."

Pietro used his walking stick to make his way around the furniture. Aaminah helped him into a seat at a large table near the fireplace. "I don't suppose you have any food, Niccolo?" Pietro called after their host. "We've been eating nothing but berries and squirrels."

While Niccolo was out of sight, Giacomo huddled with Milena and Savino. "Anyone else get the sense that Niccolo's not giving us the whole story?" he whispered.

Milena nodded. "There's definitely something off about him."

"*Way* off," Savino added. "What if he's actually working for Nerezza?" He cast a furtive glance around the room. "I mean, maybe his 'family of collectors' doesn't even exist and he actually stole all this stuff from artists after he turned them over to Nerezza."

Giacomo shivered. "You think that might be true?"

"That's just Savino's paranoia talking," Milena said.

"You have to admit, after what happened with Signor Barrolo, Pietro might not be the best judge of character," Savino argued.

"What are you three whispering about?" Pietro said.

"Nothing!" With a glare, Milena signaled to Giacomo and Savino that their conversation was over. "We were just admiring Niccolo's collection. It's very impressive."

"So, so impressive," Savino parroted.

The clatter died down in the next room, and Niccolo emerged with a stack of cups and a teakettle, along with a plate of crackers and moldy cheeses. "This should stave off the hunger. I wasn't expecting guests, so my stores are a little low. While you all get settled in, I'll head into town to stock up."

Giacomo and Savino shot each other worried looks. If Niccolo went into the village alone, there was a chance he'd inform on them.

"Maybe Savino and I could go with you," Giacomo suggested.

Niccolo pulled a key from his pocket and unlocked one of the cabinets. "It's safer if I go alone." He took a handful of gold *impronta* from a chest, locked the cabinet, and turned to leave. "If I show up at the market with a couple of travel companions, people are going to start talking. And we don't want that."

Savino grabbed Giacomo's arm and pulled him down the hall. "Come on, we can't let him leave."

"Where are you boys going?" Pietro hollered, but they were already at the back door.

Outside, Niccolo was hitching two horses up to a decrepit covered wagon. Once he finished, he took a seat on the cart and grabbed the reins.

Savino and Giacomo skirted the horses and climbed onto

the bench next to Niccolo. Nero landed on Savino's shoulder while Mico circled overhead, chirping worriedly. "You're probably going to need an extra pair of hands to carry all that food," Savino said.

"Or two," Giacomo added.

Niccolo glared at the boys. "I can handle it fine on my own. Now, leave me be."

Mico flitted around Niccolo, his chirps turning to angry squawks. "Shoo!" Niccolo swatted Mico away, but Giacomo's Genius darted closer, jabbing his beak at Niccolo's chest, where the outline of a round pendant was visible under his dingy tunic. Niccolo swiped again, but Mico avoided the strike and dove down the front of Niccolo's tunic, sending the man into a violent squirming fit. "Ah! Get out, you meddling miscreant! It's not safe!"

"Mico, that's enough!" Giacomo patted down Niccolo's tunic, trying to grab Mico.

"Hands off!" Niccolo shoved him away, and Giacomo fell backward off the cart, slamming to the ground with a *thud*.

Zanobius was still collecting firewood with Enzio a little way from the house, but upon seeing the sudden violence, they both came running up the path.

Mico shot out of Niccolo's collar, his talons yanking the necklace's chain. The clasp snapped, and Mico flew away with a black pendant trailing behind him.

Niccolo scrambled out of the cart and fell to his knees. "Give that back!"

The rest of the group ran outside to see what all the commotion was about.

"What's going on?" Pietro asked.

Niccolo gasped for air. "Help . . ."

Pietro looked concerned. "Niccolo? What's wrong?"

Aaminah went to Niccolo, flute in hand. "You're going to be all right," she told him as Luna fluttered onto her head, ready to assist. "Try to take deep breaths."

Niccolo pointed at Mico, his voice weak. "My necklace . . . I need it back . . ."

"Mico! Drop it! Now!" Giacomo whistled, and Mico finally released the pendant. It fell into the grass with a soft *thump*. As Giacomo picked it up, his breath caught. At first glance, the pendant had looked like a polished octagonal stone, nearly the size of Giacomo's palm. But on closer inspection, Giacomo noticed a pale glimmer emanating from within.

Giacomo's stomach fell. "Is this . . . ?"

"Give it here!" Niccolo wrested the gem from Giacomo's grasp and frantically fastened the necklace back on. He rubbed the gem, which glowed purple.

"How could you?" Giacomo said, disgusted. "You took your Genius's gem off its crown?"

"No wonder you were lying about Furio," Zanobius said, dropping the sticks he had gathered. "You're just as bad as Ugalino!"

"You two don't know what you're talking about," Niccolo shot back, still catching his breath.

"Niccolo, why are you keeping your Genius's gem tied around your neck?" Pietro demanded. "Tell me. This instant."

Niccolo let out a heavy sigh. "I was able to escape Nerezza. But Furio didn't. All I have left of him is his gem."

An icy chill shot through Giacomo. "You're . . . you're a Lost Soul."

Niccolo nodded and the others fell silent, shock visible on their faces.

"I'm so sorry, Niccolo," Pietro said. "I didn't realize . . ."

The last time Giacomo had encountered a Lost Soul, the man had stabbed him and left him for dead. Giacomo slowly backed away from Niccolo.

"How long ago did your Genius die?" Aaminah asked.

"Fifteen years," Niccolo said softly. "Furio's gem is the only thing that's kept me from meeting the Creator all this time. When I touch it, I'm able to regenerate myself a little. But the gem is highly volatile." He looked at Giacomo. "That's why I didn't want your Genius near it. One crack, and the remaining energy could escape."

Pietro put a hand on Niccolo's shoulder. "Why did you lie about Furio? You should've told us."

"Because the practice of keeping your Genius's gem after its death has always been frowned upon. And in this empire, the only beings more feared than Tulpas are Lost Souls." Niccolo brushed away Pietro's hand and climbed back onto his cart.

Niccolo was right. His whole life, Giacomo had been terrified of Lost Souls. It had started with his mother and father. They had never been violent toward him, but when they lost their Geniuses and their loving gazes had withered into vacant expressions, it had been as painful as a slap across the face. At the time, Giacomo had thought that some evil sickness had taken hold of his parents and sucked the love out of them.

Niccolo flicked the reins, and the horses whinnied. "I'll be back by nightfall," he said as the cart pulled away. The horses trotted down the hill, kicking up a cloud of dust behind them.

Pietro wagged a disapproving finger at Giacomo and Savino. "When Niccolo gets back, you both owe him an apology."

Savino protested. "But, Master Pietro, we thought—"

"That I was foolish enough to lead you all into Nerezza's hands again?" Pietro sounded on edge.

Giacomo and Savino traded guilty looks. "No," Giacomo said. "Of course not."

"Niccolo is a trustworthy man," Pietro assured them. "He was one of my brightest students, a rare artist who excelled at both painting and sculpture."

GARRULOUS'S JOURNALS

With Niccolo gone for the day, Milena and her friends headed back inside to go through the items he'd offered them. Milena was looking forward to a change of clothes, but she was most excited about the trunk of art supplies.

She chose a brush with a long black handle and bristles that tapered to a fine point. From Milena's shoulder, Gaia stretched her neck down to inspect it and sang her approval. Milena arced the brush through the air, and an intricate spiral pattern radiated from her Genius's gem, filling the villa with a viridescent light. Relief washed through Milena now that she and her Genius had reestablished their connection. She couldn't help but smile.

The floor creaked, and Milena turned to find Zanobius standing next to her. "It's stunning," he said.

"You must have seen Ugalino create patterns much more complex than this," Milena said.

"Yes. But you have a much finer, delicate touch."

"Thank you."

Savino entered and grabbed a carving tool from the trunk. With a steely look, he aimed the tool's curved blade at Zanobius. "Everything all right in here?" Nero ruffled his feathers and squawked.

"We're fine," Milena said. "Point that somewhere else, will you?"

Savino lowered the carving tool, but his glare held firm.

"I'm sorry if I disturbed you," Zanobius said, backing out of the room.

"You don't have to leave," Milena said, but Zanobius was already gone. She erased her pattern and turned to Savino. "Why'd you have to go and do that?"

"Do what?" Savino said, feigning innocence.

"Make Zanobius feel so unwelcome."

"You had second thoughts about his joining our group, same as I did," Savino argued.

"I know, but I've been observing him. He's much more intelligent and perceptive than we gave him credit for."

"Still, none of us should be alone with him," Savino said, then relaxed his hardened expression into a soft smile. "I was only looking out for you."

"Thanks," Milena said, appreciating Savino's intent. "But you don't need to keep your guard up all the time. Not everyone's out to get you." She gently touched Savino's arm, but he immediately stepped out of reach and began rifling through the trunk.

"I wonder if there are more carving tools in here," he muttered.

"Anyway . . ." Milena said, her jaw tightening. "Good talking to you."

She left the room, and as soon as she turned the corner, she collided with Giacomo, who was crouched over. With yelps of surprise, they fell into shelves full of small glass sculptures. One bobbled and rolled onto the floor, shattering.

"Sorry!" Milena said.

Giacomo righted himself, and they both stared down at the glittering shards.

"Should we tell Niccolo?" Milena asked.

With a sweep of his foot, Giacomo kicked the broken pieces under the shelf. "I doubt he'll notice if one tiny sculpture is missing."

"What were you looking for, anyway?"

"A globe. I figured Niccolo must have one hiding here somewhere."

"Giacomo . . ." Milena said, not hiding her disapproval.

"What? I need to figure out where the next Sacred Tool is hiding. Using a globe in combination with the Wellspring worked last time."

"Not exactly," Milena argued, reminding Giacomo that the looking device he had made to find the Compass had pointed them in the wrong direction. "And now that we're wanted fugitives, we can't risk wandering around Zizzola without knowing exactly where we're headed."

"Good point," Giacomo conceded. "But then how do we get a lead on the other Sacred Tools?"

Milena pointed to a room across the hall that was cluttered with towers of books. "That looks like a good place to start."

But she hadn't been prepared for the disorder that plagued Niccolo's library. The books weren't sorted by subject or author. Treatises on perspective were lumped in with volumes on herbal remedies. Cosmological theories were intermixed with anatomical studies. Before she could even hope to determine what books might be of value, Milena realized that she would have to reorganize.

Every so often, one of her friends would pass by, showing off their latest find from Niccolo's trove. Savino appeared in a black leather jacket and brown pants that he'd discovered, prompting Giacomo to run off and search the armoire. He returned a few minutes later in a pristine red tunic, looking thrilled to be rid of his dirty, tattered one.

Enzio stomped down the hall with a longbow and a quiver of arrows slung across his shoulder, hollering about doing some target practice outside.

Aaminah ran in, excitedly showing off a lute she'd rescued from a dusty old chest full of musical instruments. It wasn't long before she had tuned the lute's strings and was strumming a lively melody. Luna flitted around the villa, yellow shapes cascading from the gem in her crown.

Finally, just as Milena was beginning to lose hope of finding any useful information, she chanced upon a stack of ten small volumes tucked away on a shelf, hidden behind a clutter of other books. The spine of each volume was embossed with the letters *P.G.*

Milena knew those initials. Tingling with anticipation, she opened the first volume and found an inscription:

> *I set out on my journey tomorrow, anxious about what lies before me. The lands of Zizzola are full of innumerable mysteries and strange wonders. May these journals stand as my*

humble attempt to chronicle the unknown and
unlock the secrets of our world.

It was signed:

Poggio Garrulous

Milena grabbed the rest of the volumes. "I think I found something!"

Bleary-eyed, Giacomo looked up from a thick tome about ancient navigation methods. "I hope it's more enlightening than what I'm reading."

Milena laid out the journals on the floor in a neat row. "These are Poggio Garrulous's journals, written when he explored the world."

"Haven't you already studied his writings? I thought Signor Barrolo had lots of books about him."

"I've read descriptions of Garrulous's travels—it's where I first heard the Sacred Tools mentioned—but they were always second- or thirdhand accounts. These are the originals!" Milena flipped through the pages, her heartbeat quickening. "Signor Barrolo had tried to obtain the journals, but not even his black-market connections could track them down."

"If they're so valuable, why are they in Niccolo's library collecting dust?" Giacomo asked.

"You've seen how he keeps this place. I bet he doesn't even know they're here." Milena passed Giacomo the second volume. "This might be the break we need to find the other Sacred Tools. Start reading."

After a few minutes Giacomo said, "Uh . . . Garrulous really liked writing about moss and mushrooms."

"It's fascinating, isn't it?" Milena said, her eyes fixed on the page. "He really had a talent."

Giacomo yawned. "A talent for boring people to death. Where are all the tales of adventure? For a guy who explored the world, Garrulous seems pretty dull."

Milena bristled. "I think his mind was quite brilliant."

Giacomo shrugged and tossed aside volume two, then picked up a journal farther down the row, cracked it open, and flipped through the pages. Suddenly, his eyes went wide. "Look, it's the Straightedge!"

"Let me see." Milena grabbed the journal out of Giacomo's hand. Garrulous had drawn the Straightedge and described how it could amplify a Genius's power a hundred times over. She'd encountered similar claims in other writings about the Sacred Tools.

She read on, then stopped. "Wait, that can't be right . . ."

"What is it?" Giacomo asked.

Milena flipped to the first page to check the inscription, then glanced up at Giacomo. "This volume was written when Garrulous traveled through Rachana."

Giacomo stared back, dumbfounded. "Rachana?"

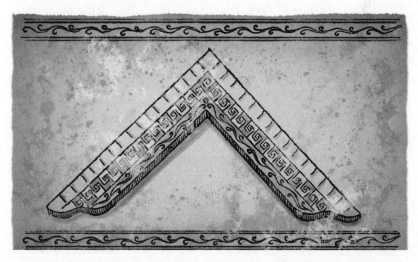

Milena gathered her friends around the table by the crackling fire to show them Garrulous's journals. She explained her theory that the Creator's Straightedge might be in Rachana.

"You must have read it wrong," Savino said dubiously. "Everyone knows the Creator used the Tools to bring the world into being, starting with Zizzola. Why would one of the Sacred Tools be in enemy territory?"

"When the world was first created, the three empires didn't exist," Pietro said, scratching his tangled beard. "States and borders came much later, when clans began to lay claim to different territories."

"That's right," Milena said, following her teacher's logic. "When the Creator finished his work, he could've scattered the Sacred Tools around the world, long before there was a Rachana."

Giacomo's doubtful expression matched Savino's. "Did Garrulous write anything about where it would be found? Did he actually see the Straightedge?"

Milena deflated. "Not as far as I can tell. I think he was transcribing legends he had heard during his travels." She looked to Zanobius, who stood leaning against the wall. She was aware that his memory was still hazy, but he might know something. "Ugalino searched for the Sacred Tools for years. Did he ever question whether they might be somewhere besides Zizzola?"

Zanobius stared into the fire for a moment. "Now that you mention it, I think that's why he took us to Katunga. He suspected we might find some clues about the Tools there. Sorry, I can't recall much beyond that."

Enzio leaned back in his chair. "But if the Straightedge really is in Rachana, don't you think the Rachanans would have used it against Zizzola by now?"

"Not if they haven't found it," Milena argued.

"And there's the peace treaty," Aaminah added. "Even if they did have it, they're not allowed to start a war."

"Hasn't stopped them in the past," Savino said. "Rachanans can't keep their word. All they want to do is fight, conquer, and pillage."

Aaminah gave him a disapproving look. "But they haven't done any of that for a long time. Maybe they've changed."

"People don't change," Savino insisted.

"Some people can," Zanobius said quietly.

"I'm sure Savino wasn't referring to you," Giacomo said, casting a glare in Savino's direction. "Your situation is completely different."

"Sadly, all great civilizations have been built on blood," Pietro interjected. "Rachana is no exception. Neither is Zizzola. But I found Samraat Jagesh to be an honorable leader who genuinely wanted to put an end to war between our two empires."

"Hold on," Milena said. "You met the samraat of Rachana? When?"

"A long time ago. I wasn't much older than you are now. As the empire's official court artist, I had the privilege of accompanying Emperor Callisto and his Council to the historic signing of the fifteenth armistice."

Milena couldn't believe what she was hearing. "So you've been to the samraat's palace?"

"I have." Pietro cracked a smile. "And it makes Nerezza's palace look like a hovel."

From outside came the sound of a rattling cart and horses neighing.

"Food's here!" Giacomo bolted from the room. The group filed out to meet Niccolo, leaving Milena and Pietro alone.

Milena sighed and stacked the journals. "I don't know . . . Maybe Savino and Giacomo are right. These probably won't lead anywhere."

"Ignore the naysayers," Pietro offered. "Follow your spark of inspiration and see where it leads you."

Heartened, Milena picked up the journals. "Thank you, Master Pietro. I will."

LAW OF CONTAGION

That night, Giacomo and his friends crowded around the table while Niccolo prepared dinner. Milena was still off in the library combing through Garrulous's journals and had yet to join them.

After what felt like an eternity, Niccolo finally emerged from the kitchen with two platters of food. One held a pile of burned meat, the other a heap of noodles covered in a pungent brown sauce. "I probably should have warned you. I'm not much of a cook."

Normally, Giacomo might have been picky, but he was so hungry he devoured his food without a second thought.

"Now, I only bought enough food to last you all a couple of weeks, maybe three, if you ration," Niccolo said. "I got a few shifty looks today, so I told folks I was stocking up for winter."

"But it's spring," Savino pointed out.

"You think I don't know it's spring?" Niccolo said defensively. "Most folks think I'm out of my mind anyway, so they won't give it a second thought. But if I use the same excuse twice, people will start getting nosy."

Niccolo took a seat at the head of the table and nibbled on a piece of bread. Even though living as a Lost Soul had blunted his taste for food, Niccolo's appetite for wine hadn't abated. He and Pietro took turns filling each other's jeweled goblets while Pietro told Niccolo how he had found refuge with one of Nerezza's Council members, then fallen back into teaching when Savino and Milena came into his life, and now felt anger and guilt at Baldassare's betrayal.

"And he's the one who lied to you about my being dead?" Niccolo asked. "Why?"

"He probably didn't want me to try to find you," Pietro reasoned. "Turned out, he kept me in the dark about a lot of things."

"I see . . . But there's still one thing I don't understand. If Nerezza knew where you were hiding all these years, how come she never went after you? She's hardly a merciful woman."

"No, but she is a cunning one." Pietro brooded, swirling the wine in his goblet. "After eliminating so many Geniuses, she didn't exactly have any artists left to help her. She used me as an unwitting ally to find and train a new generation, all so she could get her hands on the Sacred Tools."

Giacomo waited for Pietro to finish, then asked, "So, Niccolo, how can you afford all this stuff, anyway?"

"Don't be rude, Giacomo," Pietro scolded.

"I'm just curious."

"It's all right, Pietro. My family history was bound to come up sooner or later." Niccolo turned back to the group and grinned. "My last name is Abbate."

Giacomo's jaw hung slack. Everyone in Virenzia knew of the Abbates—generations of wealthy merchants and bankers who had once been generous patrons of the arts. "As in the richest family in the empire?"

"It was. Until I tarnished the name," Niccolo said heavily.

"Because you stood up to Nerezza?"

"That's right." Niccolo downed the rest of his wine and stared into the empty goblet.

"What happened? Was there a big fight? Did Nerezza attack you herself, or did she send her army? How did you get away and end up here?"

"Leave it be," Pietro said, cutting off Giacomo's flurry of questions. "No use dredging up painful memories when the past can't be changed."

"The future, however, has yet to be shaped," Niccolo looked across the children's faces. "Under Pietro's tutelage, you all could play a crucial part in creating what lies ahead."

"If I'm creating it, then I want Zizzola to be free. I want to stop Nerezza from hurting anyone again," Giacomo said defiantly.

"It's a noble goal," Niccolo said. "How do you plan on achieving it?"

"Well, we've already got the Compass. Next, we find the Straightedge. Mico is too weak to fight Nerezza's Genius now, but if his power were amplified, I might have a shot at taking her down."

"The Straightedge isn't meant to be a weapon of destruction," Pietro cautioned. "Its true power is creative. According to legend, the Creator used it to grow crops in drought-stricken lands, hold back flooding rivers, even cure the ill."

Aaminah leaned in. "Is that really true?"

Giacomo guessed Aaminah was thinking of her mother, whom she hadn't been able to save. In the hands of a great healer like Aaminah, the Straightedge could help so many others.

"Do you have any leads yet?" Niccolo asked.

Giacomo was about to tell him about Garrulous's journals when Milena entered.

"I think I might." All eyes turned to her as she walked in front of the hearth.

Niccolo glanced at the book in her hand. "What do you have there?"

"You don't recognize it? It's one of Poggio Garrulous's journals," Milena said.

"Didn't one of your ancestors fund Garrulous's journey?" Pietro asked.

"Ludovico Abbate," Niccolo confirmed. "I knew the journals were part of my family's collection, but I never realized they'd ended up here."

"Listen to this," Milena said, then began reading. "'The Creator's Compass is believed to be a powerful tool that allows the artist to create a portal of light through which he or she might travel great distances in the blink of an eye.'"

Giacomo fidgeted in his chair. "We already know that. What about the Straightedge?"

"I'm getting to that," Milena said crossly, then kept reading. "'However, I have encountered a few mystics during my travels who claim that the Compass may also be able to create a portal to the sacred.'"

Giacomo glanced down at the Compass leaning against his

chair, the firelight glinting off its golden handle. "'Portal to the *sacred*'? What does that mean?"

"As in the Sacred Tools," Milena said. "What if the Compass could create a portal to the Straightedge and the Pencil?"

Giacomo's heart jumped. "Master Pietro, do you think that's possible?"

"I suppose Garrulous could be referring to the Law of Contagion," Pietro said. "What do you make of it, Niccolo?"

"My thoughts exactly," Niccolo said.

"I don't remember reading about that law in any of Baldassare's books," Milena said. "What is it?"

"A very ancient belief that once two objects, or people, have been in contact, an energetic bond is formed between them," Pietro said.

In a flash, Giacomo returned to the moment when he had realized he was a Tulpa and pulled the Creator's Compass from its sacred geometry shield. "Could the Law of Contagion explain why I seem to have a connection with the Sacred Tools?" he asked. It might also account for the bond he felt with Zanobius, despite having known him for only a short time.

"Possibly," Pietro said. "Tulpas are sacred geometry incarnate. Your parents created you by tapping into the same energetic forces that run through the Sacred Tools."

"So if this Law of Contagion thing really works, I could use the Compass like a divining rod to home in on the Straightedge."

"But it's probably thousands of miles away," Milena pointed out. "Even if there is some kind of energetic bond between the Tools, it would be really weak."

There's another way, Giacomo thought. *But it'll be risky.*

"I'm not talking about tracking it down on foot," Giacomo said. "I know a shortcut: through the Wellspring."

Nerezza found Giacomo in his dreams that night, as she had each night since he'd fled Virenzia. This time she chased him through Niccolo's packed villa and out the back door, where Victoria was waiting for him. The bird-Genius gripped Giacomo's friends in her talons. They shouted for help and Giacomo tried to go to them, but Victoria's gem blazed violet, then fired. The beam consumed him.

Giacomo shot up in his bed and caught his breath, telling himself that he and his friends were safe, that Nerezza wasn't going to find them. But reassuring himself didn't help much, and he lay awake the rest of the night.

When night finally waned, Giacomo went from room to room, rousing everyone from bed. With the Compass slung over his shoulder, he led them up and down the rolling hills until he found a clearing far away from the villa. Flitting joyfully alongside the other Geniuses, Mico chittered at the oncoming dawn. Giacomo wished he felt as carefree as his Genius.

Giacomo recalled the other times he'd summoned the Wellspring's devastating power—Milena screaming as she was burned by its intense heat, Ugalino vanishing into its whipping winds . . . He had gone over his decision hundreds of times in his head—either Ugalino perished or thousands of Zizzolans did. Still . . .

He shook off the guilty memories and focused on the task at hand.

The night before, Giacomo had laid out his plan. He had reminded everyone that when he had been trapped in Duke

Oberto's camera obscura, the Wellspring had opened, allowing him to see across physical space to the Cave of Alessio. Giacomo believed he could use the Creator's Compass to guide him through the Wellspring again—this time to glimpse wherever the Straight-edge was.

While Zanobius and the other children retreated a safe distance down the slope, Pietro remained on the hilltop with Giacomo and their Geniuses. Mico fluttered around Tito's head while the lumbering owl Genius hooted his annoyance.

"Ready when you are," Pietro said, raising his brush.

Giacomo took a deep breath and gripped his pencil tightly.

Pietro arced his brush in front of him; the square gem in Tito's crown lit up, and the great Genius beat his wings once, thrusting his head forward. A beam of orange light shot out from the gem and formed a large circle that hovered several feet away, its edges shimmering.

Giacomo mimicked his teacher's actions, drawing a ring in the air. Mico chirped, and his tiny gem cast a glimmering red circle. With a wave of his arm, Giacomo moved his circle closer to Pietro's, as he'd been taught to. When the two circles collided, the combined energy released a shower of sparks, followed by a low hum. Then, as the circles overlapped, forming the almond-shaped eye of the mandorla, bright beams shot out and a rush of hot wind slammed into Giacomo, nearly toppling him.

Squinting, Giacomo stared into the familiar light storm of the Wellspring and unsheathed the Compass. "I'm going in."

"Be careful," Pietro said.

"I'll be all right," Giacomo assured his teacher, despite his own shaky confidence.

While Pietro kept his Genius's beam fixed on the mandorla so the Wellspring stayed open, Mico hovered above Giacomo and projected a latticed sphere around them both to act as a shield. Then, with the Compass pointed in front of him, Giacomo stepped through the radiant eye of the mandorla and into the maelstrom.

The winds crashed against the glowing shield, but Mico's barrier held. Giacomo glanced back, but he'd already lost sight of Pietro through the veil of colors. He peered forward, through the undulating swaths of greens, reds, and blues, but there was no sign of the Straightedge, either.

Maybe I'm not as connected to the Sacred Tools as I thought.

And now, unmoored from the physical world, dizziness overcame him, and Giacomo began to fear he might never find his way back. He gripped the Compass's handle tighter and closed his eyes, trying to block out the howling gale.

To Giacomo's surprise, the Compass began to vibrate, and when he opened his eyes, the circular pattern on the handle was lit up. The tip of the Compass bobbed up and down, tugging at him like it was animated by an unseen force.

"Mico, I think it's working!"

His Genius chirped excitedly. Giacomo relaxed his grip, letting the Compass guide him deeper into the storm.

Out of the cacophony came a voice. It began as a whisper that Giacomo couldn't quite make out, but gradually it grew louder, until Giacomo could understand it.

I was trying to help you, Giacomo. And you left me to die in here!

Giacomo's entire body went cold. The voice unmistakably belonged to Ugalino.

Soon, you will become a Lost Soul, like me!

Giacomo wheeled around, expecting Ugalino to appear, but all he saw were the waves of color crashing around Mico's shield. The voice faded back into the storm.

Ugalino's gone, Giacomo told himself. *He can't hurt me.*

The Compass began to shake violently. It jerked left, dragging Giacomo with it. Suddenly, the storm was swept away, and he found himself inside a strange tunnel that glowed red from rivulets of lava trickling down the rocky walls.

Mico's gem dimmed, and the lattice shield he'd created scattered into specks of light.

"Where are we?" Giacomo said, his muscles tensing. Mico hovered close, trilling warily.

The Compass jolted again, pulling Giacomo through the tunnel and into a triangular cavern full of sharp black rocks that jutted from the floor and ceiling like fangs. In the shadows, the light glinted off a shiny surface. Giacomo made out the L shape of the Straightedge.

He gasped. "Mico, we found it . . ."

But Giacomo still had no idea where in the world he was. He'd have to make his way out of the tunnel and try to get his bearings so he could find this place again in the physical world. Before he could turn to go, a new voice echoed through the chamber. It sounded hoarse and strangled, though, and Giacomo couldn't make out what it was saying.

Then, out of the darkness, a figure—more skeleton than man—emerged. He had stringy gray hair, sunken cheeks, and sallow skin. His neck was as thin as a finger, and his teeth were rotted and yellow. His black eyes stared out like two immense voids. And he was clutching the Straightedge in his bony hand.

The skeletal man shrieked, raising the Tool like a sword, and Giacomo was suddenly overwhelmed by intense agony. The man started to bring down the Straightedge, aiming to strike Giacomo's skull, and Giacomo was powerless to stop it. He was frozen

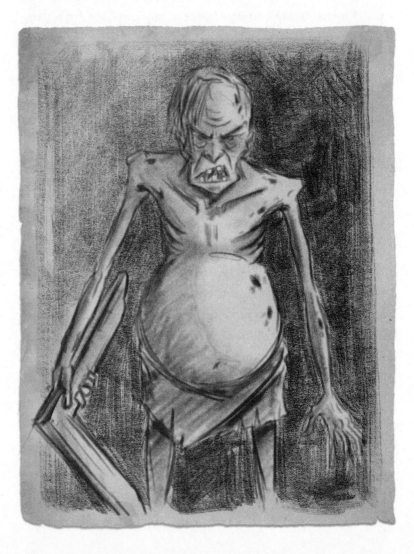

in his anguish until, at the last moment, Mico's screech moved him to action. He lifted the Compass to block the blow, and the Sacred Tools collided, setting off a blinding blast of energy that hurled Giacomo from the cavern and back into the Wellspring's maelstrom.

He clutched the Compass close, stumbling through the murky mess of colors. Somewhere, Mico called to him with a frantic song, but Giacomo could no longer see his Genius. The winds were scorching now. Tulpas could survive in the Wellspring, but not for long. "Pietro! Help!" Giacomo screamed, but the raging storm swallowed his voice. He tucked his body into a ball and braced for the end.

Then, out of nowhere, two huge hands reached under Giacomo's arms and picked him up.

"I've got you!" Zanobius shouted. He hugged Giacomo close, shielding him from the tempest.

"I can't leave without Mico!"

The last thing Giacomo remembered hearing was, "Don't worry, he's safe . . ."

When Giacomo came to, he was on his back and staring up at clouds floating through the sky. One by one, his friends' concerned faces popped into view.

Zanobius helped him sit up, and Giacomo grimaced. His head throbbed.

"Are you all right?" Aaminah said.

"I think so . . ."

Mico landed on his hand, chittering with relief, and Giacomo looked around. The grass had been scorched. Zanobius's naked chest was covered with welts and scrapes, and Giacomo could feel the burns on his own skin where the wind had whipped him. Once again, the Wellspring had done its damage. But fortunately, everyone was all right.

"Thank you, Zanobius."

"You should thank your Genius," Zanobius said. "Mico shot out of the Wellspring, screeching like mad. I knew you were in trouble."

"What happened in there?" Pietro said.

"I saw someone . . ." Giacomo said, still shaken. "He attacked me with the Straightedge."

"Who was this man?" Pietro asked.

"I got the feeling he was a Lost Soul, only much worse." Giacomo described the man's disturbing appearance. "I could feel his torment in my bones."

Milena looked troubled. "Then this Lost Soul has already found the Straightedge?"

"That's what it looked like," Giacomo said. "And he definitely didn't seem willing to part with it."

"Where's the Lost Soul keeping it?" Savino asked.

"I . . . I'm not sure. In a cave somewhere."

"What is it with Sacred Tools and caves?" Savino grumbled.

"At least we know what's waiting for us out there," Milena said. "We can start preparing."

"If I'm going anywhere near that Lost Soul, I need to get back to my sacred geometry lessons," Giacomo said.

Pietro nodded. "I was about to suggest the same thing."

SAVINO'S SCULPTURE

Zanobius wove between the mighty stones along the hillside, his master's disembodied voice echoing in his head.

You will never forget the lives you have taken! Your soul will never be at peace!

When he had heard Ugalino calling to him in the Wellspring, Zanobius had told himself he was hearing things, that the howling winds were playing tricks with his mind. But the longer he had been free of the storm, the more convinced he had become that Ugalino's words were true.

"You all right?" Enzio stepped out from behind one of the stones.

"Yes, of course." Zanobius stopped and showed Enzio the faint crisscrossing scars where the winds had slashed him. "My healing abilities work quickly."

"I don't mean your injuries." Enzio looked back toward the villa. "I've been up there watching you pacing these hills all afternoon. Something's bothering you."

"It's Ugalino," Zanobius admitted, but he kept what he'd heard in the Wellspring to himself for fear the others might believe his master still held some sway over him. "He used to say that once he was gone, it would be the end of me too."

"He only told you that so you would be dependent on him." Enzio leaned against one of the stones. "My father used that trick on me all the time. If I ever spoke up against him, he threatened to throw me out on the street, promising I wouldn't last a day without his generosity. But here I am, doing fine without him. And you don't need Ugalino, either."

That was easy for Enzio to say. Defiance seemed to be in his nature. Zanobius had witnessed the boy denouncing his own father and withstanding Ugalino's power, surviving an attack that should have killed him. Enzio possessed reserves of inner strength Zanobius could only hope to find within himself.

He looked down at the stump where Ozo had sliced off his arm. "My healing abilities only go so far. He was the one who always put me back together again."

A beautiful tune floated on the breeze, catching Zanobius's attention.

Enzio gazed off in the direction of the music. "You want to prove you're truly free from Ugalino?"

"Yes. It's the only way I'll find any peace."

"Then figure out a way to get your arm back without him."

Zanobius followed the music until he found Aaminah playing the lute for Giacomo, who was reclining against the trunk of an ancient oak. While he basked in Luna's healing light, Giacomo drew in his sketchbook. Back at the Cave of Alessio, Zanobius had watched Aaminah's beautiful music bring Enzio back from the brink of death. It seemed her talents extended to Tulpas.

Zanobius waited for Aaminah's final note to trail off before he approached her. "I was wondering, since Ugalino's gone, do you think your music can help me?" Zanobius held up the stump of his amputated arm.

Aaminah looked hesitant. "I've never created a body part out of nothing."

"How about if you had a new arm to attach?" Zanobius asked.

Zanobius tracked down Savino, who was sitting on part of the villa's broken wall and whittling a piece of wood, his Genius stationed at his side.

Initially, Savino scoffed at Zanobius's request to sculpt him a new arm. But after some gentle prodding from Giacomo and Aaminah, he relented.

"Fine. I guess it'll give me something to do while Giacomo figures out where the Straightedge is." Savino headed inside to gather art supplies and get Niccolo's permission to carve up one of the monoliths.

"Find me when you're ready," Aaminah said to Zanobius, strumming the lute. "Once Savino's done with the arm, hopefully my music can bond it to your body." She skipped off.

Savino returned a few minutes later with a long measuring stick, a hammer and chisel, and some good news. "Niccolo gave me these and said we can use whatever block of stone we want."

Zanobius was surprised to hear that Niccolo had agreed to help and wondered if he was getting used to having a couple of Tulpas under his roof.

Zanobius followed Savino around the grounds while he studied the different stones.

"Too big . . . too small . . . too many cracks . . ." Finally, Savino settled on a pale rock about waist high that was smooth on one side and rough on the other. He tapped his pencil against his pursed lips and said, "The color won't match your skin exactly, but I can work with this."

Zanobius lifted the stone and carried it closer to the villa, then placed it carefully on a tree stump.

Savino measured the lengths and widths of one of Zanobius's arms and hands for comparison, then sketched it from different angles and in various positions. "I have to say, Ugalino may have been a terrible person, but he was an amazing artist. I'll do my best to match your other arms."

"Thank you for taking the time to do this," Zanobius said, rotating his wrist so Savino could get a better view of the good arm. "I know you're still adjusting to my being around, so I didn't think you'd agree to it."

"Milena thinks I need to start being more open-minded about you."

"I see . . . So you're trying to impress her?" Zanobius asked innocently.

The tip of Savino's pencil snapped. "What? No, it's not like that." He sharpened his pencil with a knife. "Now, quit moving, you're messing up my drawings."

Once he was ready to start sculpting, Savino traded pencil and sketchbook for the hammer and chisel. Zanobius had often watched Ugalino work and was fascinated by how an artist could begin with nothing but a blank canvas or a mound of clay and transform it into something beautiful. He stood by, eagerly waiting for Savino to begin chiseling away.

Instead, Savino circled around one side of the stone, then back again, over and over. He kept referring to the studies he'd made in his sketchbook, looking unsure of himself. "I've never worked with such an intimidating piece of stone before. I usually mold clay until I figure out the form."

"Don't overthink it," a voice said.

Savino and Zanobius turned to find Niccolo heading toward them. He brushed past Zanobius on his way to Savino, then slapped the smooth side of the rock. "Inside here is a statue waiting for you to discover it."

"And how do I do that?" Savino asked.

"It's like sacred geometry. First, picture the image in your mind. Then use the hammer and chisel to chip away the parts of the stone you don't want."

"I already have the image." Savino pointed to the drawings he had made. "My problem is envisioning my lines taking shape in the stone," he complained.

"When Furio was still with me, he would help me with that part."

"How?"

Niccolo gestured to Savino's sketchbook. "Nero can take your flat sketches and give them depth."

"Pietro never taught me that," Savino said.

"Pietro was a master painter. He'll be the first to admit sculpting was never his forte."

With his Genius on his shoulder, Savino gripped his sculpting tools. Nero's gem lit up and cast a cone of blue light on the stone.

Lines took shape to show a three-dimensional form. Savino whooped with excitement. "It's one of my sketches! Inside the stone!"

Zanobius looked over Savino's shoulder. "Why can't I see anything?"

Niccolo gave him a sidelong glance. "It's only visible to the artist," he said, then clapped Savino on the back. "Now, put that hammer and chisel to use!"

Embracing his newfound confidence, Savino finally began chiseling. Zanobius watched with excitement as dust exploded from the stone.

Keeping his eyes on Savino, Niccolo stepped to Zanobius's side. "I take it Ugalino never explained his artistic process to you?"

"He didn't allow me to study sacred geometry," Zanobius replied.

"Probably because he didn't want you to understand your true nature. I'm sure he feared you'd figure out a way to break free of him."

"Did you ever meet Ugalino?" Zanobius asked.

"No. But I knew artists like him, so wrapped up in their own egos they couldn't be bothered to help their fellow man." Niccolo turned away and headed into the house. "I hope the new arm works out for you," he called back.

THE TETRAD

Milena took a seat next to Giacomo on a small bench under the shade of the enormous old oak. Nearby, Pietro was leaning on his walking stick, about to begin Giacomo's lesson. Mico buzzed back and forth while Gaia pecked the ground, hunting for bugs. Tito was roosting up in the tree's thick branches, asleep as usual.

"Now, Giacomo, since you've already studied the monad, dyad, and triad, today I'd like you to focus on the tetrad," Pietro began. Then he hobbled to the oak and eased himself between two giant roots. He propped his feet up and leaned back against the trunk, saying no more.

"Are you feeling all right, Master Pietro?" Milena asked. "I thought we were about to start."

A grin emerged from Pietro's beard. "We are, Milena. The class is yours, whenever you're ready to begin."

"What?" Even though Milena knew a lot about sacred geometry and had served as Pietro's assistant before, she'd never guided the lessons. "But I'm not Giacomo's teacher."

"You are now," Pietro said.

Milena looked at Giacomo, who met her worry with a smile. "There's no one smarter than you, Milena. You're going to do great."

"Giacomo's right," Pietro said. "Of all the students I've instructed over the years, you are one of the most extraordinary. I can't think of anyone better suited to carry on my teachings."

"Carry on . . . ? No, don't say that. You're not going anywhere," Milena said, her voice rising.

Pietro's face wrinkled into a reassuring smile. "I didn't mean it like that. I promise, I'm not ready to meet the Creator quite yet."

Milena exhaled with relief, feeling foolish. Ever since she'd left her own family behind and begun studying with Pietro, he had become like a grandfather to her. And after Baldassare's betrayal, Pietro was the only adult she could really rely on. If anything *did* happen to him . . .

She brushed away the dark thought and took a couple of calming breaths, praying that her lesson wouldn't be an embarrassing disaster. She wished she'd had time to prepare. Training Giacomo was an enormous responsibility. She would try her best not to let Pietro—or herself—down.

Milena stepped before Giacomo, smoothed her dress, and straightened her posture. "The tetrad is symbolized by the square and the number four, and it represents solidity, stability, and strength. Now, constructing a square is a little more complex than the other shapes you've mastered."

"It can't be that hard," Giacomo teased. "I've drawn squares before."

Milena narrowed her eyes and crossed her arms. "Well, yes, anyone with a pencil and a piece of paper can sketch a square. But you should understand by now that in order to have your Genius project it, you'll need to learn how to instantly visualize the square's construction in your mind's eye."

"I know, I know . . ." Giacomo brought out his handheld compass. Then he opened his sketchbook and looked up at her. "Ready when you are."

"The first step is to bring the mandorla to light." Milena circled her brush twice in the air. Gaia swooped off the ground and stretched her long neck, projecting two overlapping green circles from her gem.

"Next, add two lines: one horizontal and one vertical." Milena's glowing marks formed a cross in the eye of the mandorla. "Then you add a smaller circle inside the eye. Finally, you bring the square to light by connecting the points where the cross and circle meet."

Giacomo stared at her through the translucent shape that hovered between them like a stained glass window. "Got it," he said, and used the handheld compass to construct a square in his sketchbook.

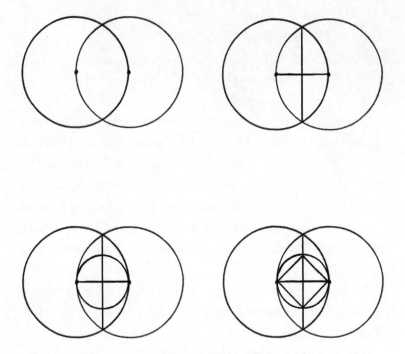

As Giacomo made his final mark, Mico's gem lit up, casting a red square next to Milena's green one. Its edges vibrated and hummed.

"Not bad for my first try," Giacomo bragged.

Milena stiffened. *Well, that was presumptuous of him.* She gave him a supportive smile anyway. "Great work. But if that Lost Soul guarding the Straightedge attacks you again, you're not going to have time to pull out your sketchbook. Keep working on the square until you and your Genius act as one."

* * *

As the week progressed, Milena spent every waking moment with Giacomo and Mico, overseeing their practice. Ever since Giacomo had walked into Pietro's studio, he'd proved a quick learner who possessed a natural connection to sacred geometry. It had taken her months of trial and error to reliably imagine a square and have Gaia project it; Giacomo and his Genius mastered the same skill over the course of a few days. That Giacomo was a Tulpa explained some of his innate ability, but still, Milena was impressed and, though she hated to admit it, a little jealous.

But Giacomo wasn't satisfied with simply practicing. One morning, Milena found him among the monoliths, itching to test his artistry against Enzio's archery skills.

"I bet you can't hit me," Giacomo goaded.

"What's going on here?" Milena demanded, stepping to Enzio's side.

Enzio slowly notched his arrow. "Giacomo wants me to use him for target practice."

"I need to know I can defend myself against an actual threat," Giacomo said, placing himself in front of a standing stone about twenty feet away. Mico hovered over him. "I'm ready, Enzio."

Milena jumped between the boys. "This is foolish, Giacomo. Did you ever think you might get hurt?"

Giacomo waved her away. "I'll be fine. Enzio's not even that good a shot."

Enzio raised his bow at the challenge. "My father made me take lessons when I was a kid."

Milena whirled around to face Enzio. "Don't you dare draw that bow!"

"Don't tell Enzio what to do!" Giacomo shouted. "And don't tell me what to do, either. Pietro might have made you my teacher, but we're not in class right now."

Milena held her ground.

"Fine, if you won't move, I will." Giacomo ran to his right, holding his pencil at the ready. Before Milena could stop him, he turned and yelled, "Enzio, shoot!"

"No!" Milena shouted, but it was too late.

Enzio had drawn his bow, and with a *twang*, he released his arrow on target.

Milena winced and held her breath.

Giacomo made four quick marks, and Mico beamed a shimmering red square in front of Giacomo's head and torso. The arrow ricocheted off the shield and dropped harmlessly in the grass.

As Mico's projection faded, Giacomo grinned boastfully. "See, Milena? I told you I'd be fine. Guess I'm ready to start learning about the pentad."

Milena tensed, trying to keep her cool. "There's still more you need to understand before we move on to the next form."

"Like what?" Giacomo said, exasperated.

"Can you name all the Universal Solids?" Milena said, knowing full well the question would stump Giacomo.

"I'd be happy to," Giacomo said defiantly. "First, there's the uh . . . I think the cube is one?"

Milena tapped her foot. "Four more to go."

Giacomo threw up his arms in surrender. "All right, you got me. But who cares? How is knowing a bunch of names going to help me master sacred geometry?"

"Oh, I don't know," Milena said, her voice rising. "The Universal

Solids only happen to be the energetic building blocks of everything in the universe."

"I'll keep that in mind." Giacomo looked unconvinced.

She gave him a hard stare. "You have so much power inside you, Giacomo. But you don't have the first clue how to use it."

Milena wheeled around and marched away.

THE COLLECTION

From her royal box, Nerezza gazed down at the amphitheater's stage, where rows of muscular men stood still as statues, the sun glinting off their tan, oiled torsos.

"Meet your crew," Minister Strozzi said.

"Impressive," Nerezza replied. "But are you sure they'll be able to manage? This is no ordinary ship."

"And these are no ordinary crewmen," Strozzi assured her. "The Marinai will have no trouble powering your vessel. I selected them especially for their strength and endurance."

Satisfied, Nerezza ordered the Minister of War to make sure they were ready to leave as soon as she received word of Giacomo's location.

"The Marinai are also known for their lack of discipline," Xiomar's gravelly voice cautioned.

Strozzi flinched, startled by Xiomar's arrival. Nerezza turned to find the hunchback looming in the doorway.

"What are you doing here?" she demanded.

Xiomar bowed demurely. "My apologies. I only came to offer my counsel."

Strozzi seethed. "Your counsel isn't needed. I will make certain that the Marinai follow orders."

Xiomar nodded. "Still . . . It never hurts to have a fallback. I've found that even the most unruly subjects can be controlled with just a few drops of sacred brimstone."

Strozzi turned to Nerezza. "The only power his potions have is to make men dull and weak. I need the Marinai at full strength."

"I agree," Nerezza said, then turned back to Xiomar. "I've no doubt Minister Strozzi will keep the Marinai in line. You're both dismissed."

Strozzi shouted down at the crewmen, ordering them to clear the stage. The Marinai turned and marched away as one, their steps moving in rhythm with Nerezza's heartbeat.

But Xiomar's words thrummed inside her too. *It never hurts to have a fallback.*

What if Giacomo refused to help her obtain the Sacred Tools?

He had never properly learned obedience. Or respect. He'd already proved himself to be strong-willed. *That's the problem with artists having Geniuses*, Nerezza thought. *It makes them too unpredictable.* And Nerezza hated unpredictable.

"Minister Xiomar, wait."

Xiomar paused in the doorway and looked back, peering around his massive hump. "Yes, Your Eminence?"

"The sacred brimstone you spoke of . . . Do you think it would work on a Tulpa?"

"It is unlikely," Xiomar said, coming back into the room. He rubbed his pointed chin. "If it's Giacomo you're concerned about, I would need to create a much more powerful elixir to ensure his submission."

"But it's possible?"

"To know for sure, I would need access to your collection."

Nerezza scowled. Xiomar knew that room of the palace was off-limits. But if he had a method to secure dominance over Giacomo, she was willing to let him in. "Just this once," she said.

A slight smile crept across Xiomar's lips.

Nerezza and Xiomar approached a large bronze door beneath the palace, guarded by two soldiers. She motioned them to move aside, then spun the dials of a cylinder on the door handle until the correct sequence of symbols clicked into place. The door unlocked with a metallic *thunk*, and she led Xiomar into a dark antechamber.

"Through here," Nerezza said, parting a thick velvet curtain.

Whenever she entered this space, Nerezza felt like she was stepping into the heavens. The gems glittered all around her like stars. She imbibed their energy, transforming it into inspiration. Some of her most brilliant ideas—such as the design for her new ships—had been conceived while gazing at her collection.

Awestruck, Xiomar studied a large, octagonal red gem on a pedestal. The jewel was at least the size of his head. "Is this . . . ?"

"The Segretti gem," Nerezza proudly informed him. "One of my greatest challenges, but in the end, even Segretti's Genius succumbed to Victoria's overwhelming power."

Xiomar turned to take in the rest of the collection. "Now, where might I find the Ghiberti gems?"

"This way." Nerezza strode to the back of the room, past

displays containing more brightly colored gemstones. When Baldassare had first informed her of Giacomo's arrival at his villa, he had also told her his parents' names: Orsino and Amera Ghiberti. They had been part of a rebellion that had tried and failed to overthrow the government. When Nerezza had generously offered the couple amnesty in exchange for their service, they refused, so she executed their Geniuses and added their gems to her growing hoard. Soon after, the Ghibertis wasted away and their son was sent to an orphanage.

Nerezza had forgotten all about the Ghibertis until Giacomo declared himself a Tulpa and catapulted Orsino and Amera's names back into her awareness.

The day after Giacomo and his friends fled the city, Nerezza had scoured her collection until she found the Ghiberti gems in a small glass case tucked away in the back of the room.

"Here they are," Nerezza said.

Xiomar leaned in, studying the two near-identical gems, which were elongated octagons, pink in hue, about three inches in diameter. They did not look especially impressive at first glance. Xiomar gripped one of the gems between his long yellow nails and held up an eyepiece to inspect it. "The power used to create Giacomo is contained in these gems."

"And you can extract it?"

"I'll need to perform some tests to be sure." Xiomar lowered the eyepiece. "Tampering with a Genius's gem is a volatile process. It takes patience and a steady hand."

"And assuming you succeed?"

"Any trace of rebellion will be erased from Giacomo," Xiomar assured her. "He will be compelled to comply with your every order."

SETBACK

Shortly after sunrise, Zanobius helped with the morning chores, as he had since their arrival. It was the least he could do to thank Niccolo for allowing him to stay.

Zanobius went to the well, hoisted the bucket out of the deep, and unhooked it from the pulley. When he rested it on the edge of the stone wall, the surface of the water rippled in expanding circles like a Genius's sacred geometry projection.

A loud chirrup caught his attention. Luna zipped around the side of the house, followed a moment later by Aaminah, who was running toward him with her lute.

"Zanobius! Zanobius!"

His nerves went on high alert. "What's wrong?"

"Nothing," Aaminah said, hopping up and down. "Savino stayed up all night and finally finished the sculpture! Come look!"

Giacomo, Enzio, and Milena were already gathered at the tree stump when Zanobius arrived. He found Savino with Nero on his shoulder, the Genius's gem pulsing a dim blue. Before them stood a flawless replica of Zanobius's arm and hand carved in stone.

"What do you think?" Aaminah said.

Before Zanobius could answer, Savino said, "I still have a few finishing touches to make." He stepped around his sculpture, studying it from all sides, then leaned in, using a steel file to smooth the stone's surface.

Savino had perfectly captured the structure and musculature of Zanobius's thick arms; the hand, frozen in a clawlike grip, appeared so realistic that when Zanobius moved his own fingers, he half expected the sculpture to move too. If Zanobius hadn't witnessed Savino's steady progress over the past week, he would have assumed Ugalino had somehow returned from the dead to create it. "The resemblance is remarkable," Zanobius complimented him.

Savino nodded his thanks as he filed one last groove in a knuckle. Then he stood back and wiped his brow. "Okay, I think it's done. One of my better efforts, if I do say so myself. Try it on."

With his two left hands, Zanobius picked up the stone and held its roughly hewn base up to the stump of his right arm.

Savino leaned in and inspected the area where the sculpture touched skin. "Looks like it matches up." He wiped his dusty hands on his tunic. "Aaminah, it's time to work your musical magic."

Zanobius took a seat on the tree stump, and Aaminah plunked down in the grass in front of him, cradling the lute in her lap. She strummed a chord, her fingers dancing across the strings. Luna fluttered in front of Zanobius, launching bursts of yellow circles,

squares, and triangles from the gem in her crown. The light floated down and seeped into Zanobius's new arm.

"Can you tell if it's working?" Giacomo asked.

"It feels . . . tingly," Zanobius said.

Savino turned to Aaminah. "That's a good thing, right?"

Aaminah shrugged. "I think so."

Gradually, the stinging sensation became a soothing warmth that spread from Zanobius's elbow to his shoulder. Zanobius let go of the stone arm and it hung from his body, its edges melding seamlessly with his flesh. "It's fused!"

Aaminah kept playing for a while longer, and when the last of Luna's light faded, Savino said, "Try wiggling your fingers."

Zanobius concentrated on his new hand. Despite his best effort, the fingers were unresponsive. "I can't move them."

"Maybe try a different song, Aaminah," Savino urged. "Something more intense. That last tune sounded too light and airy."

"I like light and airy," Aaminah grumbled.

For the next hour, Aaminah plucked and strummed, her fingers never stopping. She played intense songs, calm songs, fast songs, and slow songs, but nothing seemed to work.

Finally, Luna's light began to flicker and dim. Her feathers drooped, and she landed in the grass. Aaminah's fingers were red and blistered when she pulled them off the strings and her body sagged with fatigue. "I'm sorry, Zanobius. I was afraid this was going to happen."

"Thank you for trying," Zanobius said politely, hiding his disappointment. He cradled the stone appendage, its weight now feeling like a burden.

"Don't worry, we'll get that arm turned to flesh and moving," Giacomo said, trying to sound reassuring.

"How?" Zanobius said.

But Giacomo couldn't give him an answer.

That night, Giacomo walked the villa grounds. He had tried to sleep, but every time he drifted off, his nightmares returned. Only this time, it wasn't Nerezza who haunted his dreams, but the skeletal man who'd brutally attacked Giacomo with the Straightedge.

To take his mind off his distressing vision, Giacomo turned his attention to the problem of Zanobius's arm.

I have to be missing something, Giacomo thought. Savino had replicated Zanobius's arm masterfully and Aaminah's skills were unmatched, so why hadn't Zanobius been healed completely?

Then it hit him: maybe Ugalino was the missing piece. What if Zanobius couldn't fully heal because his creator was gone?

And whose fault is that? A wave of guilt smacked into Giacomo.

Under the light of the crescent moon, he spotted a hulking silhouette perched on the roof like a gargoyle.

"Zanobius?" Giacomo stepped closer, craning his neck to see the Tulpa. "What are you doing up there?"

Zanobius gazed into the distance. "Someone needs to keep watch, and since I don't sleep . . ."

"You've been doing this every night?" Giacomo was touched by Zanobius's loyalty. No one had asked him to guard the villa; he'd taken the responsibility upon himself. "Mind if I join you?"

"Come on up."

Giacomo went back inside and climbed up the creaky stairs to the top floor. He slipped out a small window and shimmied down the roof. Zanobius was leaning back on his three good arms. The stone arm hung at his side, a dead weight.

"I was wondering . . . Have you ever lost a limb like this before?" Giacomo asked.

"I seem to remember losing a leg to a particularly vicious cat-Genius, though the details elude me. And there was a time when Ugalino and I had a run-in with a pack of wolves. I think I lost three hands that day."

"And what did Ugalino do to fix you?"

"Same as Savino did—he would sculpt me a new body part."

"Right . . . But how did he get it to fuse with you and make it work again?"

Zanobius furrowed his brow. "I'm trying to remember . . . I think he lit up my patterns."

The symmetrical tattoo on Zanobius's chest was made up of several circles connected by a web of crisscrossing lines. Giacomo's hand went to his own chest, knowing it held the same pattern, though it wasn't visible all the time, as Zanobius's was. He had seen his markings illuminated only once, with the help of the Creator's Compass.

"Was it like when Ugalino wiped your memory?" Giacomo asked.

"No, I don't think so." Zanobius pondered again. "When Ugalino healed me, he only lit up certain shapes within the pattern."

"What kind of shapes?"

"There was a cube, I think. A few others. He called them a name—something to do with a solid . . ."

"The Universal Solids?" Giacomo blurted out.

"Yes, that was it. Do you know them?"

Giacomo's mind began to race. What had Milena said?

The Universal Solids only happen to be the energetic building blocks of everything in the universe.

Suddenly, it all clicked into place. Attaching the arm had been only a first step. What Zanobius needed now was help from the universe to spark it to life.

"I think I have an idea to get your arm moving, but first I need another lesson with Milena." He paused. "Do me a favor, and don't tell anyone what we talked about."

"Why not?" Zanobius asked.

Because Milena thinks I don't have a clue how to use my powers.

"Because even though everyone is being nice to us, let's face it, we're still Tulpas in their eyes—different. It's better if we keep this between us, at least for now."

Zanobius nodded his understanding. "Giacomo, I have to tell you something . . . When we were in the Wellspring, I heard Ugalino's voice."

Giacomo shivered. "What did he say?"

"That I'll never be able to forget the lives I've taken. That my soul will never be at peace."

"I heard him too," Giacomo admitted.

Zanobius's eyes filled with fright. "Then it wasn't only in my mind? He's really still out there?"

"No, he's gone," Giacomo said. "It must have been our guilt playing tricks on us."

"Probably." Zanobius sighed. "But what he said was true. I can't forget all those people I've killed. I don't know how to put that behind me. I'm not even sure I should."

Giacomo keenly felt Zanobius's pain. He was haunted after taking one life. Zanobius might have been responsible for dozens of deaths. Maybe more.

"You'll drive yourself mad unless you find a way to forgive yourself."

"Maybe someday I'll be able to . . ." Zanobius hung his head. "But I don't know how right now."

The chirps of crickets filled the long silence. Finally, Zanobius looked back at Giacomo. "Can I ask . . . What did he say to you?"

Giacomo could barely utter the words. "He told me I would become a Lost Soul."

Zanobius put a hand on his shoulder. "As long as I'm with you, I won't let that happen."

UNIVERSAL SOLIDS

The next morning, Giacomo took Niccolo up on his offer to lock the Compass in one of his cabinets. It had become a burden to carry it everywhere, and it would be safer hidden away until they were ready to move on.

With the Compass secure, Giacomo whistled for Mico, and together they wandered the villa grounds. They found Milena sitting under the old oak, reading from another of Garrulous's journals.

"What's the latest with Signor Garrulous and his wild, worldly adventures?" Giacomo said, trying to act casual and friendly.

Milena didn't even look up. "I'll let you know if I find anything that might be helpful to our mission." Her voice was cool.

Giacomo pressed ahead. "I was thinking about what you said before . . . I'd like to learn more about the Universal Solids."

Milena glanced up, an eyebrow raised. "You still want me to be your teacher?"

"I'm sorry about the other day. You were right. I still have a lot to learn about my powers."

Milena studied him for a tense moment, as if she were gauging his sincerity. To Giacomo's relief, she shut the journal and got to her feet. "Let's get to work."

Giacomo took his seat on the bench, but as Milena was about to begin, Zanobius wandered by.

"Sorry, I didn't mean to interrupt," he said.

"Actually, it's good that you're here," Milena said. "Could you help me with a demonstration?"

"Of course. What do I have to do?"

"Stand there." Milena pointed to a spot on the ground several feet away. "I'm going to have my Genius project some shapes in front of you." She looked at Giacomo. "To understand the Universal Solids, we need to move beyond the point, line, and surface, into the third dimension of volume."

While Zanobius took his position, Milena described how each of the five Universal Solids originated out of the pattern emblazoned on Zanobius's chest and back. She called it the *Creator's Pattern*.

Giacomo looked at Zanobius. "Did you know the pattern had a name?"

Zanobius shook his head. "Ugalino never mentioned it."

Milena swiped her brush, and Gaia projected some glowing lines a few inches in front of Zanobius's chest. The green overlay lined up with some of the lines in the Creator's Pattern. It looked like a Y inside a hexagon. "The first Solid is the six-sided hexahedron, commonly known as the cube." Milena waved her brush again, and Giacomo marveled as she transformed the two-dimensional lines into a three-dimensional form.

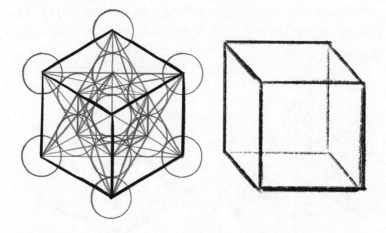

Zanobius also looked impressed as he stared down at the glimmering shape hovering in front of him. Milena let the cube fade away, then drew a new set of lines. Like before, the two-dimensional outline perfectly overlaid Zanobius's tattoos. "This one is called the icosahedron." Once again, she pulled two dimensions into three, bringing to light a Solid with twenty triangular facets.

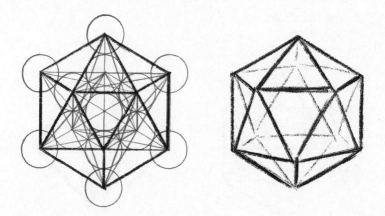

With a flourish of her brush, Milena next drew the outline of a triangle and transformed it into a pyramid. "And this is the tetrahedron."

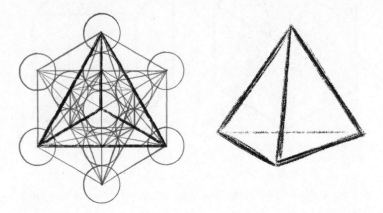

Gaia projected another design—a triangle inside a hexagon. "And I'm sure you'll both remember this shape." As soon as Milena's lines became three-dimensional, Giacomo recognized the octahedron.

"That's the shape the Creator's Compass was locked inside," Giacomo remarked.

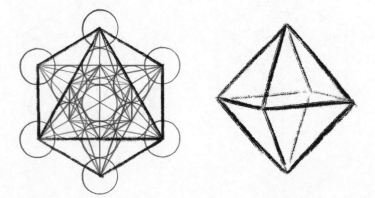

"The fifth and final Solid is the dodecahedron." Milena's green lines re-formed one last time, into a rounded shape with twelve pentagonal faces. "The ancients referred to it as the element of the cosmos."

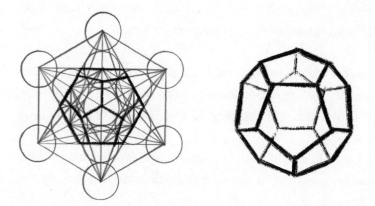

As the final Solid faded away, Giacomo's gaze fell on Zanobius's stone arm, and Pietro's words came back to him.

Tulpas are sacred geometry incarnate . . .

His mind flashed to the duke's camera obscura—that twisted Tulpa-making machine. Giacomo remembered seeing the Creator's Pattern and the Universal Solids projected on the wall inside the obscura, though he hadn't realized their significance at the time.

There was also the Tulpa cipher he'd found and later destroyed. It had depicted a four-armed, four-legged man surrounded by drawings of the Solids and the Creator's Pattern.

If Giacomo's hunch was right, he'd just figured out a way to bring Zanobius's arm to life. As soon as the lesson was over and Milena went back to reading, he pulled Zanobius aside.

"Just give me some time to master all the forms, and then we'll get your arm moving," Giacomo said, keeping his voice low.

Zanobius looked uneasy. "How?"

"I don't think it's an accident that you and I are both marked with the Creator's Pattern. Tulpas aren't only connected to the Universal Solids; we were created out of them."

Zanobius waited patiently as Giacomo spent the next few days under Milena's guidance, learning to construct the five Universal Solids in his sketchbook until he and Mico could reliably bring them to light.

One night after dinner, Giacomo pulled Zanobius aside. "After everyone goes to sleep, meet me under the old oak. I'm ready."

Zanobius stayed perched on the roof until he heard the last bedroom door shut and the glow from the candles was dim in the windows. Once the villa had fallen silent, Zanobius crept down the wall and slunk away toward the old oak.

As he approached, he could see the tree's leaves shimmering red.

"Giacomo?" he whispered.

"Over here," Giacomo whispered back.

Zanobius rounded the trunk and found Giacomo crouched behind the tree. Mico was perched on his shoulder, and the faint red light was coming from the Genius's gem.

"Did anyone see you?" Giacomo asked.

Zanobius glanced back toward the house. "I don't think so."

But then they heard hushed voices and the patter of footfalls coming up the hill.

"Hide!" Giacomo pulled Zanobius behind the tree with him. They tried to cover the light from the Genius's gem, but Zanobius heard a chirp—and it wasn't Mico. In the next instant, a bright yellow beam was shining in their eyes.

"Luna found Mico!" Aaminah announced, running up the hill, followed shortly by Savino, Milena, and Enzio.

Giacomo sighed and shuffled out to meet them.

"What are you doing out here, Giacomo?" Aaminah asked innocently.

"Nothing, just some late-night practicing," Giacomo said.

"Oh," Aaminah said, sounding confused. "Then why did Milena make me use Luna to track you down?"

"Because he's up to something." Milena approached, glowering at Giacomo and Zanobius. "I saw you both sneak away from the villa."

"Maybe we wanted some space," Giacomo said pointedly.

Milena looked from Giacomo to Zanobius. "One of you tell me what's going on."

Zanobius was the first to break under Milena's stern glare. When he revealed how Giacomo planned to jump-start his healing by lighting up his patterns with the Universal Solids, Savino's face lit up.

"Really? Do you think it will actually work?"

Milena elbowed Savino. "Don't encourage him."

Savino rubbed his arm, frowning at her. "Let's at least hear Giacomo out." Savino turned to Giacomo. "What do the Universal Solids have to do with Zanobius's arm?"

"I think you were right that Aaminah's music wasn't intense enough," Giacomo said.

"Hey," Aaminah complained.

"No, I'm not criticizing your playing. But you were only able to mend Zanobius on the surface. To bring his arm to life, he needs to tap into a stronger kind of energy." Giacomo pointed to Zanobius's chest. "And the Creator's Pattern is a channel to that energy."

"You didn't create Zanobius," Milena said. "You don't know what might happen if you light up his patterns."

"Come on, let him try," Savino protested. "If it means my sculpture doesn't go to waste, then what's the harm?"

Milena held up her scarred arm. "Because this is what happens when Giacomo isn't in control of his powers."

"That was an accident," Giacomo said.

"How did you get hurt?" Zanobius asked.

"The first time Giacomo opened the Wellspring, it burned me," Milena said bitterly.

"And I still feel terrible about it," Giacomo said. "Why do you think I went to you for more lessons? I'm trying to be careful. You've seen me practicing."

"And you need a lot *more* practice before you mess with the Creator's Pattern. Give that to me and let's go back inside." Milena lunged forward, reaching for Giacomo's pencil.

Giacomo pulled away. "No!"

"This is just like with the target practice. This time, I'm going to get Pietro before you do something stupid." Milena turned to the others, who hadn't moved. "Aren't you coming with me?"

Savino, Aaminah, and Enzio shook their heads.

"I want to see if this will work," Aaminah said.

"Giacomo's theory makes a lot of sense," Savino added.

"Zanobius needs our support," Enzio argued. "We should give it to him."

Milena grumbled in exasperation and stormed off toward the house.

Zanobius lifted his stony appendage and pictured his fingers curling, his wrist flexing. "I'm ready if you are."

With a whistle, Giacomo summoned Mico into action, then drew the first shape in the air.

Mico cast a beam of red light from his gem, projecting a cube that hovered inches from Zanobius. Giacomo moved the shape closer until its vibrating edge touched Zanobius's chest. With one more sweep of his pencil, Giacomo pushed the cube into Zanobius, and the corresponding lines on the Tulpa's tattoos lit up.

A pleasant warmth flooded through Zanobius. "I think it's working."

Giacomo swiped his pencil in front of him, forming the lines of the icosahedron. Mico projected the form, and Giacomo gently guided it into Zanobius's chest too. He followed with the tetrahedron and octahedron. Savino, Enzio, and Aaminah watched, eyes wide with anticipation.

With each new shape, Zanobius felt a fresh wave of heat radiate through him. His arm began to tingle, like a thousand fireflies were buzzing inside it. With a *crack*, his thumb moved.

"Keep going!" Zanobius urged.

Finally, Giacomo lit up the fifth Solid—the dodecahedron. *The element of the cosmos.*

With the final pattern ablaze, Zanobius's whole being began to vibrate. Another *crack*. More fingers moved. Then, finally, the entire hand came to life.

Aaminah let out a squeal of excitement. "I can't believe it!"

Giacomo smiled proudly. "When Milena sees this, she's going to owe me a huge apology."

But the odd thing—the thing Zanobius sensed but that the children couldn't know—was that the hand was moving on its own. Zanobius focused and tried to assert control over it, but it defied his mental commands. He watched, powerless, as it balled into a fist.

An icy chill shot through his arm, extinguishing all traces of warmth. The glowing lines of the dodecahedron spread out, filling his entire chest pattern with a deep purple glow. Zanobius tried to warn the children to get away from him, but his throat seized. Giacomo's expression transformed from elation to confusion, then to fear.

Without meaning to, Zanobius lunged at Giacomo.

His vision blurred.

Someone screamed.

Then the world went black.

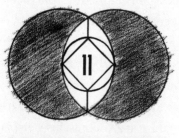

BROKEN APART

SCREEEE!

Mico darted into the sky, joining the other Geniuses, who were also squawking in alarm.

"What happened?"

"Watch out!"

"Zanobius, what's wrong with you?!"

Giacomo was vaguely aware of all the noise and shouting, but his focus was on Zanobius, who was now lumbering toward him.

"Zanobius! Stop!" Giacomo commanded, stumbling backward.

But Zanobius wouldn't obey. He yanked Giacomo up by his tunic and held him off the ground. It was hard to see in the darkness, but now that he was up close, Giacomo could swear that Zanobius's blue eyes had turned strangely black. But before he could tell for sure, Zanobius had flung him into the tree trunk.

Giacomo crumpled to the dirt, his head foggy. The world spun. Somewhere, Mico let out a pained squeak.

"Zanobius . . ." Giacomo said weakly, scrambling back against the oak. "Please . . ."

Zanobius lunged again but was hit from the side by sharp spikes of blue light that sent him reeling.

"Stay back!" Savino shouted, pointing his chisel in Zanobius's direction while Nero circled above him.

"Don't hurt him!" Giacomo called out.

"You'd rather he kill you?" Savino snapped back. He jabbed his chisel again. Nero dove at Zanobius, his gem blazing.

The Genius circled Zanobius and coiled a glimmering spiral around him, but before it was complete, Zanobius smashed through the blue light and resumed his advance.

"This isn't you!" Giacomo said. "Take back control!"

Ignoring Giacomo's plea, Zanobius brought down his four fists, hard and fast. Giacomo rolled left an instant before Zanobius pounded the earth, then clawed his way across the grass, coughing.

Nero swooped by for another assault, hitting Zanobius with jagged squares of light. Zanobius staggered and roared, and the next time Savino's Genius arced around, Zanobius leaped and batted him out of the air. Savino cried out and hit the dirt as Nero spiraled and crashed.

"Savino!" Aaminah, who had been watching in shock as the nightmare unfolded, ran to him. Giacomo looked for Enzio, but he had disappeared.

With Zanobius closing in again, Giacomo spotted his pencil in the grass and dove for it. He snatched it up and made a wild, arcing motion. Mico wobbled in front of him and beamed a wave of light that crashed into Zanobius, driving him back.

If I can stop his tattoos from glowing, maybe I can put an end to this, Giacomo thought.

Zanobius fought through the streaming light, then dropped to all eight limbs, galloping straight at Giacomo. Giacomo drew a square shield, and Zanobius ran into it headfirst, but he was stunned for only a moment. Giacomo brought up square after square, but Zanobius anticipated each one, jumping over or around them. Before Giacomo realized it, Zanobius was upon him and had him pinned to the ground.

"Let me go!" Giacomo begged as Zanobius lifted him up by his collar once again. "I know you don't want to do this!"

Zanobius's stone hand locked around Giacomo's throat and squeezed.

Giacomo's windpipe felt like it was about to be crushed. His eyes grew heavy, and he knew he wouldn't last much longer. He wanted to tell Zanobius that he was sorry, that this was all his fault, but he had no breath to form the words. Giacomo's head rolled back. The stars turned blurry . . .

CRACK!

Giacomo's ears rang.

There was a flash of green, and Zanobius's new arm shattered into fragments. As Giacomo dropped to the ground, cool air rushed back into his lungs and the world returned to focus.

"Giacomo, are you all right?" Milena shouted.

"I . . . I'm fine." His throat felt raw.

Behind Milena, Niccolo crested the hill with Enzio. Tito announced his arrival with a deafening hoot and swooped down with Pietro on his back.

Zanobius groaned and staggered, holding his head. His chest and back patterns pulsated with light, then dimmed. When Zanobius opened his eyes, Giacomo was relieved to see they had become blue again. Zanobius stared in disbelief at the chunks of stone around him and stepped toward Giacomo.

"What . . . what happened?"

"Keep away from him!" Milena warned. She raised her brush, ready to strike again.

"No, don't!" Giacomo shouted, throwing himself in front of Zanobius. "He's not dangerous anymore."

Giacomo glanced back at Zanobius. "You're not, right?"

Zanobius stared back, looking confused and scared, like he had no idea he had nearly ended Giacomo's life.

Zanobius felt a lightness on his right side. His broken arm lay in pieces across the ground. His head was throbbing, and his chest burned. Hazy, horrific images of what he had done replayed in his mind: swatting Nero out of the sky, trying to crush Giacomo, nearly choking him to death.

"Zanobius, did you hear me?" Giacomo said. "You're not going to hurt anyone else, right?"

To Zanobius's great relief, the darkness that had overwhelmed him was draining away. He shook himself out of the trance. "No . . . I'm all right."

"Well, Nero and I aren't!" Savino shouted, limping across the grass, cradling his wounded Genius in his arms. "What happened to you?"

"I don't know," Zanobius said.

"I'm so sorry. I didn't think you would react like that. I thought—" Giacomo reached for him, but Zanobius pulled away.

"I told you it wasn't safe," Milena snapped. She turned to Pietro. "I warned him!"

With a grim expression, Pietro pointed his walking stick in Giacomo's direction. "You were supposed to be studying sacred geometry, not experimenting on Zanobius."

Giacomo crossed his arms and turned away from his teacher. "It doesn't matter. Zanobius is back to normal."

"Are you sure?" Savino glared at Zanobius. "How do we know you're not going to attack one of us again?"

"He won't," Giacomo insisted.

"I'm not a threat," Zanobius said, but even as the words came out, he knew they sounded hollow. Ugalino had planted the seed of brutality within him, and there didn't seem to be any way to get rid of it.

Ugalino was right, he told himself. *I'll never be at peace.*

"We can't risk it," Savino said. "Zanobius, I think you need to leave."

"What?" Giacomo said. "No way."

"I agree with Savino." Milena went to his side and stroked Nero's head. "This could have been any one of our Geniuses."

"And next time might be worse," Pietro said.

"No!" Enzio stepped next to Giacomo, facing off against Savino, Milena, and Pietro. "Don't drive Zanobius away after all he's done for us."

"Like what?" Savino said incredulously. "I know you think you owe him some life debt, but you don't."

Aaminah joined Enzio and Giacomo. "Zanobius should stay," she agreed. "He wasn't in control. You can't hold that against him."

"That's exactly the problem." Milena threw up her arms in frustration. "We can't predict when he'll snap again."

As the children continued to argue, Zanobius found himself agreeing with both sides. If he stayed, there was a chance he might hurt someone again. Or worse. But when he imagined heading off into the world alone, it felt like stepping into a terrifying black void.

I have no master. No home. I don't belong anywhere.

"You can't make him leave!" Giacomo shouted.

"Watch me," Savino hollered back.

"That's enough!" Niccolo shouted, silencing the children. Zanobius waited for him to cast his lot in with those who wanted him gone. To his surprise, Niccolo stuck up for him. "The decision belongs to Zanobius."

"Why does he get to choose?" Milena asked.

"Everyone should have a chance to determine their own fate," Niccolo said.

"I'm sorry I used the Creator's Pattern like that," Giacomo said, his eyes full of sorrow. "But don't leave because of my mistake."

Zanobius put his hand on Giacomo's shoulder and felt him flinch. *Even my fellow Tulpa fears me now,* he thought sadly.

"It's not your fault," Zanobius assured him. "I let you take that risk. And Milena is right. Next time, something else might make me lose control—something none of us can predict." Zanobius looked around at the group. "I already have enough blood on my hands. I don't want them stained with any of yours."

Giacomo gripped his wrist tightly, desperately. "Don't go. Please . . ."

Zanobius knelt down to hug Giacomo. "I'm sorry, but I have to." When he pulled away, Giacomo's eyes were wet.

He looked over everyone's faces one last time. Those who had insisted he leave cast firm stares, while Enzio and Aaminah looked hurt. "Thank you all for letting me be a part of your group," Zanobius said. He turned to Niccolo and gave him a nod of appreciation. "And thank you. For reminding me who's in control."

The sun rose over the distant mountains, turning the sky pink. Zanobius headed toward the dawn and didn't look back.

SEED OF REBELLION

After Zanobius left, Giacomo couldn't bear to be around anyone. He spent the day outside, alone with only his Genius. Mico flitted from tree to tree as Giacomo channeled his sadness and anger into his drawings, sketching the jagged mountain peaks.

Though they had known each other only a few weeks, Giacomo had felt a deep bond with Zanobius. He was the only one in the world who could truly understand what it was like being a Tulpa. Now that he was gone, what did that mean for Giacomo's future? The scar on Milena's arm stood as proof that Giacomo was also a potential danger to his friends. If he made another mistake, would Savino, Milena, and Pietro cast him out too?

That night, when he couldn't sleep, Giacomo flipped through his sketchbook. He stopped on the images he'd drawn earlier that day of the mountains to the east. Zanobius had headed in that direction when he left. *He's only a day out*, Giacomo thought. *Maybe I can catch up to him.*

Before he had a chance to talk himself out of it, Giacomo got out of bed. He cupped Mico in his hands and snuck into the kitchen, cramming his satchel with food. Then he packed his art supplies and headed for the door.

On his way through the dining room, he stopped at the cabinet containing the Compass and used the key Niccolo had given him to unlock it. He grabbed the Compass, then thought twice about taking it since the others would need it to complete the mission. While Giacomo deliberated, a voice interrupted him.

"Going somewhere?"

With a startled gasp, Giacomo wheeled around to find Niccolo in the shadows, sitting in an elaborately carved chair that looked like a small throne.

Giacomo put the Compass back down. "No . . . I just . . . I couldn't sleep."

Niccolo leaned forward into the candlelight, fixing a skeptical glare on Giacomo. "So you thought you'd take a nighttime walk with a satchel full of food and the Creator's Compass?"

"Is this what you do with your nights? Lurk in the shadows to make sure none of us leave?"

"Believe me, I'd love to be snuggled in bed right now." Niccolo's hand went to his gem. "But I don't sleep much anymore."

"Oh," Giacomo said. "Sorry."

"I assume you were off to find Zanobius?" Niccolo asked bluntly.

"It's my fault he's gone," Giacomo said. "He shouldn't be out there on his own."

"Zanobius is capable of taking care of himself," Niccolo said. "But you still have an important mission to finish. Your friends need your help to find the other Sacred Tools."

"How come Zanobius gets to choose his fate, but I don't?" Giacomo challenged.

"That's a fair question," Niccolo said. "Ultimately, what you do is completely up to you. But there are some things you need to know, things I should have told you when you arrived." He gestured to a chair next to him. "Please. Sit."

Curious to hear the man out, Giacomo dropped his satchel on the table and took a seat. Mico started awake and let out an annoyed chirp, ruffling his feathers. Giacomo shushed him back to sleep.

"Do you know where evil begins, Giacomo?"

It was not what Giacomo had expected Niccolo to say. He thought about the most evil person he knew—Nerezza. "I guess some people are just born that way?"

Niccolo shook his head. "People don't come into this world knowing evil. They learn it. They take all their shame, self-loathing, and fear and hide it away in the darkest recesses of their souls. We all do this to some degree, but for a few, those negative emotions can begin to fester until they consume a person's entire being."

That describes Nerezza perfectly, Giacomo thought.

Niccolo tented his hands at his chin. "This evil begins to spread from the host, infecting anyone it encounters. Some people are strong enough to resist, but many are not, and soon the wickedness has spread across an entire empire, too powerful to overcome."

"Are you saying Nerezza's reign is like a plague?" Giacomo asked.

Niccolo nodded, then continued. "Nerezza's villainy began long before she started killing Geniuses. When she first became Empress, she felt vulnerable. She used the power of her throne to spread lies and put down anyone who spoke against her. If enough people had acted early on, her tyranny might have been stopped, but like so many, I stood by and did nothing—said nothing—while Nerezza's cruelty coursed through the empire."

"Why didn't you try to stop her back then?"

"Because I was selfish and scared. I didn't want to sacrifice my own artistic goals or my family's noble reputation. I believed that others more talented and brave than I would bring down Nerezza."

Niccolo explained that what finally pushed him to act was learning that Nerezza had hunted down and killed Pietro—or so he believed at the time. Seeking revenge, Niccolo decided he would attack Nerezza while she was giving a speech in the piazza.

Giacomo's heartbeat quickened. "Were you afraid?"

"Terrified," Niccolo said. "Before I could even get close enough to do anything, my nerve gave out. I tried to sneak away, but Furio and I were captured by a group of soldiers and dragged before Nerezza. In front of the citizens of Virenzia, she decided to make an example of me."

"And your Genius."

Niccolo nodded. "Nerezza's wretched bird struck Furio down. My insides felt like they were being ripped out of me. Everything went dark, and I waited for the Creator to take me. But instead of waking up in the heavens, I came to in a comfortable bed. Furio's gem lay next to me on the pillow."

"Who rescued you?"

"A small group of rebels had also been in the piazza that day, and they risked their lives to save me. Two of them took me into their home while I healed." Niccolo paused and looked into Giacomo's eyes. "Their names were Orsino and Amera."

Giacomo went cold. "My parents? You knew them?"

Niccolo nodded. "That's why I let you all stay. When you told me who your parents were, I knew I couldn't turn you away. I owed them that much."

A riot of emotions exploded inside Giacomo. "Why didn't you tell me you knew them?"

"Because I'm not proud that I sat back like a coward while people like your parents were on the front lines, fighting Nerezza."

A lump formed in Giacomo's throat as he thought of his parents' courage and selflessness. "Did you meet me when I was a baby?" he asked.

"No. Your parents hadn't created you yet, but they told me of their intentions. Though they viewed Ugalino as an extremist, they were inspired by what he had accomplished. They understood that a Tulpa is a seed from which an entire universe may be created. Ugalino had planted a seed of fear and violence, but your parents aspired to create a different kind of Tulpa—one who could inspire courage and hope, and who would help humanity, not harm it."

"Then they should have told me what I really was!" Giacomo said, brimming with resentment.

"I'm sure they were just waiting until you were older, Giacomo. Your mother and father showed me great kindness, far more than I deserved. They never would have done anything to hurt you."

Niccolo's words soothed Giacomo, quelling the fire inside him. "How long did you stay with them?" Giacomo asked.

"Only a few weeks," Niccolo said. "My body healed, but with my Genius gone, I knew my soul would never be the same. Any fight I had left died along with Furio.

"So one night, I packed a few belongings and wrote your parents a note saying goodbye. I couldn't look them in the face and tell them I was abandoning the rebellion. I snuck out of Virenzia through the sewers and made my way back here, to my family's villa." Niccolo stared blankly out at the room, and a quiet sadness hung in the air. In the hearth, the last flames flickered and died.

"Maybe you can choose a new fate," Giacomo suggested. "Once we figure out where the Straightedge is, you can help us go get it. Come with us. Help us take down Nerezza."

"Then you've made your decision?"

Giacomo took the memories of Zanobius and his desire to see him again and packed them away in a trunk inside his mind. Perhaps he and Zanobius would reunite one day, but for now Giacomo needed to focus on the greater good. "Yes," Giacomo said. "I'm not going to abandon the mission."

Niccolo smiled and straightened, as if casting off a heavy yoke. "Then I'd like nothing more than to join you."

MILENA'S DISCOVERY

The quest to find the Sacred Tools had come to a standstill, and Milena seemed to be the only one who cared. Following Zanobius's departure, she had spent the day reading through Garrulous's journals, eager to find proof that the Straightedge was in Rachana. So far, though, she'd only found descriptions of Rachana's culture and history.

> *Rachana's heroes are the great and powerful*
> *warriors who have served as protectors of all*
> *that is noble and sacred to the Rachanan people.*
> *These warriors pride themselves on their*
> *strength, both of body and of spirit.*

And as fascinating as the information was, nothing she read would likely persuade the others to leave the comfort of Niccolo's villa and forge into potentially hostile territory. Still, she had a gut feeling that Garrulous's journals would ultimately prove helpful, so she kept up her research.

The morning after Zanobius left, she tucked a couple of volumes under her arm and, with Gaia perched on her shoulder, Milena wandered the villa, looking for a quiet, cozy place to read. Pietro was still sleeping upstairs, and his grating snores echoed through the house. Milena went downstairs to the library, but Savino and Enzio had claimed the room. They sat on the floor, hunched over a game board, and Milena recognized the three concentric squares with black and white stones as belonging to the Mill Game. She had played it with her sisters when she still lived back home.

She moved on to the dining room, where she found Giacomo slumped over the table, head on his arms, fast asleep. Milena wondered what made him so tired—had he lain awake thinking of Zanobius's attack, as she had? She could ask, but they had barely spoken two words to each other yesterday and she didn't feel like trying to make conversation now.

Outside, Aaminah was running through the grass, playing the lute while Luna plunged through the air. As much as Milena admired Aaminah's carefree spirit, all the noise was too much this early in the day.

Milena made her way up one hill and down another until all she could hear was the leaves rustling in the breeze. She breathed deeply, taking in the cool, crisp air.

Finally . . . quiet.

With Gaia looping gracefully through the sky, Milena propped herself against one of the monoliths and cracked open volume five of Garrulous's journals. It began with an account of Rachana's polytheistic belief system.

*I am slowly coming to terms with the fact that
my faith in a single Creator has limited
my view of the vastness of the universe. The
Rachanans worship ten deities, and each god
embodies one of the ten sacred geometry forms.
This has led me to conclude that perhaps our
beliefs aren't so different. Rather, they are like
two branches growing from the same tree.*

Milena felt the same way Garrulous must have—intrigued, but confused. The idea that the Creator was the only god in the universe had been ingrained in her since childhood, so the notion that there could be multiple gods flipped her worldview upside down.

As she read on, Milena was particularly taken with Garrulous's descriptions and drawings of the horse-Geniuses and thought how incredible it would be to see one in person.

*On the backs of their armored, winged horse-
Geniuses, the Rachanan warriors soar through
the sky, wielding a type of dagger they call a
katar and igniting brilliant displays of sacred
geometry from the gems in their Geniuses'
armor.*

Milena was absorbed in the journal for what must have been hours, because by the time she looked up, the sun had moved from her left to her right. Gaia flapped her wings, squawking plaintively.

"Just a few more pages, and then we'll go," she said.

Milena turned to the next entry, and her heart went still. Staring back at her was the image of a skeletal man with hollow eyes, a stick-thin neck, and a distended belly—exactly like the figure Giacomo had described seeing in the Wellspring!

Milena quickly gathered the other books. She was about to head back to the villa to share her discovery with Giacomo, but he found her first.

"There you are!" he called out, coming up over the rise with Mico trailing behind him. "Aaminah said she saw you leaving the house this morning, but she didn't tell me you were way out here."

"Giacomo, listen to me, I need to tell you something."

"No, I need to say something first," Giacomo insisted.

"Whatever it is, it can wait. Look!" She shoved the journal in his face, and as soon as he saw the drawing, Giacomo's eyes registered shock.

"That looks like the Lost Soul who attacked me!" Giacomo snatched the journal out of Milena's hands and began to read aloud. "'The Rachanans believe that Pretas are ghosts who haunt the place where they died. An experienced guru can usually guide a Preta to its next life, but if a Preta hungers for something vital, such as power, it will cling to this world with every piece of its soul and torment anyone who crosses its path.'"

"Pretas sound even worse than Lost Souls," Milena commented.

Giacomo gazed up from the journal, a haunted look in his eyes. "That means you were right all along. The Straightedge really is in Rachana."

"It certainly looks that way."

"Milena, I'm so sorry . . ."

"It's all right. I wasn't totally sure about the Straightedge being in Rachana, either, until I saw this drawing."

"No, I mean I'm sorry about not listening to you before," Giacomo said. "That's what I came to say. Pietro made you my teacher for a reason, and I didn't respect that. If I had, maybe Zanobius would still be here."

Milena sensed his sincerity and sadness. "Thank you for saying that. And I know it was hard to see Zanobius leave, but in the end, I think it was the best decision for all of us."

Giacomo shrugged and gazed down at his feet. "I guess so."

Standing there with his slumped shoulders, bowed head, and downcast eyes, Giacomo looked not like a powerful Tulpa, but a lost, scared boy. Still, Milena couldn't entirely forget how untamed and unpredictable his abilities were. "I have to ask . . . Do you think what happened to Zanobius could happen to you?"

Giacomo's eyes flicked up with a spark of uncertainty, then he stared off into the distance. After a long silence, he turned back to her, his posture straight, his expression full of resolve. "It's not going to happen to me," he said confidently. "Now, come on, let's go tell the others we're heading to Rachana."

But as they turned to walk back together, they heard shrill

squawks and a deep hoot coming from the direction of the villa—
Nero and Tito were sounding the alarm. Gaia stretched her neck
and let out a throaty call, joining their cries, and Mico zigzagged
through the air, chirping frantically.

Giacomo froze. "Something's wrong."

Milena clutched her brush. "Let's go."

They raced back to the villa, and as they crested the hill, Milena
gasped. An enormous ship crept across the sky, its sails billowing
in the wind, the Zizzolan Empire's black-and-white flag flapping
from the mast. It looked like the warships Milena was used to seeing docked in the Bay of Callisto, only this one had two enormous
wings extending from its hull, slowly beating up and down.

Nerezza had found them.

ESCAPE

Giacomo stared aghast at the approaching behemoth, his mind reeling. "Have you ever seen a flying ship before?"

"Never." Milena grabbed the back of Giacomo's tunic and yanked him behind a large stone. "I guess Nerezza is more creative than we give her credit for. But how did she track us down?"

Giacomo scanned the sky but didn't see any sign of Nerezza or her Genius. "I have no idea."

A dozen ropes uncoiled from the ship's deck, and a rush of black-armored soldiers descended, climbing the fifty or so feet down. They hit the ground and encircled the villa. A small team broke off and stormed the house, kicking down the front door.

Almost immediately after, Giacomo heard shouts coming from behind the house—the soldiers must've chased his friends out the back door. He couldn't see what was happening to them, but bursts of blue, yellow, and orange lit up the sky, so he knew they must be putting up a fight.

"We have to get closer," Giacomo whispered.

Milena pointed to the line of monoliths leading to the house. "We'll use those as cover."

They darted from stone to stone and made their way toward the sounds of the battle, which were intensifying: Geniuses shrieked, music rang out, energy crackled, swords clanged, and gunfire erupted.

Giacomo reached the final stone and crouched behind it, and heard Milena stop right behind him. From their new vantage point, they now had a clear view of the back of the villa where Savino, Aaminah, and Pietro stood with their backs against a crumbling brick wall.

Several dozen soldiers with swords drawn were pressing in on them, but the artists wielded their tools and, circling above, their Geniuses rained down attacks on the advancing army. From one of the upper windows, Enzio leaned out and drew his bow. He fired an arrow that pinged off a soldier's breastplate, then notched another.

Giacomo held up his drawing pencil, ready to add his power to the mix.

But just then, with a *crack*, the back door burst open, and Giacomo's attention swung from Enzio to Niccolo, who bolted across the grass. He carried the Compass in its leather sheath, which was tucked under his arm. A line of soldiers peeled away from the group to chase after him. Niccolo was quick, and it looked like he might get away, but a few soldiers were still descending from the floating ship. A long-haired soldier swung down on a rope dangling from the hull and dropped into Niccolo's path. The man wore black armor and carried a long sword, but the scar running down the side of his face made Giacomo realize the man wasn't an ordinary soldier.

He was Ozo.

The mercenary charged and clotheslined Niccolo, sweeping him off his feet. With a grunt, Niccolo slammed to the ground, and Ozo snatched the Compass from his hands.

"Give it to me!" a booming voice demanded.

A familiar portly figure strode forward.

"Oh, great. Signor Barrolo is here too," Milena muttered.

Baldassare swiped the Compass from Ozo and unsheathed it, regarding it with a devious smile. Giacomo seethed. Baldassare hadn't fought and bled to obtain the Compass. He had no right to it.

Giacomo had started to lurch forward to try to take back the Compass when Milena grabbed his wrist. He was about to protest that they should *do* something, but when he looked at Milena, her eyes were on the sky.

A harsh screech assaulted Giacomo's ears. From the clouds, Nerezza and her grotesque Genius swooped down and circled the villa.

"She's only showing her face now?" Giacomo grumbled. "What a coward."

"No, she's a strategist," Milena said. "She was keeping her distance so Tito wouldn't sense her before the ship arrived."

Victoria flew straight at Pietro's owl, jaws primed to gnash. Her fangs clamped down on Tito's wing, and she flung him away like he was a rotten piece of meat. With a thunderous crash, Tito hit the ground, kicking up a cloud of dust. By the house, Pietro collapsed with a cry, clutching his own arm, so strong was their connection.

"Pietro!" Aaminah cried, and Savino turned toward their fallen teacher.

The second Savino's and Aaminah's attention faltered, the soldiers moved in. Two tackled Savino and wrested his carving tools away; a third knocked Aaminah to the ground and smashed her lute against the wall. Its strings snapped, and with an out-of-tune squeal, the instrument died.

Ozo grabbed Savino by the collar. "Where's Zanobius?"

"In the house," Savino said through gritted teeth. Giacomo was impressed by his quick thinking.

The lie worked. Ozo rushed inside, where he would soon find countless places for someone to hide among Niccolo's antiques.

Victoria landed with a heavy *whoosh*, and two burly soldiers helped their leader dismount. The train of Nerezza's black robe followed her like a long shadow. She stalked toward Niccolo, who was still lying flat on the ground.

"Niccolo Abbate, I believe you have something that belongs to me."

Niccolo's hand went to his gem. As it glowed, his face flushed with color. Buoyed by the surge of energy, he rose to his feet and yanked off his necklace. The chain dangled from his raised fist. "Return the Compass and let everyone go!"

A sudden coldness hit Giacomo's core, and he grabbed Milena's arm. "No . . ."

Milena blanched. "He wouldn't . . ."

Nerezza's confidence cracked, and she stepped away from Niccolo. "Take the necklace from him!" she ordered.

The two burly soldiers marched toward Niccolo, who closed his eyes and bowed his head, as if offering a prayer to the Creator.

"Get down!" Giacomo yelled, pulling Milena with him.

Niccolo cast his gem at the ground, and it erupted in a blinding purple flash. Victoria screeched and retreated skyward. Without his Genius to channel the energy, wild lengths of light snaked out of Niccolo's shattered gem and thrashed chaotically, taking out any soldier within fifty feet. One blazing strand lashed Nerezza, toppling her down the hill; another struck Baldassare, causing him to drop the Compass. Within seconds, nearly the entire army had been neutralized—temporarily, at least.

As the last traces of purple light flickered away, Niccolo swayed. His knees buckled, and he collapsed.

"I have to help Niccolo!" Giacomo shouted. Scrambling to his feet, he bolted from behind the stone.

"I'll get the Compass!" Milena called after him.

By the time Giacomo reached Niccolo, soldiers were beginning to stagger to their feet. Giacomo dropped to his knees and propped Niccolo's head on his lap.

Niccolo groaned, and his eyes fluttered open. "Giacomo . . . Get out of here . . ."

"No, we had a deal. You were supposed to come with us."

"I chose . . . my fate . . ." Niccolo's voice grew weak, until it was barely a whisper.

Giacomo wanted to tell Niccolo that there were other ways to finally *do* something, better ways to honor his parents' memory than self-sacrifice. But as Giacomo stared into Niccolo's half-lidded eyes, the life drained from them, and the lesson was for him alone. Niccolo let out a soft exhale and went limp.

"Be at peace," Giacomo said softly. Mico let out a sad trill.

A gruff voice broke the silence. "Where's Zanobius?!"

Giacomo wheeled around to find Ozo marching toward him. Grieving would have to wait. Giacomo jumped up and jabbed his pencil at the air. Ozo dodged Mico's streak of light and kept coming.

"Where are you hiding him?!" Ozo demanded.

Giacomo knew he couldn't use Savino's ploy a second time. "Zanobius isn't here! He's gone!"

"You're lying!" Ozo lunged, swinging his sword. Giacomo felt the blade nick his arm, and he stumbled backward. Mico swerved a little as he looped through the air.

His heart pounding, Giacomo sprinted for the first place he saw that offered cover: Niccolo's house.

He barreled through the front door and down the hall, veering into the labyrinth of antiques. Behind him, Ozo's boots clomped across the wooden floor, coming fast.

Giacomo ducked behind a stack of chairs, then wriggled into the narrow space between two armoires. He cupped Mico in his hands and whispered to his Genius to stay quiet.

The footfalls slowed. Giacomo spied the mercenary through a tiny opening between the stacks of furniture. Ozo came to an abrupt stop only a few feet from Giacomo's hiding place.

"Come out, Giacomo!" Ozo shouted, hurling aside a chair with so much force that it splintered against the wall. Ozo bored through Niccolo's collection, and Giacomo winced as more furniture thudded and crashed around him.

"Tell me where Zanobius is, and this all ends!" Ozo shouted, then pushed over a mirror to look behind it. Glass shattered, and shards skittered across the floor.

If Giacomo stayed put, it was simply a matter of time before Ozo rooted him out. His only option was to make a break for it and try to regroup with Milena and the others outside.

Out of the corner of his eye, Giacomo glimpsed a familiar figure slink from the shadows and raise a bow. Enzio took aim at Ozo and let his arrow fly. With a meaty *thunk*, the arrow lodged in Ozo's shoulder, between the plates of his armor. The mercenary roared and spun around, stalking toward Enzio.

Giacomo waited for Ozo to pass, then he thrust out his pencil. Mico hit the armoire with a pulse of light and it toppled, crashing onto Ozo, who let out a muffled yell.

Giacomo burst from behind the pile of broken furniture. "Enzio, come on!"

Together, they tore down the hall and bolted out the back door. Giacomo found Pietro sitting against the wall, clutching his arm while Aaminah played a soft tune on her flute, which she kept hidden in her boot for emergencies.

"Where have you been?" Savino snapped. He stood guard, once again wielding his carving tool, ready to strike if more soldiers came their way. Most were still recovering from Niccolo's attack.

"Sorry," Giacomo said. "Have you seen Milena?"

"I'm coming!" Milena shouted. She sprinted toward Giacomo, Compass in hand.

With no time to waste, Giacomo passed the Tool from Milena to Pietro. "We need you to make a portal to the Rachanan palace," Giacomo urged.

"Why do you want to go there?" Savino demanded.

"Because that's where we're going to find the Straightedge," Milena explained. "I found this drawing in Garrulous's journals—"

"You can explain later!" Enzio interrupted. "I'll go wherever, as long as it's not back home with my father." He nodded toward Baldassare, who had retreated to a safe distance and was shouting at soldiers. From behind the hill, Victoria rose up, wings heaving. Nerezza sat on her Genius's neck, her torn cloak flapping in the wind. On her order, the army began advancing. A line of handgunners dropped to their knees, leveled their weapons, and lit the fuses on the guns' barrels.

Anticipating the attack, Milena and Giacomo quickly drew up sacred geometry shields before the guns flashed and boomed. The metal balls ricocheted off the shields, then fell harmlessly away. The handgunners reloaded as the next wave of soldiers advanced.

"Rachana it is!" Pietro hollered. "Now, help me up." Savino and

Giacomo hoisted their teacher to his feet. Tito staggered over to them, his wing drooping at his side.

Pietro concentrated for a moment, like he was drawing up a deeply buried memory, then he opened the Compass and spun it. The portal swelled, burning brightly. Savino, Giacomo, and Enzio provided cover while Milena and Aaminah helped Pietro through. Their Geniuses followed.

"You two go!" Enzio shouted, firing off another arrow. "I'm right behind you!"

Savino and Nero disappeared into the brightness, Giacomo and Mico on their heels. As the light enveloped him, Giacomo turned back to check on Enzio, horrified to discover Ozo heading their way.

"Enzio, look out!" Giacomo shouted, but his warning came too late. The last thing Giacomo saw before the current of light swept him away was Ozo knocking Enzio to the ground and barreling toward the portal.

Luminous waves surrounded Giacomo, carrying him through space. A few seconds later he was launched out the other side of the portal, where his fall was broken by something soft. Mico poked his head out of the sand and chirped with annoyance.

Giacomo staggered to his feet and snatched the Compass away from Pietro, holding its legs to the circle of light. "I have to close it right now!"

"What about Enzio?" Milena asked, looking worried.

"He's not going to make it," Giacomo said sadly, then he offered Enzio a silent apology and spun the Compass. But before the portal vanished, Ozo dove out of the light and somersaulted past Giacomo. He rolled to his feet, sword at the ready, Enzio's broken arrow still lodged in his left shoulder.

"I know you're hiding Zanobius! Where is he?"

"I already told you, I don't know!" Giacomo shouted.

Ozo moved toward Giacomo, but Savino slashed his carving tool, and Nero projected a lattice of blue that coiled around the mercenary, stopping him in his tracks.

"Let me out of here!" Ozo demanded. He struck his sword against the light, but the steel shaft bounced back, spitting sparks.

With the mercenary detained, Giacomo and his friends turned their attention to Enzio's predicament.

"What's going to happen to him?" Aaminah said, her voice full of concern.

"Enzio will be all right," Giacomo said, trying to ease the guilt gnawing at his gut. "Baldassare wouldn't let any harm come to him . . . right?"

"Except Enzio knows where we were going," Savino pointed out. "What if he tells Nerezza?"

Giacomo shook his head. "No . . . he wouldn't."

"How can you be sure?" Milena asked.

I can't . . .

"Because he hates his father and Nerezza as much as we do," Giacomo insisted. "The best way we can all help Enzio now is to see this mission through."

"I agree," Pietro said. "And let's always remember the sacrifice Niccolo made to save us all. He was a hero." After a moment of silence, Pietro spoke again. "Now, tell me, how does the palace look? Still as magnificent as I remember?"

Giacomo scanned his surroundings, finding nothing but rolling dunes dotted with scrubby trees. He plodded through the sand and up a slope. "Uh . . . I don't see a palace."

"That's not a good sign . . ." Pietro muttered.

Giacomo's heart sank. It was midday, and the sun was scorching. He was about to resign himself to being stranded in the middle of a desert when he reached the top of the dune and stared down at an impressive fortress, its massive stone walls in the shape of a ten-pointed star. And at its center stood a spectacular white stone palace with dozens of spires and archways. Atop the main structure sat an enormous dome that reflected the sun in a blazing golden glow.

"We made it . . ." Giacomo said in awe. "We're in Rachana."

THE HOLDOUT

From atop her Genius, Nerezza stared down at Niccolo's lifeless body. Years ago, after Niccolo's failed assassination attempt against her, Nerezza had driven the Abbate family to ruin as punishment. Niccolo had somehow eluded her all this time, but no longer. With a flick of her brush, she cast a violet beam at the shattered hull of Niccolo's gem. She drew it toward her, grasping it from the light. Once she returned to the palace, she would add it to her collection, where it rightfully belonged.

"We searched the villa," Minister Strozzi announced. "There was no sign of where Giacomo might be headed."

Nerezza had watched Ozo follow the boy into the portal. *He will know where I can find Giacomo.* But Ozo was one swordsman against five artists and their Geniuses. The likelihood of his getting a message to her seemed near impossible.

"What about Zanobius?" Nerezza asked. She hadn't seen him at all during the battle.

"There's no sign of him, either, I'm afraid," Strozzi said.

Where could he have gone? Nerezza wondered, shaken by the thought of the Tulpa wreaking havoc somewhere in her empire at that very moment.

"Shall we bury the body?" Minister Strozzi asked, glancing down at Niccolo's corpse.

"No," Nerezza said. "Leave it be. Victoria is getting hungry."

Strozzi's wrinkled brow hinted at his revulsion. "Yes, Your Eminence." He ordered his soldiers back to the ship, which hovered between two rolling hills.

Nerezza turned her attention to Barrolo's son, who struggled to escape the grip of two of her mightiest soldiers, Luca and Luigi. She had plucked the twins from an orphanage at the age of ten after witnessing them carrying a tree trunk a hundred yards like it was nothing. Barrolo stood alongside them, whining that they should release his boy.

"Where did Giacomo go?" Nerezza demanded.

Enzio met her with a defiant stare. "I don't know."

"Did he and his friends discover the location of the other Sacred Tools?"

"If they did, they didn't tell me." Enzio's chin jutted out, and his eyes darted away, exactly like Barrolo's did when he was lying. *Like father, like son.*

Nerezza edged closer. "Tell me where they went, or I'll let Victoria pick you apart."

The great bird bared her fangs and growled. The boy's eyes flashed fear, but he didn't break.

"If you think I know something, then you're not going to feed me to your Genius," he challenged.

Barrolo pleaded with Enzio. "Son, tell the Supreme Creator where Giacomo went and we can return home. If not for me, for your mother."

Mention of his mother seemed to hit a nerve with the boy. Enzio looked down sadly, then after a moment, his expression hardened again. "I'm not going back home."

Baldassare served Enzio a sharp smack across his cheek. "You will learn respect!"

Enzio spat in his father's face. "Make me."

Barrolo's face turned red. Nerezza noted that the son seemed stronger than the father. Perhaps some time in the company of her Minister of Security would change that.

"Lock him up belowdecks," Nerezza ordered.

Luca and Luigi picked up the thrashing Enzio and carried him to the ship.

"You don't need Enzio, Your Eminence," Barrolo argued. "Just give me some time. My black market connections led us to Niccolo. It won't be long before they help us find Giacomo again."

"Your son knows something, and I aim to discover what," Nerezza said. "He belongs to me now."

"No!" Barrolo blustered. "You . . . you can't!"

"Keep talking and you'll be walking back to Virenzia!"

Barrolo immediately fell silent, his face twisted into an angry scowl. He whipped around and stormed up the gangplank.

Once the injured had been tended to and everyone was aboard, Nerezza ordered the ship back to Virenzia. Its great mechanical wings heaved, pushing the groaning beast skyward. As Nerezza led her army back home, she told herself this was only a temporary setback, one that she would remedy in due course.

And though Enzio had proved more rebellious than Nerezza had anticipated, it was only a matter of time before he told her what she wanted to know. Everyone had a breaking point.

SAMRAAT AJEET

At the sight of the Rachanan fortress, Giacomo suddenly felt vulnerable in this desert with no cover. He scanned the cloudless sky, expecting warriors on horse-Geniuses to swoop down at any moment and surround the group. Thankfully, none appeared.

"We can't just walk up to the samraat's front gate, knock, and expect to be welcomed inside." Savino clutched his carving tool as Nero's projection continued to spiral around Ozo.

"But Pietro's been a guest at the palace before," Milena said.

"Last time, I was there by invitation," Pietro said, shaking his head. "Simply by stepping on Rachanan soil, we've already violated the peace treaty, but hopefully I can persuade Samraat Jagesh to hear us out."

"You want to get into that fortress so badly? I'll get you in," Ozo offered.

"And why would you help us?" Giacomo asked.

Ozo looked across the empty landscape. "Because I'm not

interested in sticking around in this dust bowl. I want you to send me back to Zizzola." His eyes went to the Compass.

"So you can keep hunting Zanobius?" Giacomo said angrily. "No way."

Milena grabbed Giacomo's arm and pulled him aside. "This might be our best chance at getting past those gates," she said in a hushed voice. "Since Ozo's from Rachana, the guards might listen to him. The longer he's with us, the more of a danger he is to you."

Giacomo considered Milena's idea. Zizzola was a big place. If Giacomo lied about the direction in which Zanobius had been headed, the chances of Ozo tracking him down were slim. Giacomo glared at the mercenary through his shimmering prison. "Let him go, Savino. I think we have a deal."

With Ozo now free, the group trudged down the dunes until they came to a wide street paved with flagstones in repeating hexagonal patterns. To Giacomo's left, the sun glimmered off the surface of a river leading to a distant city. The group turned right, following the road until it ended at the fortress's towering arched entrance. The bronze doors barring their entry were covered with panels that depicted warriors amid battle, flying on horse-Geniuses. The outer wall was constructed with gigantic blocks of stones that interlocked like pieces of a puzzle. High above, a dozen warriors in gold helmets and armor patrolled the battlements.

One of the warriors stopped and looked down. She shouted something in Rachanan, and a moment later, archers appeared on the wall, aiming arrows down at them.

"She's ordering us to stop or they'll shoot," Ozo translated.

The group halted, and Pietro stepped to Ozo's side. "Please

inform the Rachanans that Pietro Vasari has arrived and humbly asks to speak with His Excellency Samraat Jagesh and—"

Ozo cut him off. "I'll do the talking, old man."

For the next five minutes, Ozo and the woman in charge argued back and forth. More than once, Ozo threw up his arms in frustration and muttered, "She's impossible!" Giacomo began to worry that trusting Ozo to talk their way in might have been a terrible mistake.

Finally, the woman motioned for two of her fellow warriors to follow her and they disappeared from their post.

"What did she tell you?" Giacomo asked. "Are we going to get to talk with Samraat Jagesh?"

"Not likely . . ." Ozo said. "According to her, Samraat Jagesh died two years ago."

Pietro sighed heavily. "That doesn't bode well."

A metallic groan rang out, and the gates slowly swung open, revealing the female warrior and her counterparts. Behind them, a line of silver-armored warriors were mounted on horseback, but there was still no sign of any horse-Geniuses. Instead of swords, the warriors all clutched oversized daggers with horizontal hilts, called katars, according to Milena.

The woman uttered something to Ozo, who in turn translated: "Her name is Lavanthi, granddaughter of the late Samraat Jagesh. Her father, Samraat Ajeet, is willing to meet with you."

On the other side of the fortress's gate, Giacomo discovered an environment worlds apart from the barren landscape outside. Here, there were lush gardens with countless varieties of colorful flowers, perfectly manicured bushes, and trees with singing birds. Impressive stone fountains flanked long reflecting pools, where

frogs croaked on lotus flowers. In the center of the fortress, raised high on a platform, was the samraat's palace, shimmering like a mirage. Giacomo couldn't wait to draw it—assuming he would be around long enough to do so.

Ozo stuck out his arm, stopping Giacomo. "I held up my end of the deal. Now send me back to Zizzola."

But before Giacomo could take the Compass off his back, Lavanthi barked another order.

"She's demanding we all turn over our weapons," Ozo explained.

The artists grudgingly surrendered their pencils, carving tools, and brushes. Aaminah gave her flute to one of the gold-clad men, who tossed it into a sack with the other items. Lavanthi glared at Ozo and pointed at his sword. Ozo argued back. Giacomo guessed he was trying to explain that he wouldn't be staying, but the warriors didn't seem to care. While two men pinned Ozo's arms behind him, Lavanthi unstrapped his sword belt, disarming him. Next, Lavanthi reached for the sheathed Compass slung across Giacomo's back. To her eye, its handle must have looked like the hilt of a sword.

Giacomo backed away. "Ozo, tell her this isn't what she thinks. It's not dangerous."

Lavanthi raised her katar, pointing it at Giacomo's chest. He didn't need a translator to understand she was serious. Without further argument, he handed over the Compass.

Giacomo shrugged at Ozo. "Sorry, I guess your trip is going to be delayed."

Ozo glared back, jaw clenched.

Lavanthi whistled sharply, and from behind a tall row of hedges, three winged horses in protective armor lazily trotted out. Their gems were embedded in the crowns of their faceplates, but the creatures didn't at all resemble the majestic, powerful horse-Geniuses of legend. These Geniuses were emaciated, their heads slung low, their featherless wings drooping like sails on a windless day.

Aaminah gasped and grabbed Giacomo's arm. "What's wrong with them?"

Mico let out a wary trill. Giacomo shivered as a haunting thought fixed in his mind. "They look like Lost Souls . . ."

Lavanthi and her fellow warriors mounted their frail horse-Geniuses and escorted Giacomo and his friends down the central path between two long reflecting pools and up the palace steps. Once they reached the top, Lavanthi dismounted and hollered at the group.

"Your Geniuses have to wait outside," Ozo informed them.

Until Giacomo knew what was afflicting the horse-Geniuses, he wasn't eager to let Mico and the bird-Geniuses out of his sight. "She already took our tools," he complained. "Our Geniuses won't harm anyone."

But arguing was pointless. If they wanted to speak with the samraat, they had to follow Lavanthi's orders. Mico and the other Geniuses fluttered up to the eaves. Tito stayed on the ground, still nursing his wing.

As the group headed toward the palace doors, Giacomo pulled Ozo aside, keeping his voice low. "By the way, would you mind not mentioning that I'm a Tulpa? I don't want the samraat flying into a rage before we have a chance to get the Compass back."

"Sure. But the minute you do, you better send me back to Zizzola." Ozo clomped away.

Lavanthi led everyone through the immense palace halls and Giacomo marveled at the intricate sacred geometry mosaics that adorned the floor, the walls, and the arched ceilings. They passed by bronze-clad warriors holding spears and stepped into a huge chamber that was even more opulent than the rest of the palace. Torches mounted on columns cast everything with a warm glow. On a dais in the center of the room, an older man with dark skin and a short white beard sat on a golden throne covered in jewels and topped with a canopy. Giacomo assumed this was the man they had come to meet: Samraat Ajeet.

He wore long red robes embroidered with silvery spiral patterns. Atop his head sat a dome-shaped headpiece that tapered to a point. On the walls hung dozens of large-scale portraits of regally posed men and women in similar garments. Each one stared at the viewer with the same severe expression as the man currently settled on the throne. Giacomo wondered if having a sour temperament was a requirement for becoming a samraat.

Lavanthi dropped to one knee and bowed her head to the samraat. Then she rose and spoke to him, periodically gesturing at the new arrivals.

As he listened, Samraat Ajeet regarded Giacomo and his friends with a scrutinizing gaze. The look—full of malice—was one Giacomo had recognized on the faces of other adults who

abused their authority: his cruel caretakers at the orphanage, the nasty soldiers who patrolled the streets of Virenzia, and, most prominently, Nerezza herself.

Giacomo met Ajeet's gaze with a spiteful look of his own. He wanted the samraat to know he wasn't intimidated by him. Ajeet refused to look away, even once his daughter had finished bringing him up-to-date.

Giacomo broke first when he sensed someone else watching him. He turned his attention to a young, slender man standing off to the side. A few sprigs of hair sprouted from the man's chin, and his lip showed the faint beginnings of a mustache. In stark contrast to his lavish surroundings, he wore an unadorned pale yellow robe and head wrap. His dark brown eyes fixed on Giacomo, studying him intently. But unlike Ajeet's harsh expression, the young man's gaze was full of curiosity, as if he recognized Giacomo and was trying to place where they'd met. Giacomo was confident they had never crossed paths.

Pietro shuffled forward, his walking stick clacking against the marble floor. "Ozo, please thank His Excellency for meeting with us," he said with a polite bow. "And let him know what an honor it is to be visiting his great empire again."

Ozo began to translate, but Samraat Ajeet cut him off and, to Giacomo's surprise, replied in Zizzolan. "We may speak directly. My father insisted I learn your language to keep the peace between our people—a requirement I regret not passing on to my own daughter. Now, if it is true you are the great Pietro Vasari, then the honor is all mine. But my father told me Pietro died many years ago."

Pietro chuckled. "Rumors have a way of spreading far and wide, even across the sea, apparently. I assure you, I am Pietro Vasari and I am very much alive, though perhaps a bit worse for the wear."

"My father admired your talent. He even displayed some of your paintings in the palace halls."

"And may I offer my condolences, Your Excellency. Samraat Jagesh was not only a champion of the arts, but also a champion of peace and justice."

"Thank you. He was a great leader, open-minded and diplomatic," Ajeet mused. "But even he would view your arrival here as a violation of the treaty between our empires."

"Perhaps . . . But he would still hear me out before turning us away," Pietro argued, a hint of his familiar gruffness coming through.

After a moment of consideration, Ajeet nodded. "Then tell me, why are you here?"

"As your daughter probably told you, my students and I have Geniuses. This has made us targets of Supreme Creator Nerezza. We've been on the run from her."

"And you want me to offer you protection?"

"A roof over our heads and some food is all we require," Pietro said.

"I'm sorry for your predicament," Ajeet said in a tone Giacomo found insincere. "But the safety of my people comes first. The last thing I need is for Nerezza to show up with her army, searching for you and your Geniuses. I cannot offer you aid."

"Your Excellency," Giacomo blurted out. "We're not a danger to you or your people. Nerezza has no idea we're here."

"The answer is no!" Ajeet said sternly, then barked an order at Lavanthi in their native language. She stepped in front of the group and raised her katar, then pointed at the door, directing them to leave.

"You can't send us back to Zizzola!" Giacomo shouted at Ajeet.

Pietro grabbed his arm. "That's enough, Giacomo. Show some respect."

"Why? He's not showing us any," Giacomo muttered.

"Wait." The young man who had been observing Giacomo stepped forward. "I have a few questions."

"I've made my decision, Guru Yaday," Ajeet snapped. "I don't need your counsel in this matter."

Giacomo looked at the young man with new interest. *He's a guru?* But how could someone so young be an adviser to a samraat?

"But, Your Excellency, don't you find it odd that Giacomo was able to travel through the empire, apparently unnoticed, without horses or supplies?" the guru asked. "And according to Lavanthi, they walked up to the gate, seemingly from out of nowhere. Who could survive the harsh conditions of our desert and approach without being seen?"

"We . . . we flew here on Pietro's Genius," Giacomo said, trying to cover.

"All six of you flew on the back of one Genius? I doubt that." Yaday pointed to the Compass slung over Lavanthi's shoulder, and she handed it to him. He gazed at the circular pattern on the handle, then pulled off the sheath. He gasped and turned to Ajeet. "I knew I sensed a powerful energy when they entered. Look!"

Ajeet leaned forward, peering at the golden Tool. "Could that really be . . . ?"

Yaday snapped the Compass open and held it reverently up to Ajeet. "The Compass of the Gods," Yaday pronounced.

"No, that's the *Creator's* Compass," Giacomo corrected. "It's one of the Sacred Tools."

"You call it by one name," Guru Yaday said, "but in Rachana, we know it as one of three Divine Yantras—powerful instruments used by our ten gods to keep the great world turning."

Savino snorted dismissively. "Sorry to disappoint you, but we found the Compass in Zizzola, so it can't belong to your gods."

Yaday turned to Giacomo. "How did you come across it, exactly?"

"Well . . ." Giacomo cleared his throat, then gave an abbreviated account of how he, Savino, Aaminah, and Milena had followed a trail of clues through Zizzola—clues that eventually led them to the cave in the mountains where they discovered the Compass. He introduced Ozo as the man who had been hired to protect them on their quest and purposely left out any mention of the Wellspring or Tulpas.

Once Ajeet heard Giacomo's account, his brow wrinkled. "Pietro, it seems you didn't tell me the whole story. Why are you really here?"

Before Pietro could answer, Giacomo spoke up. "It's true, we came looking for more than a safe place to hide. We think one of the other Sacred Tools might be somewhere in Rachana."

"You seek the Straightedge," Yaday said knowingly.

Giacomo and Milena shared elated smiles. "We were right," Milena said. "It is here!"

"And you intend to steal it?" Ajeet's voice rose in anger.

"No . . . Well, not from *you*," Giacomo tried to explain. "From the Preta who's guarding it."

Ajeet's and Yaday's faces became terribly confused. "Preta?" Ajeet said. "What are you talking about?"

Giacomo described his vision: the Straightedge in the cavern with lava, and the skeletal spirit who'd attacked him to protect it.

Ajeet waved Yaday over to him and the two men conferred privately. Every few seconds, one or the other would shoot Giacomo a look of grave concern, causing him to wonder if he would be forced to return to Zizzola empty-handed. Finally, Yaday stepped to the edge of the dais and gazed down at Giacomo.

"You've already acquired the Compass, and now you've been able to visualize the Straightedge . . . How is it that such a young artist seems to be linked so closely with the Sacred Tools, as you call them?"

Giacomo didn't like where this line of questioning was headed. "I got lucky, I guess?"

"No, there is something different about you." Yaday approached, circling Giacomo. "You have a powerful aura as well."

Giacomo shrank from Yaday's probing stare. "Probably just the Compass's energy rubbing off on me."

Yaday stopped and leaned in, his face inches from Giacomo's nose. "What are you, Giacomo?"

Giacomo's breath caught. *How could Yaday know the truth?* It was as if the guru were looking not just into his eyes, but into his soul, as well. Giacomo felt a warmth spread across his chest and glanced down, half expecting to see the Creator's Pattern glowing.

When Giacomo had announced to Nerezza that he was a Tulpa, he'd known it would make him a target. The words had been an act of rebellion against Nerezza, a commitment to finding the Sacred Tools and ending her reign. So why was he so nervous to tell the truth to these strangers?

Maybe because once they know, Lavanthi will run me through with her dagger? he thought darkly.

"I'm a Tulpa," Giacomo said, releasing a huge exhale.

Yaday's eyes brightened and he let out a tiny gasp. "I never thought I'd have the honor of meeting a Nirmita," he said.

As soon as Yaday said the word, Lavanthi and the other warriors in the throne room all stared at Giacomo, looking stunned.

"Nirmita?" Giacomo asked, self-conscious, but thankful they hadn't immediately attacked him.

"In our language, it means 'the one who has been created,'" Yaday explained, then turned to Ajeet. "This would seem to change the situation, Your Excellency."

"Indeed . . ." Ajeet rose to his feet and opened his arms. "Welcome to Rachana, Giacomo."

THE LEGEND OF VRAMA

Samraat Ajeet strode from his throne room, beckoning Giacomo and his friends to follow.

"I'm not really in the mood for a tour," Ozo grumbled, holding his injured shoulder.

"Lavanthi can take you to the healers," Yaday offered. "They'll tend to your wound."

"Anything to get me away from this lot," Ozo said, casting a sidelong glare at Giacomo.

While Ozo and Lavanthi disappeared down a long hall, Samraat Ajeet led the rest of the group out the back of the palace and onto a large terrace overlooking the grounds. The sun hung low in the sky, turning it a brilliant orange. Off in the distance, Giacomo spotted a lumbering elephant.

Savino leaned over to Giacomo. "I don't get it," he said in a hushed voice. "The samraat finds out you're a Tulpa, and he invites us to stay?"

Giacomo shrugged. "It wasn't the response I expected, either. But if it helps us get closer to the Straightedge, I'm not about to argue with him."

"And what did Yaday mean, 'This would seem to change the situation'?" Savino said. "What do Ajeet and his guru want from you?"

Yaday stepped over to them. "Is there a question I can answer?"

"No," Savino said brusquely. "We're fine."

Ajeet directed everyone's attention across the manicured lawns to a collection of buildings with red tiled roofs. "Our elite warriors and their Geniuses live over there," Ajeet explained. "But the stables aren't as full as they once were . . ."

A stable boy approached, leading an armored horse-Genius with a dull grayish coat. Like Lavanthi's Genius, this one was bone thin, with sagging wings. The Genius groaned as Ajeet took its reins. "It's all right, Kavi."

"Is this your Genius?" Giacomo asked.

Ajeet nodded and stroked the horse's neck. "Shortly after I took the throne, I noticed Kavi was becoming lethargic and irritable. His wings molted, and he lost the strength to fly. Finally, his power waned altogether, and he was unable to project the simplest of shapes. If something isn't done to save him, he will soon die, as many other Geniuses already have."

"Can I pet him?" Aaminah asked.

With a nod, Ajeet stepped aside.

Aaminah let Kavi sniff her hand, then she gently laid it on his snout. Kavi whinnied softly. Aaminah hung her head, and her eyes filled with sorrow. "I can feel his suffering." She looked up at Ajeet. "I'm a healer. Maybe I can help. How did Kavi and the others get so sick?"

"It's not a sickness, exactly," Ajeet said.

"At first, that's what we thought too," Yaday explained. "Our own healers worked night and day, but nothing they did seemed to help. Then we got word that Geniuses in other cities had fallen ill too, and we began to suspect there might be another force at work. Thanks to Giacomo's insight, we now have an idea who's likely behind the demise of the Geniuses—Vrama."

"Who's that?" Milena asked.

"He was Rachana's first samraat," Ajeet said.

"And based on Giacomo's description of the Preta he saw, we believe it's him," Yaday said.

"But how did he get the Straightedge?" Giacomo asked. "And how is he using it to make your Geniuses powerless?"

"Follow me," Yaday said. "Once you hear Vrama's story, things should become clearer."

Back inside, Yaday took them to a hidden alcove underneath a staircase. He pulled a key from his pocket and unlocked the door. Behind it, stone steps wound into darkness. Torch in hand, Yaday guided them downward.

They entered a vast underground chamber buttressed by rows of thick, worn columns. Frescoes covered the rock walls, but instead of being painted, the images had been carved into the stone. More torches were mounted on the walls, and Yaday lit them one by one. The room filled with flickering light.

"This was the original throne room," Ajeet explained. "Here, the early samraats reigned during the age of the monad. Centuries later, the current palace was built over it."

Yaday moved toward the far end of the room, using his torch to illuminate another carved stone wall. This one was more elaborate than the others. "This relief depicts the story of how the ten gods gave Vrama possession of the Divine Yantras—or the Sacred Tools, as you know them."

Across the top of the relief were carvings of ten male and female figures clad in intricately patterned robes. Each god held a long staff topped by one of the ten sacred geometry shapes, from the monad's circle to the decad's ten-sided decagon.

Giacomo's eyes were drawn to the center of the image, where a man in a warrior's armor flew on a horse-Genius, ringed by rays of light. The Compass, the Straightedge, and the Pencil hovered above him.

Giacomo had been taught that the Creator had controlled the Tools. Still, this new theory was intriguing. "Why did the gods give Vrama the Sacred Tools?" he asked.

"At the beginning of our current time cycle, the gods began a search to find the bravest, wisest, and mightiest warrior to lead the people," Yaday explained. "To help them determine who was worthy of this great honor, they held a competition." Yaday pointed to the bottom of the carving, where warriors and their horse-Geniuses clashed with one another. "Vrama emerged triumphant, so the gods declared him the first samraat of Rachana and granted him the use of the three Divine Yantras."

"For many years, Vrama used the Yantras for the betterment of Rachana and its people, as any samraat would aspire to do," Ajeet cut in. "The Compass allowed him to travel to all corners of the empire so he could help solve disputes between warring tribes; the Straightedge amplified his Genius's powers, allowing Vrama to cure droughts and protect coastal villages from storms; with the Pencil, he designed and built temples across the growing empire and devised a crop-irrigation system that put an end to famine. With Rachana now peaceful and prosperous, the gods returned to take back what belonged to them."

"But wielding so much power had corrupted Vrama, and ruling Rachana wasn't enough for him," Yaday said. "He wanted to over-throw the gods and take their place. So Vrama used the Yantras to make his palace fly, and he ascended to the heavens."

"Hold on," Savino interrupted. "I was following you until the part about the flying palace. Now I know this is all made up."

"Yet you believe a single Creator came to Zizzola and used the Sacred Tools to bring into being everything in existence," Yaday challenged.

Savino crossed his arms and huffed. "Sounds more believable than Vrama soaring into space in a giant palace and warring with a bunch of gods."

Giacomo nudged Savino. "Will you just let him finish? I want to hear the rest."

Yaday brushed off Savino's comments and continued. "Vrama and the gods clashed for seven days and seven nights. Eventually, the gods took back the Compass and the Pencil, but Vrama clung to the Straightedge. So the gods opened a portal and cast Vrama and his palace back to earth, where they crashed in a fiery explosion. The force was so great the ground erupted in hundreds of different places, creating all of Rachana's volcanoes." Yaday passed his torch over an image of lava-spewing volcanoes circling a giant crater.

Ajeet picked up the tale, pointing to the carving of the crater.

"Over the ages, the crash site became myth, a mystery that my predecessors and their gurus sought to unravel. Then, a couple of years ago, the Straightedge's resting place was revealed to Guru Pankaj during one of his meditations."

Yaday nodded slowly, his expression traced with sadness. "My teacher persuaded Samraat Jagesh to assemble a team of warriors and lead a mission to retrieve the Straightedge. They never returned."

Ajeet explained how he had led a search party, hoping to find his father and the others. Instead, he discovered an enormous caldera that apparently had formed after one of Rachana's many volcanoes erupted and caved in. Everyone had perished in what appeared to have been a tragic accident. Refusing to put any more lives at risk, Ajeet called off the search for his people and the Straightedge. But before returning home, Ajeet and his warriors performed a funeral ritual for those they had lost—Samraat Jagesh, Guru Pankaj, and the warriors, including Lavanthi's husband.

Aaminah gasped. "How horrible . . ."

Ajeet turned to Giacomo. "Not long after, our horse-Geniuses began to weaken. At the time, we thought it was a coincidence, but now it seems clear that my father's death was no accident. Your vision confirms our worst fears: Vrama still haunts the site where his palace crashed, and he killed my father and our people for trespassing."

"No wonder he was so furious when he saw me," Giacomo said.

"I read that Pretas are tied to the place where they died," Milena said. "If Vrama can't leave the caldera, how is he harming the Geniuses?"

"He has to be using the Straightedge in some way," Ajeet said.

"But I thought it could only amplify a Genius's power, not take it away," Giacomo pointed out.

"Vrama has had thousands of years to hone the Straightedge's capability," Yaday said. "It seems he's devised a way to alter and extend its power."

Giacomo shivered. *Could Vrama drain Mico's power?* "If that's true, then Vrama is unstoppable."

"Not necessarily," Ajeet said, a gleam in his eye. "Isn't that right, Yaday?"

Yaday froze, like Ajeet had put him on the spot. He looked down, scratched the few hairs on his chin, and sighed. "There is a way to vanquish him for good . . . But it will be extremely dangerous." He glanced up at Giacomo. "For both of us."

Giacomo looked between the samraat and his guru, unable to imagine how this was going to end well for him. "But you two just got through telling me how Vrama killed a bunch of Rachana's best warriors. Why would I want to go anywhere near that caldera?"

"Because our Geniuses will go extinct if Vrama keeps hold of the Straightedge," Ajeet said.

"And your abilities allowed you to acquire the Compass," Yaday added.

"But it was trapped inside a glowing shape, not in the clutches of a murderous, half-dead warrior-ghost-man!" Giacomo argued.

Aaminah grabbed his arm. "Giacomo, Geniuses are suffering. We have to help."

Giacomo looked to his teacher, who had been leaning against a column this whole time, quietly listening from the shadows. "What do you think I should do, Master Pietro?"

"You were brought into this world too late to help save Zizzola's

Geniuses," Pietro said. "But in Rachana, you have the chance to make a difference."

Part of Giacomo wanted to get Mico and his friends' Geniuses as far away from the threat of Vrama as possible, but he knew he wouldn't be able to live with himself if he abandoned Rachana in its time of need.

Giacomo met Ajeet's expectant gaze. "I'll do whatever I can to stop Vrama," he said.

"We all will," Aaminah added, then turned to Milena and Savino. "Right?"

"Of course," Milena said. "There's no way I would let you two face something like this alone."

"Sure, I'll help," Savino said. "On one condition."

"What's that?" Ajeet asked.

"Once Giacomo gets the Straightedge from Vrama, you have to give us back the Compass and let us leave with the Sacred Tools."

Ajeet considered the request, then bowed his head. "Once Vrama is defeated and our Geniuses regain their power, the Sacred Tools are yours. You have my word."

Giacomo emerged from the palace's bowels, overwhelmed by the task ahead of him and exhausted from the harrowing events of the day. It seemed hard to believe that just this morning, they'd been fighting Nerezza and her sky-ship army.

A team of brightly dressed servants greeted the group outside, where Giacomo and his friends were reunited with their Geniuses. Yaday explained that they would be taken to their quarters.

The servants escorted everyone along a path that ran from the palace and wound through another lush garden. A few minutes later they arrived in a tree-lined courtyard lit by lanterns. Mico took a dip in a trickling fountain, while Gaia, Nero, and Luna perched on the roof of a gazebo. Tito roosted in one of the trees, nursing his injured wing. Ringing the courtyard was a two-story building with long, covered balconies that led to dozens of doors.

With a chorus of "good nights," Giacomo and his weary friends shuffled off to the rooms assigned to them.

Giacomo collapsed onto the canopied bed and nestled his head into the pillow. He'd begun to drift off when the image of Ajeet's sickly horse-Genius trotted into his mind. Giacomo tossed and turned. With a gentle trill, Mico came to rest next to him. Giacomo cradled him close, grateful for his Genius's health and praying it would last.

WONDERS WITHIN

BONG! BONG!

Giacomo startled from his slumber and squinted at the morning light pouring through the windows. With a groan, he pulled himself out of bed, got dressed, and staggered into the courtyard as the last bell chimed from the palace. Four servants wearing purple-and-red outfits greeted him with synchronized bows, then directed him to the gazebo, where bowls and plates full of brightly colored foods crowded the table. One of the men poured tea into a beautifully painted cup. Giacomo bit into a piece of thin, crispy bread and washed it down with the tea, which tasted sweet and spicy at the same time. One by one, the rest of the group emerged from their rooms and joined Giacomo for breakfast.

"It all smells delicious," Pietro said, easing himself into a chair. One of the servants ladled some yellowish soup into a bowl and set it in front of him.

"Here, Master Pietro," Milena said, handing him a spoon.

Savino wrinkled his nose. "Are you sure it's safe to eat?"

Aaminah slurped up some noodles. "Tastes safe to me."

"I think we can trust Ajeet not to poison us," Giacomo said. "Quit being so paranoid."

The servants passed around the food, and Giacomo made sure to sample every dish. His taste buds were delighted by all the new flavors, but the enjoyment abruptly ended the moment Ozo lumbered out of his room. He had traded his black Zizzolan armor for some colorful Rachanan robes, and his shoulder was wrapped with a bandage. Giacomo had secretly hoped the mercenary would have slipped away in the middle of the night. No such luck.

Ozo stomped into the gazebo, swiped a plate stacked with sweet flatbread, and slumped into a chair. He kicked up his sandaled feet and set them on the table. "Good morning," he uttered in a tone that was not entirely unpleasant, then tore into the bread like a ravenous animal.

Giacomo traded surprised looks with his friends. "Uh . . . good morning?" he replied.

"Sounds like you had a restful sleep," Pietro said.

Ozo tore into another hunk of bread. "Best in years." But because his mouth was full of food, it came out, "Beef in ears."

A long, awkward silence hung over the breakfast table, with no one quite sure what to make of Ozo's sunny mood. Finally, Giacomo spoke up. "We didn't get the Compass back yet. I guess you're stuck here with us for now."

Ozo shrugged off the bad news. "It's probably best for me to lay low for a while, anyway. I could use the time to heal up."

"You're not angry?" Giacomo asked in disbelief.

"Pass me those noodles, would you?" Ozo said, ignoring the question.

Out of nowhere, a little girl no more than six years old clambered up the steps of the gazebo. She wore a helmet far too big for her and dragged a katar behind her. "Ozo! Ozo!" she yelped.

"Who's she?" Milena whispered across the table to Giacomo.

"No idea," Giacomo whispered back.

Ozo leaned down to her and tilted up her helmet enough to see her big brown eyes. He greeted her with a chuckle.

A woman's voice shouted a harsh word in Rachanan from across the courtyard. The little girl flinched and ducked behind Ozo. Giacomo spotted Lavanthi marching their way, her black hair tied in a long braid that trailed behind her. Yaday followed, arms pumping, trying to keep pace.

Lavanthi made straight for the girl, her steely expression breaking only for a moment as she and Ozo nodded hello to each other. She snatched away the helmet and katar from the girl and ushered her from her hiding place with a stern scolding.

Aaminah went over and with a huge smile said, "I'm Aaminah. What's your name?"

The girl stared back blankly, then looked up at Lavanthi.

"Her name's Soraya," Ozo said. "She's Lavanthi's daughter. We met last night while Lavanthi was tending to my shoulder."

Giacomo remembered that Lavanthi's husband had been one of the warriors who died in the caldera and felt an immediate kinship with the girl. He knew how hard it was to lose a parent.

Lavanthi spoke in Rachanan to Ozo, who translated. "Soraya wants to be a warrior like her mother, but Lavanthi keeps reminding her she's still too young."

Soraya gave a vigorous wave. Aaminah smiled and waved back. "Hello, Soraya. Nice to meet you."

Yaday stepped forward, his hands clasped in front of him. "Sorry to interrupt, but I'm here to inform you all that Samraat Ajeet is gathering warriors for the mission to Vrama's caldera. He wants to leave within the week."

"I'll make sure they're ready," Pietro said. "But please let Ajeet know I'll be staying behind. My days of adventuring are long past."

"Of course," Yaday said. "But as of now, only Giacomo will be joining the warriors."

"What?" Giacomo said. "That wasn't the deal we made with Ajeet. My friends have to come too."

"The samraat must first determine whether they will be worthy additions to the mission," Yaday explained.

"Worthy?" Giacomo sprang from his seat, boiling with anger. "If it wasn't for Milena, Savino, and Aaminah, I'd probably be dead right now. How's that for worthy?"

"I understand, but Samraat Ajeet needs to assess their strengths and weaknesses." Yaday turned to Giacomo's friends. "You'll need to report to the training fields later this afternoon for your first evaluation."

"And who is going to be evaluating us?" Milena asked edgily.

"That honor belongs to Lavanthi," he said, gesturing toward her. Lavanthi regarded Milena with a cold stare, then turned her attention to Soraya, who was tugging at her armored skirt and babbling something in Rachanan. Lavanthi patted her head, then spoke to Ozo, who wolfed down the rest of his breakfast.

"Lavanthi said she'll see you later. Until then, we'll be taking a walk in the gardens," Ozo said, wiping his mouth on his sleeve and rising from the table. "Apparently, Soraya needs help feeding some baby ducklings in the pond." Ozo followed Lavanthi and her daughter and left the courtyard.

Once they were out of earshot, Giacomo turned to his friends across the table. "A walk in the gardens? Baby ducklings? What's gotten into him?"

"Isn't it obvious?" Aaminah said. "Ozo's in love."

Giacomo practically choked on his food. "In love? That's ridiculous, no one falls in love overnight. Especially someone like Ozo."

"They can if it's true love," Aaminah said wistfully.

"Who cares about Ozo's love life?" Savino grumbled. "What's really ridiculous is this evaluation. Ajeet should be begging for our help."

"Yaday, perhaps I could have a word with the samraat," Pietro said, wiping his hands on a cloth napkin. "My students are more than capable—"

"Samraat Ajeet was very clear on the matter," Yaday said, cutting him off. "Whoever wishes to accompany Giacomo must first be tested."

"What if I refuse to go on this mission without them?" Giacomo challenged. "I bet Ajeet will change his mind then."

"Refuse? No . . . no, I wouldn't advise challenging the samraat's decision," Yaday said nervously, as if he'd had some experience in the matter.

Milena glowered at Yaday. "Excuse us," she said, and pulled Giacomo aside into a huddle with Savino, Aaminah, and Pietro.

"I'm getting the sense that this evaluation isn't exactly optional," she said, keeping her voice low.

"Even if we pass this test, there's no guarantee Ajeet will take us," Savino whispered. "I bet it's all a ploy to keep us off the mission so when Giacomo gets the Straightedge, Ajeet will have an easier time stealing it from him."

"I'm willing to do whatever I need to if it means we're able to help save the Geniuses," Aaminah added.

"I don't see that you have much of a choice," Pietro advised.

"Giacomo will need you by his side; so for now, you'll have to play by Ajeet's rules."

Savino sighed. "Fine . . ."

They all turned back to Yaday. "We'll see Lavanthi at the training fields," Milena said.

"One request," Aaminah added. "I don't suppose you have an instrument I could borrow?"

"I'll have one of the servants bring something by," Yaday said.

Milena looked at Giacomo apologetically. "I guess we won't be able to start your lessons again until tonight."

Yaday cut in. "No need to worry about that. Samraat Ajeet has requested that I prepare Giacomo for the mission myself."

"You?" Giacomo said incredulously. "I mean, no offense, but Milena's been teaching me."

Milena glared at Yaday. "I assume Samraat Ajeet was clear on this matter too?"

"Very," Yaday said with finality, then waved Giacomo forward. "Come. We have a lot of work to do and very little time."

Giacomo glanced back at Milena, looking for . . . what? Her approval? Her permission?

"Go," Milena said, then she wheeled around and headed back toward her room. "I'm going to get ready for this absurd evaluation."

"Good luck . . ." Giacomo offered, knowing it was little comfort.

"Now, if you'll follow me, we can get started," Yaday said, whisking Giacomo away from Pietro and his friends.

"Through here." Down in the palace's ancient underbelly, Yaday ducked into a small opening in the wall Giacomo hadn't noticed the day before. The narrow passage led to a round, rocky chamber that looked like a dank cave. Yaday secured his torch in a sconce, then moved to the center of the room, where he dropped some logs into a sunken hearth, kicking up sparks. Mico chased the floating embers up to the ceiling.

Being underground reminded Giacomo of his old sewer hideout back in Virenzia. "Is this where you live?"

"Yes, every guru who has served the samraat has called this room home. I left my village when I was only a boy to study here at the palace with Guru Pankaj." Yaday indicated a small shrine, where melted candles and wilted flowers surrounded a painting of a jovial, round-faced man with a white beard. "My teacher is still with me in spirit."

Giacomo often felt the same way about his parents. "Do you ever get lonely down here?"

"All the great gurus have lived solitary lives," Yaday said, sidestepping the question. But the faraway look in his eyes was all too familiar. In Giacomo's old sketchbooks, the many self-portraits he had drawn during his years in hiding wore the same expression.

Yaday put a kettle of water over the fire. "Now tell me, where are you in your studies?"

Giacomo slumped and gazed into the flames. He explained that his Genius had shown up only a few months ago, but since then, he'd made a lot of progress in his sacred geometry skills. For now, he didn't mention his budding ability to access the Wellspring for fear that Samraat Ajeet might somehow exploit it.

"And have you always known you're a Tulpa?" Yaday inquired.

"Not until recently."

"You've lived your whole life not truly knowing what you are?" The fire crackled and popped.

"I know I still have a lot to learn," Giacomo said defensively, "but you don't even have a Genius. What do you know about fighting with sacred geometry?"

"Not much, I confess. I approach sacred geometry from a spiritual angle."

"And how is that going to help me get the Straightedge from Vrama?"

"Using ordinary weapons or sacred geometry to battle a Preta only destroys it momentarily," Yaday explained. "The more you try to fight, the fiercer a Preta becomes."

Yaday went on to say people became Pretas mainly because they had lived lives corrupted by jealousy, lies, or greed. The longer a Preta remained earthbound, the harder it was to release its hold on this world, especially if it clung to an item of great power.

Like the Straightedge.

"Then how do we defeat Vrama?" Giacomo asked.

"Ordinarily, a guru such as myself would persuade a Preta to depart the physical plane by offering it something it craves, such as food or water, or a particular object. If the person's death was sudden, reuniting a Preta with a loved one can sometimes give it a sense of closure."

It was strange the way Yaday would talk about Pretas only in general, and not specifically about Vrama—as if he was avoiding some key information. It made Giacomo nervous.

"But Vrama already has the object he wants," Giacomo pointed out, trying to get to the bottom of it. "I doubt a snack is going to persuade him to part with it. And assuming Vrama ever had any loved ones, they would've died a very long time ago."

"That's correct."

"Then what are we going to offer him?"

Yaday took a deep breath and looked up grimly. The flickering flames reflected in his eyes. "You, Giacomo. You're the offering."

Giacomo jumped back and pointed his pencil at Yaday. Mico swooped in to help, his gem already starting to glow.

Yaday raised his hands in surrender. "Let me explain."

"I think I've heard enough." Giacomo backed toward the passageway. It had turned out that Savino had been right to be paranoid.

"Please, don't go," Yaday insisted. "I need your help to save Rachana's Geniuses."

"Then find another Tulpa—or Nirmita—to help you."

"The last known Nirmita left this world hundreds of years ago," Yaday said. "You're the only one who can help right now."

Giacomo thought of Zanobius but didn't mention him. "I can't. Not this way."

"You're afraid—I understand." Yaday's gaze drifted toward the portrait on the shrine. "I was terrified after my teacher's sudden death. I had so much still to learn from him, and I didn't think I was ready to become a guru to a samraat. But in time, I learned to stop letting my fears control me, and instead, learned to control them."

Yaday's story gave Giacomo pause. *If I could control my fears, maybe my nightmares will finally stop.* "How did you do it?" Giacomo asked.

"I can show you," Yaday offered. "Does that mean you're willing to help?"

Giacomo lowered his pencil, hoping he wasn't making a grave mistake. "I'm listening."

"Excellent," Yaday said, letting out a relieved sigh. "If you stay open-minded to what I'm about to teach you, I promise you'll come out unharmed." Yaday then described how a Preta who had been around as long as Vrama usually hungered for one thing: to regain physical form. It was impossible for Vrama to take over a human body, but he could assume control of a Tulpa.

The explanation did nothing to quell the horror swirling through Giacomo.

"We only need to make him *think* you're offering yourself freely," Yaday assured Giacomo after reading his expression. "To transfer his soul, Vrama has to abandon his Preta form. Once he's vulnerable, I can cast him out through a purification ritual." Yaday opened a wooden cabinet and removed a small clay jar. "But you'll need to focus on maintaining a calm, clear mind. If you don't, Vrama will feed off your darkest emotions and take you over completely."

"And how am I supposed to stay calm with a Preta about to devour my soul?"

Yaday opened the jar and sprinkled some dry leaves into a mortar, then ground them with a pestle. "Are you familiar with meditation?"

"No, not really."

Yaday pulverized the leaves into a green powder that he poured into the now-boiling kettle. "It is a way to clear away all distractions, self-doubts, and mental limitations. Even the most powerful warriors practice meditation to strengthen their body-mind connection. The warrior's katar is the spark to sacred geometry's fire—"

"Like my pencil," Giacomo interrupted.

Yaday nodded. "But the mind is what controls the flames. To resist Vrama, you must learn this control too. Are you ready to get started?"

Every muscle tensed as if Giacomo's body was warning him not to do this. He looked at Mico, who was perched on his finger. "What do you think?" The Genius chirped brightly, which Giacomo took as a good sign.

With a metal hook, Yaday pulled the kettle off the fire and filled two cups with steaming liquid. He handed one to Giacomo and gestured to a cushion on the floor. "Please, sit and relax." Yaday sat across the fire from him.

Giacomo sniffed the tea. It smelled like sweet flowers. Mico dipped his beak into the cup and took a drink. "That's not for you," Giacomo scolded.

"Actually, the tea will help you both relax." Yaday sipped from his cup.

Giacomo brought the cup to his lips and swallowed. Warmth seeped through his body and into his fingers and toes. The knots in his muscles melted. His eyelids felt like they were made of lead.

"Close your eyes, focus on your breathing, and let my words guide you," Yaday said, his voice tranquil and smooth.

With each breath, Giacomo's stomach and chest gently rose and fell. But almost immediately, doubts and distractions began to crowd his mind. *What do you think you're doing? This is stupid . . .*

Ajeet's only using you . . . It's never going to work . . . I'm hungry . . . But I just ate breakfast . . .

"When thoughts arise, let them float away like clouds in the breeze," Yaday interjected.

Giacomo tried not to think, but every time he released one thought, a new one popped up. Soon, he was trapped in an endless loop of thinking about not thinking.

This is maddening, Giacomo thought, then caught himself.

Stop thinking.

There it was again.

ARRGH! This is impossible!

Yaday must have sensed Giacomo's internal struggle. "Relax your mouth, your jaw, your brows . . ."

Giacomo brought his awareness to his face, which had hardened. He took a deep breath and exhaled. Like wax softened by a candle's flame, the tension melted away.

"Sometimes it helps to focus on a simple image," Yaday said.

In his mind, Giacomo summoned a familiar shape—a single point of light surrounded by a circle, which he saw each time he practiced sacred geometry. Almost immediately, his limbs, his muscles, his whole being seemed . . . weightless.

"Now, staying calm, I want you to imagine a painful or fearful situation," Yaday said.

"Why?"

"Save your questions for later. For now, simply perceive."

Giacomo focused on the circle's rippling surface where a faint image began to appear. The circle swelled larger and the shape filled his whole vision. Before he knew it, Giacomo was back in the piazza by Nerezza's palace.

"Mico, what's going on?" Giacomo looked around and discovered that his Genius had vanished.

A racking pain vibrated throughout his body. His head throbbed, and his heart felt like it was being ripped out of his chest. A singular thought consumed him: *I'm going to die . . .*

He brought his hands to his face, and to his horror, they were red and sticky.

Behind him, someone screamed. Giacomo whirled around to find Milena sprawled on the ground, her clothes blood-soaked. Savino, Aaminah, Enzio, and Pietro huddled around her. Savino pointed at him, shouting, "You did this!"

Giacomo stumbled back, reeling. He couldn't have hurt Milena. He never would do something like that.

Unless . . .

With a start, Giacomo pulled himself from his meditation. He was panting, and sweat trickled down his face.

Yaday gazed at him from across the fire. "It's all right, you're safe. What did you see?"

"I . . . I had become something awful. I attacked Milena . . ." He couldn't help but be reminded of Zanobius's violent breakdown at Niccolo's villa.

"It sounds like you're afraid of losing control," Yaday said. "That's precisely the kind of fear Vrama could feed off."

"How do I get rid of it?" Giacomo asked desperately.

"You've already taken the first and most important step—acknowledging the fear."

THE SFUMATO FOREST

Since he required neither rest nor food, Zanobius walked nonstop for two days and nights after leaving the villa. With no destination in mind, his four feet carried him over Zizzola's green hills, across windswept valleys, and through the snow-dusted mountains. The last thing he wanted was a confrontation, so he was careful to steer clear of farmhouses or villages. But Zanobius knew he couldn't roam for eternity. He needed to find someplace to live far away from any humans, where he could escape the terrible things he'd done.

Your soul will never be at peace . . .

Zanobius shook off his master's voice and forged on.

As another day waned and the sky glowed red with the setting sun, his journey came to an abrupt stop at the edge of a sheer cliff. Zanobius stared out in awe at the deep, wide canyon before him. A wave of feelings overwhelmed him, squeezing his chest tighter and tighter.

I'm truly all alone.

Zanobius sat and dangled his legs over the rocky edge. He gazed up at the stars blinking on until they blanketed the sky. And as he struggled to decide where to go, another forgotten memory surfaced.

A few weeks after he and Ugalino had fled Virenzia, they were flying on Ciro, soaring over an expansive forest. Zanobius suggested that it might be a good place to hide for a while.

"The Sfumato Forest is no place for me," Ugalino had said. "People believe it is infested with deadly creatures, so humans don't dare tread there."

The memory faded, leaving Zanobius with a new destination. He found the Guiding Star with his finger and drew a line across the sky until he found Laterna the Lion. He followed the constellation's southward-pointing tail and forged into the night.

When Zanobius arrived at the borders of the Sfumato Forest a few days later, he was met by a dense wall of gnarled trees. It was as if the forest had built its own defense against the outside world. Howling animals and screeching birds called to him from the woodland's shadowy interior. He shouldered his way through a tangle of barbed branches that scraped and pierced his skin, and after clearing the thicket, he waded through a bog, the murky water lapping at his waist.

Finally, he came to the heart of the forest, where trees with broad trunks towered like giants, forming a thick canopy that blocked the sun. Zanobius pressed on through the darkness, keeping an eye out for a cave or hollow tree trunk—a place he could make a new home.

A green glow lit up the forest floor, and Zanobius looked down to find a luminescent patch of mushrooms at his feet. As he continued walking, the light trailed him, moving from mushroom patch to mushroom patch. Zanobius picked up his pace, zigging and zagging, but everywhere he turned, the glowing mushrooms followed, lighting his way.

Farther on, he heard a deep growling. Zanobius stopped and wheeled around.

"Who's out there?" he bellowed.

A pair of enormous yellow eyes pierced the blackness. The growls grew louder. The eyes blinked, then moved closer. More mushrooms lit up, casting an eerie glow on a bipedal beast lumbering toward Zanobius. It was nearly twice his height, and its muscular arms and legs were matted with gray hair.

It was also headless.

The creature's bulging eyes, fat nose, and gaping mouth were embedded in its torso. It regarded Zanobius with a strange stare, then grunted a string of sounds. Leaves crunched and twigs snapped, and from between the trees, a dozen more headless creatures emerged and surrounded Zanobius.

Bracing for the creatures to lunge at him, Zanobius raised his fists, but the forest dwellers didn't return the threatening gesture. Instead, the gray-haired one asked, "What are you?"

Dumbfounded, Zanobius dropped his guard. "You speak Zizzolan?"

"I do," the creature's voice rumbled. "Now, explain who you are. None of us has seen a human like you before."

"That's because I'm not a human, I'm a Tulpa. An artist created me. Most humans think I'm a monster."

"And these humans drove you into our forest?"

"In a sense. I came here to be alone."

"Instead, you found us."

"And what are you, exactly?"

The creature's smile was enormous and toothy. "We are the Blemmyes, stewards of this forest. I am called Ch'Leeno. Did your creator give you a name?"

"Zanobius."

"Welcome, Zanobius." Ch'Leeno motioned to the other Blemmyes and spoke in a series of short grunts. As they retreated into the darkness, Ch'Leeno turned to Zanobius. "Please, join us."

Zanobius followed the Blemmyes through the forest until they reached an immense cave. Its rocky walls were covered with moss and more glowing mushrooms. Dozens of Blemmyes with various hair colors ventured from the tunnels, curiously observing their new guest. In his native tongue, Ch'Leeno introduced Zanobius to his clan, then invited Zanobius to sit on one of the rocks that with others formed a circle in the middle of the cave.

The Blemmyes ripped handfuls of moss and mushrooms off the walls and stuffed their mouths full. Ch'Leeno passed a helping to Zanobius, but he waved it off.

"Thank you, but I don't require any food."

Ch'Leeno shrugged, then swallowed his own meal in one gulp. "So Tulpas don't eat?"

"Others can," Zanobius said, thinking of Giacomo. "But my master didn't create me that way."

"He denied you a great pleasure," Ch'Leeno replied, devouring another pile of mushrooms. By the time the Blemmyes had finished their feast, the moss and mushrooms had begun growing again.

Zanobius was in awe. "Incredible."

"We live in harmony with the Great Mother," Ch'Leeno explained.

"Who is she?"

"The entire forest. She gave us life and sustains us. She offers us visions of what was, makes us aware of what is, and prepares us for what might be. In return, we protect her from those who might do her harm."

"The mushrooms . . ." Zanobius realized. "They lit up like they were tracking me."

"From time to time, humans stumble into our territory, either by accident or because they seek to harm us. Through the mushrooms, the Great Mother alerts us to their presence, and we drive them away."

The way Ch'Leeno spoke of the Great Mother reminded Zanobius of the way humans sometimes spoke of the Creator.

"If the Great Mother gave you all life, does that mean there are no Blemmye mothers and fathers?"

"We are neither men nor women. Only Blemmyes." Ch'Leeno led Zanobius to the mouth of the cave and pointed to a tree that had fallen. Several large lumps had erupted out of its bark. "Inside those growths are the next generation. Wherever a tree dies, more Blemmyes are born."

"How old are you?" Zanobius asked.

"I was birthed many centuries ago, during what humans call the age of the tetrad. But the Blemmyes have lived here for millennia, long before humankind appeared."

Zanobius asked Ch'Leeno how he could speak Zizzolan when the Blemmyes had such limited contact with humans. It turned out that a long time before, Ch'Leeno had become curious to know more about humans and their way of life, so he decided to venture to the outside world. But everywhere he went, humankind had met him with fear and violence. That sounded familiar to Zanobius.

"I soon returned to the safety of the Great Mother, but I didn't leave empty-handed." Ch'Leeno shoved aside a rock, revealing a stash of scrolls and books in the cave wall.

"You taught yourself to read," Zanobius said, impressed.

"During my travels, I did meet one young man who didn't fear me. He taught me his language and gifted me these books to continue my studies."

Zanobius couldn't help but think of Enzio, Giacomo, and Aaminah, who had stood by his side despite his having lost control. He hoped they were all still safe.

Ch'Leeno rolled the rock back in place. "What's your story, Zanobius? How come you left the human realm?"

"The artist who created me controlled my mind and forced me to do horrible things. Now that he's gone, I don't trust myself to be around others."

"I see . . ." A heavy silence hung between the Tulpa and the Blemmye. "You're welcome to stay in the forest as long as you like," Ch'Leeno offered. "In the Great Mother's arms, you will find only peace."

Zanobius nodded, grateful. "That's what I was hoping."

Zanobius found much to admire in the Blemmyes' way of life. Unlike humans, they strived to exist in harmony with their environment and one another. They didn't dwell on the past or fear what might happen in the future. As each moment transpired, they received it without judgment, content with what the Great Mother had provided them.

Taking their lead, Zanobius spent his days exploring the forest, observing his new home. The meditative walks calmed him and put his mind at ease. However, one afternoon, his serenity was broken when a thick mist swept through the forest. Worried he might get lost, Zanobius hurried back toward the Blemmyes' cave, but the fog quickly enveloped him.

Zanobius stumbled around blindly, unable to see even a few inches in front of him. From somewhere in the haze, a woman whispered to him.

To be at peace, you must never forget . . .

Was that the Great Mother speaking to him? What did she mean?

Suddenly, the fog cleared, and Zanobius found himself surrounded by bronze and marble statues. He recognized his master's old studio back in Virenzia and realized he wasn't just recalling an old, dormant memory—he was reliving it.

Ugalino burst through the door, a panicked look on his face.

"Zanobius, Nerezza found out about you!" he shouted. "We have to leave!"

They could already hear soldiers' boots thundering toward the door, so Ugalino and Zanobius raced up the stairs and onto the balcony outside, where Ciro waited to carry them away.

But someone else was waiting for them too—Supreme Creator Nerezza. She sat on the neck of her black-feathered Genius, grasping a long paintbrush. Her gaze locked onto Zanobius, and her eyes flashed with an expression that he read as fear.

No, Ugalino corrected, speaking to Zanobius through his mind. *That's the look of jealousy. She knows she will never be able to create anything as magnificent as you.*

"I will give you one opportunity to destroy your monster," Nerezza said. "If you refuse, I will destroy it for you."

"I refuse," Ugalino snarled. He raised his pencil, gesturing in a blur, and blinding white light shot forth from Ciro's crown. Nerezza and her Genius took to the sky as the stones exploded below them.

Soldiers crashed onto the balcony. Upon seeing Zanobius, they recoiled in shock but quickly recovered and leveled their spears.

I'll handle Nerezza, Ugalino told him in his mind. *You kill the soldiers.*

At first, Zanobius thought he had misunderstood his master. Ugalino had never ordered him to do anything so violent before. Zanobius tried to resist the command, but he discovered he could not.

He did not feel connected to what happened next. Bones cracked. Men screamed. Soldiers flew into the air, limbs flailing. Then came quiet. Zanobius peered down at the tangled mass of bodies littering the street, aghast at what he had done.

Zanobius, help!

He turned to find his master sprawled on the balcony, his robes torn and smoldering, struggling for his pencil, which lay out of reach.

Nerezza looked down from astride her bird-Genius, hovering overhead. She flicked her brush, and her Genius targeted Zanobius next. A violet light beamed from Victoria's gem and struck

Zanobius, throwing him into the wall. Bricks crumbled around him. He staggered to his feet, but Nerezza rained down more streams of light.

His arms shattered into dust.

His legs disappeared from under him.

Piece by piece, Nerezza blasted Zanobius into oblivion until there was only darkness.

Some time later, Zanobius regained consciousness. To his surprise, he was back in his master's studio. Ugalino sat slumped in a chair, snoring, a curved sculpting tool dangling from his hand.

"Master?"

Ugalino snapped awake. "Zanobius!" His voice was full of relief.

"What . . . what happened?" Zanobius asked groggily. "I thought Nerezza destroyed me."

"I rebuilt you. You're more powerful now, more resilient."

Zanobius stretched out his four arms and curled his fingers into fists. A new strength coursed through him.

"As long as I'm alive, Nerezza can never truly end you," Ugalino assured him.

But that didn't stop her from trying.

Eventually, word of Zanobius's resurrection made it to Nerezza, and it wasn't long before she and her army descended upon them once again. This time, there was no chance to run. They hadn't even heard the soldiers approaching when the windows of Ugalino's studio filled with a violet glow. The building crumbled around them. Nerezza had razed it to the ground.

Zanobius rose from the rubble, carrying his injured master. Ciro swooped in and took Ugalino on his back, but before Zanobius could climb on, soldiers swarmed him.

While Ugalino's and Nerezza's Geniuses clashed in the sky, Zanobius fought for his life on the streets. Eventually, he and Ugalino battled their way to the city's outer wall, where Ugalino and Ciro finally brought down Nerezza in a blaze of light. At the time, he thought they'd killed her, but as it turned out, Nerezza was rather resilient herself.

Zanobius leaped onto Ciro's back, and they soared over the mountain, leaving behind Virenzia and a trail of death and destruction. They flew into the clouds, and mist enveloped them. When it cleared, Zanobius found himself back in the forest, the memories of the soldiers he had killed fresh in his mind. Ugalino's warning came back to him.

You will never forget the lives you have taken! Your soul will never be at peace!

His master had been right. Zanobius had been foolish to think he could hide from his past. If he couldn't find serenity among the peaceful Blemmyes in a sacred place like the forest, he never would.

When Zanobius returned to the Blemmyes' cave, Ch'Leeno greeted him with a warm smile. Zanobius couldn't find it in himself to return it.

"Did you enjoy your walk?" Ch'Leeno asked.

"I think the Great Mother gave me one of those visions you were talking about."

"And what do you think she was trying to tell you?"

"I can't change what I've done," Zanobius said. "But I can try to make amends for the past. I've decided to move on."

Ch'Leeno's giant eyes widened with surprise. He translated Zanobius's words for the other Blemmyes, who responded with a chorus of disappointed groans.

"Thank you for letting me stay with you," Zanobius said. "But I realized I need to help my friends."

"You're going to return to them?" Ch'Leeno asked.

"No. I'm heading to Virenzia."

Ch'Leeno regarded Zanobius with concern. "And you think you'll find peace there?"

"Probably not," Zanobius said. "But I will find Supreme Creator Nerezza."

THE WARRIORS OF RACHANA

Wearing boots, pants, and a loose-fitting blue tunic, Milena left her room, ready to face Lavanthi and her evaluation under the blazing afternoon sun. In a matter of minutes Milena was already sweating through her new clothes.

She found Aaminah in the gazebo strumming an instrument that had a pear-shaped body and a long, tapering neck. It looked similar to a lute, but it made a more piercing sound. Luna produced strings of light that danced through the air.

"You picked that up fast," Milena commented.

"It's called a tambur," Aaminah said, her fingers tripping over the four strings before quickly gaining purchase again. "I'm still getting the hang of it."

Savino arrived shortly after, and with their Geniuses in tow, the three headed out. They found Lavanthi waiting in the center of a grassy, oblong training field, her legs splayed wide, her arms behind her back. She studied their approach with a critical gaze, as if the evaluation had already begun. Ozo stood next to her, and a line of six bronze-clad warriors were stationed behind them.

With Savino and Aaminah flanking her, Milena stepped directly in front of Lavanthi, blinking the sweat out of her eyes, refusing to show any hint of weakness.

Using Ozo as her translator, Lavanthi explained that the mark of a true warrior was being strong in both body and mind. "You will be pushed to your physical and mental limits during this evaluation," Ozo said, channeling Lavanthi's words.

Lavanthi narrowed her eyes and pointed at Gaia, who stood on Milena's shoulder.

"For these tests, you won't need your Geniuses," Ozo explained, and Aaminah gasped.

Savino threw up his arms. "Are you kidding me?"

"How is she supposed to evaluate our mastery of our Geniuses if we can't use them?" Milena said, trying to keep her anger in check.

After a brief exchange with Lavanthi, Ozo replied that sacred geometry attacks are ineffective against a Preta. Milena, Savino, and Aaminah needed to demonstrate they could handle the physical and mental rigors of the mission without relying on their Geniuses' power.

Milena traded defeated looks with Savino and Aaminah, then eased her Genius off her shoulder. With a flourish of her wings, Gaia soared skyward, Nero and Luna right behind her.

The following days became a relentless routine of sleeping, eating, and trials. Milena rose early each morning and scarfed down her breakfast. Then she, Savino, and Aaminah dragged their weary bodies to the field, where Lavanthi and her warriors presented them with that day's challenge.

They suffered through short- and long-distance footraces (where Savino demonstrated his speed and stamina), scaled walls (which Savino excelled at again), dueled with wooden swords (Savino and Milena held their own against their warrior opponents, while Aaminah was quickly disarmed), and archery (Milena's precision and patience helped her land bull's-eyes, while Savino's and Aaminah's arrows flew wildly off target).

During each challenge, Lavanthi proved to be as tough and demanding as Milena had anticipated. If Milena fell behind in a footrace, Lavanthi barked at her until she sped up; if she held a sword incorrectly, Lavanthi twisted her fingers into the proper grip. Milena bristled every time Lavanthi corrected her, but she sucked up her pride and didn't argue. Aaminah, however, let her frustration get the best of her. After each dressing-down, Aaminah kicked the dirt and pouted, or stormed off the field, or fought back tears. Lavanthi lectured her for being such a child, which only stoked Aaminah's defiance.

On the fourth day, Milena was eating breakfast in the gazebo, steeling herself for the day ahead, when Aaminah shuffled over, still wearing her nightclothes.

"Why aren't you dressed yet?" Milena asked. "We need to go soon."

With an exasperated harrumph, Aaminah took a seat. "I'm not going back on that field."

"I know it's been hard, but—"

"I tried to do my best, I really did, but that woman is horrible! And I know I'm not as strong as you and Savino, but she doesn't need to keep yelling at me about it! I can't stand to spend one more minute with her. I feel sorry for her daughter."

Milena sat next to Aaminah and put her arm around her, giving her shoulder a little squeeze. "I hated the physical trials too, but Lavanthi promised we'd start the mental tests this morning. I bet you'll do great at those."

Aaminah crossed her arms and slumped forward onto the table. "No, you're the smart one, remember? And Savino's the strong one. I'm just the overly sensitive one, which isn't much help in a fight."

"But you're much better at other things than we are." Milena pointed to the tambur lying on the table. "I mean, I doubt I could teach myself to play a completely new instrument so quickly. And I'd never trust Savino to heal one of my injuries."

Aaminah cracked a smile. "He'd probably only make it worse."

"Exactly!"

They shared a chuckle, and Milena was glad to have helped put a smile back on Aaminah's face. "I think today's challenge is about resilience," Milena said. "And I don't know anyone with a stronger spirit than you. You've been through so much, but nothing has ever broken you." Milena stood up and held out her hand. "So will you come?"

Aaminah took Milena's hand. "All right," she said, then added, "but if Lavanthi says one more mean thing, I'm leaving."

"And I'll be right behind you," Milena assured her.

Aaminah left to quickly change, and Giacomo walked up, grabbing a few slices of bread from the table without making eye contact. His avoidance bothered Milena. Ever since he'd started spending his days with Yaday, Giacomo had become distant and cagey.

"How are your lessons going with Yaday?" she asked.

"They're fine." Giacomo stuffed a piece of bread into his mouth as if to end the conversation.

"That's it? Fine? What are you learning? Did he teach you about the pentad yet?"

"Uh . . . a little . . ."

"So you're able to construct a pentagon?"

"Not exactly," Giacomo admitted.

"Then what have you two been doing every day?"

"Yaday's been teaching me to meditate," Giacomo said hurriedly, then turned from her. "I have to go, I'm late. See you later."

"Wait!" Milena called, but Giacomo was already speeding out of the courtyard. *Why is he acting so strange and secretive?* she wondered. His behavior reminded Milena of when he had been coming up with the reckless plan to fix Zanobius's arm. What was he keeping from her this time? Milena hoped Giacomo wasn't getting himself in over his head again.

She gazed down at her half-finished meal. Suddenly, the food seemed unappetizing. She pushed her plate away.

Lavanthi paced in front of her fellow warriors while Ozo translated.

"These men and women can perform feats of great physical strength. But without *inner* strength, they would all be overpowered in battle."

Milena stood at attention between Savino and Aaminah, praying that they would get through the final days of evaluation together. Gray clouds blanketed the sky, offering a cool breeze. It was a relief after the unceasing heat.

"Each of you close your eyes and look within," Ozo said, relaying Lavanthi's instructions. "Visualize the most important person in the world to you and make a mental portrait of them."

"Why are we doing this, exactly?" Savino said.

Lavanthi explained that if you are looking death in the face, physical strength alone won't be enough to save you. But if you have a motivation to live, you'll do whatever is needed to survive, no matter how dire the situation.

Milena shut her eyes and took a breath, trying to determine who motivated her the most.

Images flashed through her mind. To her shock, she first pictured her mother—a weasel-faced nightmare of a woman. Why in the world was she thinking of her? Reflecting more deeply, Milena realized that despite her and her parents' mutual disdain, she still harbored a childish longing to return home one day and reunite with her family. But would the promise of such an unlikely reunion be enough to help her endure anything? Doubtful.

Giacomo appeared next. Despite his enormous talent for getting under her skin, Milena was devoted to helping him. Enduring Lavanthi's evaluation was a testament to that. But she'd known him for only a short time. Was their bond strong enough to stave off death?

Then she saw Aaminah's sweet face—she thought of her as a little sister and would do anything for her. She brought to mind Savino—she had known him the longest of her friends, which made their connection that much stronger. And though he was exasperating at times, Milena knew his surly exterior was only a mask to hide his kindness and loyalty. Savino didn't want anyone to think he had a softer side for fear they would take advantage of it.

Next, she pictured Gaia, soaring through the sky. When Milena was a little girl, her father had done everything in his power to drive away Milena's Genius in the hope that their bond would be severed. But Gaia had returned to Milena again and again until her father finally gave up.

All of them had motivated Milena to keep going when life became difficult, but the deeper she looked, one individual eclipsed the others—Pietro.

From the moment she had stepped into his dark studio in the cellar of Baldassare's villa, Milena had felt welcomed by him. Though he could be gruff and surly at times, he only ever had her best interests at heart. He was the kind of man she wished her father could have been—protective, loyal, and kindhearted.

Pietro had always been there for Milena, and now that he was getting older, she wanted to be there for him. She needed to be, especially since Baldassare was out of the picture.

If death was coming for her, Milena was confident the thought of Pietro would inspire her to fight on, no matter how hopeless things seemed.

Milena felt a warmth come over her, and when she opened her eyes, the sun was peeking through the clouds. She glanced over at Aaminah and smiled, then gave Savino a firm nod, wondering whom they had envisioned.

"Let those images burn into your minds," Lavanthi said through Ozo. "They just might save your lives one day."

THE PIRATES OF PAOLINI

After making his way out of the Sfumato Forest, Zanobius headed east across a desolate, rocky expanse. He ignored the sharp stones that sliced the bottoms of his feet and focused instead on a plan that would get him within striking distance of Nerezza.

Marching directly into Virenzia was out of the question. Soldiers would swarm him before he made it anywhere near the Supreme Creator's palace, and Zanobius had made a pledge to himself not to harm anyone except Nerezza.

He considered sneaking into the city through the subterranean aqueducts, but because of the recent battle in the piazza, Zanobius had to assume that any potential entryway would be locked down.

An oaky smell filled Zanobius's nostrils, and he froze. Down the hill, he noticed a small village, where chimneys puffed smoke. He looked down at his bare body, his only clothing a skirt of dingy fabric. Now that he was near civilization again, it wouldn't be long before he was spotted. Ugalino never would have let him wander out in the open for this long without covering up. The village would have supplies—he'd just have to quickly get in and out.

Zanobius waited long after darkness fell, then crept down the hill and through a field of snoring cows. He only hoped the towns-people slept as soundly. He prowled from house to house, peering in windows until he finally found what he was looking for in a storage shed: a long, hooded cloak. He plucked the garment off a rusty nail and draped it over himself, ignoring that it was damp and hemmed with mud.

From somewhere inside the cloak, Zanobius heard the crinkling of parchment. Curious, he felt around until he found an inner pocket. When he unfurled the roll, his own image stared back at him from the page. The notice called for his capture—alive. The reward was 10,000 gold *impronta*.

Panicked, Zanobius shoved the parchment back into his cloak. He quickly checked his surroundings to make sure he hadn't been spotted. Then he pulled the hood low over his face and slunk away.

But as Zanobius walked farther from the village and the initial fear settled, the wanted notice inspired him to rethink his plan. This whole time, he had been approaching his problem from the wrong angle. Maybe he shouldn't hide his arrival, but make a show of it. If Nerezza wanted Zanobius alive, it was likely because she wanted to destroy him herself. He needed to use that fact to his advantage.

Zanobius had his ticket into Virenzia, and now all he needed was someone eager to collect the reward. And he knew exactly the place to find them.

Ships both large and small clogged the port of Paolini.

A few months after they fled Virenzia, Ugalino had brought Zanobius here, seeking safe passage out of the empire. In a musty old tavern, they had found the captain of a merchant vessel who was willing to overlook their status as fugitives, for the right price. Once Ugalino had stuffed the captain's pockets with gold *impronta*, he and Zanobius hunkered down in the ship's cargo hold and set sail for Katunga. Zanobius hoped to find that same captain again, but if not him, the place would be teeming with plenty of other money-hungry humans.

Zanobius made his way into town, where the pungent stench of fish and salty air filled his nostrils. The port was populated by the dregs of society: chain mail–clad mercenaries, pirates with long, tangled beards and toothless snarls, and an assortment of ruffians wearing tattered leather long coats and wielding all manner of bladed weapons. Zanobius moved past a row of ramshackle buildings, where his wanted notice hung in every window. At the end of the street, he spotted the tavern he was looking for.

Zanobius pulled his hood down a little lower and entered. He shouldered through the crowd, making his way to the back of the room. A couple of men, noticing his immense size, cast sidelong glances his way, but most were too distracted by their drinks and rowdy revelry to give him a second look.

From a shadowy alcove, Zanobius observed the faces of the ribald patrons, keeping watch for the captain of the merchant ship who had helped him and Ugalino all those years ago. Over clamorous hoots and hollers, Zanobius overheard someone emphatically insist he had witnessed statues come to life. Zanobius homed in on the voice. It belonged to an old, gray-haired man who held court with two younger men—one scrawny, the other broad-shouldered.

"They were twice as tall as anyone in here!" the old man declared, gesturing around the room.

"You're full of it," the broad-shouldered man said, then took a swig of ale.

The scrawny man slammed his fist on the table. "My father's not a liar! I saw them too!"

"One of 'em turned my older boy to stone right in front of my eyes," the old man said, and he began sobbing.

The broad-shouldered man got up, shaking his head. "Now I heard it all. Statues coming to life . . . I think you had a few too many, old man." He staggered off toward the bar.

Zanobius stood motionless. *Statues coming to life? Could these men have encountered Tulpas?* If there were others like him and Giacomo, Zanobius needed to know. He approached the old man and his son, careful to keep hidden under his cloak. "Excuse me, but I happened to overhear your story. Where did you see these statues?"

The old man looked up through his watery eyes. "Down south, guarding a chasm. Why? Who wants to know?"

"I'm sorry, my name is . . ." Zanobius paused as he conjured up an alias. "Giuseppe," he said.

"Well, Giuseppe, you can call me Little Dino," the scrawny man said. "This is my father, Old Dino." He patted the old man on the back. Old Dino raised his mug to Zanobius in greeting, then guzzled what was left in it.

"How long ago did this encounter happen?" Zanobius asked.

Little Dino shrugged. "A couple months back."

"Did the statues speak? Were you able to communicate with them?"

"Weren't really the talking type," Little Dino said. "Besides, I was too busy trying not to get killed by them."

Old Dino dropped his empty mug on the table and wiped his beard with the back of his hand. "Luckily, we were with some kids who had Geniuses. They got us across the chasm before the statues could do us all in."

Zanobius tensed. Ozo had been traveling with the children when he crossed the chasm. Could these men have been working for the mercenary who'd hunted him?

"How did the statues come alive?" Zanobius asked.

"Why're you so interested, anyway?" Old Dino snapped, eyeing Zanobius with suspicion. "They friends of yours?"

Little Dino put a hand on his father's arm, calming him. "The whole event was very traumatic for my father." He smiled apologetically at Zanobius. "Probably best if we quit talking about it."

Zanobius nodded his understanding. But he suspected that further questioning would confirm his hunch: somehow, Giacomo had unwittingly awakened the statues.

Old Dino leaned across the table, his voice becoming more agitated. "Who are you, anyway? I've never seen you in here before."

"Dad, calm down." Little Dino passed his mug to his father. "Here, have the rest of mine."

Old Dino stared deep into Zanobius's eyes. His voice dropped to just above a whisper. "*They* sent you, didn't they?"

Zanobius wasn't sure what Old Dino was getting at. "Nobody sent me. I'm just here looking for an old acquaintance."

"Liar!" Old Dino shouted. He lunged across the table.

"Dad—"

Before Little Dino could stop him, his father pulled back Zanobius's hood, exposing his marble-white skin.

"I knew it! You're one of them!" Old Dino recoiled in horror and reached for something below the table. A second later, a scythe cut through the air, slashing Zanobius's cloak clean off him.

"It's the Tulpa!" Old Dino shouted, and the tavern suddenly fell silent. Everyone's gaze locked on Zanobius. "It's going to kill us all!"

Little Dino brandished a spear with a long, jagged blade that glimmered in the candlelight. Zanobius grabbed the edge of the table and lifted, tipping it into the Dinos and the men behind them. Zanobius barreled into bodies as he made his escape, stumbling into the street.

The tavern emptied behind him, and the drunken customers gave chase with shouts of "Monster!" and "Kill it!"

Hoping to avoid a fight, Zanobius ran toward the edge of town, but he found his path blocked by a group of surly pirates armed to the teeth. Though his plan had been to be captured, this was not how Zanobius had imagined it.

Zanobius batted away the jabbing swords and spear tips. The crowd closed in. The blades came faster. Zanobius fought off those closest to him, careful to pull his punches, but the sheer number of attackers soon overwhelmed him. Metal lanced his arms, his legs, his back.

Short of killing every man on the dock, Zanobius saw no way to save himself.

Thankfully, a man's gruff, commanding voice came to his rescue. "Lay down your arms!"

"Why should we?" someone in the crowd shouted back.

"Because he's worth more alive than he is dead!" the man roared.

The blades parted, and the assailants stepped back, making way for a thickset man with a shock of white hair that transitioned into a long black beard. Rings pierced his ears and nose.

"Can't any of you ne'er-do-wells read?" He held up Zanobius's wanted notice for all to see. "Says here, the Supreme Creator wants this Tulpa captured alive," the bearded man said, his mouth spotted with gold teeth. He pointed to the pirates. "Chain him up and throw him in the hold."

"Yes, Captain Wolff," one of the pirates said.

Two other pirates shackled Zanobius's wrists and ankles with cold metal cuffs and pulled him to his feet. Despite a few hiccups, the plan had worked. To make his capture seem convincing, Zanobius struggled against his chains, but he had no intention of breaking free. Not yet.

The pirates led Zanobius up the gangplank and onto the ship, where Captain Wolff now waited on deck. He leaned in and flashed a gold-flecked smile.

"Welcome aboard, Zanobius."

LAMENT FOR THE LOST

"To get to the root of your fear, you must first sit with it," Guru Yaday said.

Giacomo sat cross-legged in the grass opposite his new teacher, who had taken him into the gardens to meditate, hoping the fresh air would help clear his mind. But Giacomo was replaying his awkward encounter with Milena in his head. He had wanted to tell her more about his studies with Yaday, but she still seemed hurt about being replaced as his teacher. He figured she would disapprove anyway, so Giacomo had hurried away before she had been able to question him further.

Yaday picked up a small, two-headed drum that had a bead tethered to each side. As he spun the drum's long handle, the stones beat out a steady rhythm, and Giacomo's distracted thoughts immediately began to settle. "Breathe in . . . Breathe out . . ." Yaday said gently.

Giacomo closed his eyes and repeatedly traced the five sides of a shimmering pentagon, attempting to find focus and calm. Yaday had taught Giacomo a little about the pentagon—a symbol of the pentad—and how it was the most spiritual of all the forms because it urged the meditator to move away from the material world and tap into the infinite world within. Or something like that. Giacomo still didn't grasp all of what Yaday had said, but if picturing a pentagon would help him deal with his fears, he was willing to give it a try.

The problem was, his imaginary line kept trailing off, squiggling this way and that. Giacomo re-formed the pentagon over and over until, finally, its shiny surface cast back his own image. He thought he was getting somewhere, but then his reflection began to transform—his skin turned marble white and his hair short-ened, then his body sprouted two more arms and two more legs. The reflection lunged forward, shattering the pentagon.

Giacomo gasped, startling himself from his meditation.

"What did you see this time?" Yaday asked.

Giacomo reached out his finger so Mico could land on it. He stroked the tuft of hair that sprouted from the top of his Genius's crown. "Someone I've been trying to forget."

"A friend?"

"His name is Zanobius," Giacomo said. "He's also a Tulpa."

Giacomo wished Zanobius was with him now, and not only because two Tulpas against Vrama would be better than one. Zanobius was the only one in the world who could truly understand what Giacomo was going through.

"Another Nirmita?" Yaday said, sounding surprised. "Why didn't he come to Rachana with you?"

Giacomo explained the violent events that had led to Zanobius's departure. "Even though it was Zanobius's decision to leave, Milena and Savino wanted him gone," Giacomo said.

"And you're afraid they'll turn on you, like they did on Zanobius?" Yaday asked.

As soon as Yaday said it, Giacomo realized the truth in the guru's words. "I guess I'm scared I'm going to end up alone again," Giacomo admitted.

"I understand," Yaday said. "Now, settle your breathing, and sit with that fear some more."

But the meditation was cut short when a pained whinny pierced the air, sending a chill through Giacomo. Mico let out a startled squawk.

"Not again . . ." Yaday shot up from the grass, and Giacomo scrambled after him. Together, they headed in the direction of the sound, hurrying out of the gardens.

They reached the main path in front of the palace, where they came upon a horse-Genius that had collapsed next to one of the reflecting pools. Giacomo froze, an ache in his chest, while Yaday shouted to some warriors at the top of the palace steps, and they immediately ran inside.

The Genius's wings lay limp across the grass, its breaths coming in labored snorts. A gold-armored warrior dropped to his knees and cradled the horse-Genius's head in his lap. Giacomo wished there was some way to help the animal. But there was nothing he could do.

People began to appear from all corners of the fortress to see what had happened. Ajeet descended the palace steps, panic spread across his face.

The samraat pushed his way through the growing crowd and

went to the warrior's side. The horse-Genius let out a heavy exhale, then fell still.

The gem on the horse-Genius's armor glowed, its light cocooning around the Genius's body until it had formed a luminescent second skin. A tinkling sound rang out, then the Genius's light-body began to come apart, transforming into radiant particles that floated off in the wind. Within minutes all that remained of the once noble creature was its diamond-shaped gem and a glimmering trail eddying across the purple-and-orange sky. With tears in his eyes, the warrior picked up the large gem and cradled it in his hands.

Ajeet bowed his head and placed a fist over his heart. The other warriors mirrored him. As the palace bells chimed, Ajeet helped up the warrior in gold and led him down the path, the crowd following. Giacomo trailed behind the Rachanans' somber procession.

As the tenth bell tolled, they all stopped at the fortress gates. Warriors lit two pyres, one on each side of the archway, and the fire's heat washed over them. Savino, Milena, Aaminah, and Pietro made their way through the crowd and over to Giacomo. "We heard a Genius died," Aaminah said, sounding worried.

"I saw it," Giacomo said. "It was so horrible."

Aaminah let out a stifled sob. Milena pulled her in and gave her a comforting hug, and then they turned to watch the ceremony.

Beneath the archway, the warrior faced Ajeet. He took off his helmet and then, piece by piece, he removed the rest of his armor until he was garbed in only a white tunic, brown pants, and sandals. Lastly, he held his katar flat across both palms and kneeled, offering the weapon to the samraat. The warrior, who had appeared so majestic and powerful in his armor, now looked so . . . ordinary.

From inside his robes, Yaday pulled out what looked like an animal bone and raised it to his lips. He blew on one end, trumpeting a wavering cry. Then he spun his two-headed drum, tapping out a steady beat. He recited a long, songlike prayer in Rachanan, and everyone bowed heads. Giacomo followed their lead.

Waves of sorrow coursed through Giacomo as he grieved not only for this horse-Genius, but also for all the Geniuses, both in Rachana and back home, that had been forced from this world too early. Soon, Nerezza would pay for her role in the demise of the bird-Geniuses. But right now, the dire threat was Vrama.

He needs to be stopped, Giacomo vowed.

When Yaday finished, the gates swung open and, speaking softly in Rachanan, Ajeet called on the man to rise. With his gem cupped in his hands, the man walked toward the blazing orange sun, leaving the fortress and his fellow warriors behind.

As the crowd scattered, Giacomo approached Yaday. "Where is that warrior going?"

The guru explained that when a Genius dies, a purification ritual is performed to help the warrior shed the shell of who they once were and embark on a journey to the Sacred Lands, at the outer edges of the empire. "There, the gods will watch over the warrior as he makes a new home among others who have suffered the same fate," Yaday said.

Other Lost Souls. Giacomo shivered despite the heat.

"You just kick them out?" he asked. "It seems so cruel."

"It sounds much nicer than how Lost Souls have historically

been treated in Zizzola," Pietro commented. "At least here, you get to keep your Genius's gem. *And* you get a proper send-off."

"Yes, it's meant to be an honor and an important rite of passage," Yaday said.

Samraat Ajeet called everyone over. "I've informed Lavanthi to ready her warriors. We leave for the caldera in the morning."

Yaday glanced over at Giacomo, then back to Ajeet. "But Giacomo and I—"

"I'll be ready," Giacomo said, stepping forward.

"Excellent," Ajeet said.

"What about us?" Savino asked, gesturing to Milena and Aaminah. "Are we going on the mission too?"

"I need to speak with Lavanthi further," Ajeet said. "I'll announce who will be joining me tonight. We'll be holding a ceremonial feast." Ajeet and Lavanthi strode back toward the palace.

Yaday pulled Giacomo away from his friends and whispered to him, "Why did you tell the samraat you're ready? We both know you're not. There's still a final step to the meditation I haven't even told you about."

"It's a week's journey to the caldera, right?" Giacomo said. "That should give you plenty of time to teach me more on the way."

"Are you sure about this?" Yaday said, his voice tinged with concern.

"Absolutely," Giacomo assured him, though in fact he was not sure at all.

A FEAST AMONG GODS

Upon returning to her room, Milena found a beautiful dress spread out on the bed, its hundreds of tiny inlaid beads shining. Her friends had also been gifted with new garments, which they were instructed to wear to the ceremonial dinner.

As day turned to dusk, the newly attired group gathered under the lanterns in the courtyard, where a cadre of guards waited to escort everyone to the palace.

The door to Pietro's room swung open and he walked out, leaning on a new cane with a gold handle. He wore long, brightly colored robes.

"Master Pietro, you look very dignified," Milena said.

Pietro ran his hand down the front of his robe. "Why, thank you. This silk feels magnificent. And so much more breathable than my old wool robes."

Aaminah tugged at her golden dress. She tripped over its hem and stumbled. "How does anyone walk in these things?"

"Slowly and gracefully," Milena advised, sauntering past. "You look beautiful, by the way."

Aaminah grimaced. "Pfft, I feel ridiculous."

Savino adjusted his blue hat. "How do I look?" he asked, fishing for a compliment.

"Like that hat's too small for you," Giacomo said, buttoning his orange-and-purple embroidered vest.

"I was asking *Milena*," Savino said, turning to her.

"You look very handsome," Milena said approvingly. "But we are Samraat Ajeet's guests, so you might want to show a little respect and button your pants."

Savino's eyes darted to his crotch, where the front of his trousers hung open, exposing his red underpants. Giacomo burst out laughing. Milena and Aaminah snickered.

Savino's face turned scarlet as he buttoned himself up. "Not funny."

"It kind of is," Milena teased.

As Milena and the others made their way through the corridors of the palace, a painting caught her eye. It was an enormous canvas that portrayed dozens of figures in the samraat's throne room. A man who Milena assumed was a young Samraat Jagesh sat under the golden canopy, his warriors and their horse-Geniuses surrounding him. Before them, Emperor Callisto stood at a table, writing on a scroll and flanked by several Zizzolan soldiers in black armor. The realistic style looked out of place among the Rachanan works, which were painted with blocks of flat color and repeated patterns.

Milena gasped as it hit her. "Pietro, there's a painting here of the peace treaty signing—I think it's one of yours!" Upon closer inspection, Milena found Pietro's signature in the corner of the canvas, confirming her hunch. "It is!"

"Not among my finer works," Pietro said dismissively as he quickly shuffled past his students. "Come, we don't want to keep Samraat Ajeet waiting."

"Doesn't that woman next to Emperor Callisto look familiar?" Savino said, pointing to a poised figure in a dark robe.

Milena focused on the woman and instantly felt a chill. "That's Nerezza when she was young."

Giacomo turned to Pietro, who had paused in the middle of the corridor. "You didn't tell us Nerezza was with you when you came here."

"Not much to tell," Pietro said, scratching his beard. "She wanted to join her father for the signing of the armistice."

"But didn't you mention to me that you used to be friends with her?" Giacomo said, probing further.

"We were once fellow students—that's all," Pietro said brusquely, then walked off toward the sounds of a crowd gathering. "Now, come, we don't want to be late."

Milena and her friends followed, hanging back. "Do you get the sense that he's not telling us the whole story?" Milena whispered.

"He's definitely hiding something," Giacomo said, eyeing Pietro with suspicion.

"But what?" Savino's question hung in the air.

Milena passed through a grand entrance and into the Ceremonial Hall, an enormous circular room. High above, the heavens were framed by round windows. The moon cast a bluish light across ten towering marble statues that ringed the room, their arms reaching up to support the vaulted ceiling. Milena recognized the figures as Rachana's ten gods from the relief sculpture.

In the center of the hall, well-dressed guests sat around the edges of a large, rectangular cloth with a decorative floral pattern, its corners held down by ornamental weights. Milena was used to taking her meals at a table, seated in a high-backed chair, never on the floor.

Milena helped her teacher sit down next to Aaminah, then took her place beside Savino, and Giacomo plunked himself down on her other side.

A row of warriors in ceremonial garb was across the cloth table from them. With lavish clothes, combed hair, and a clean-shaven face, Ozo was barely recognizable next to Lavanthi and her daughter. He and Lavanthi seemed to be in the midst of a heart-to-heart. He stared so deeply into Lavanthi's eyes as she spoke that Milena wondered if Aaminah was right—maybe there was a romantic spark between the mercenary and the warrior. Strangely, it made her aware of her own body sitting so close to Savino's, and she fidgeted with the beads on her dress.

A servant rang a bright-sounding bell, and Samraat Ajeet walked through an archway at the back of the room in vibrantly colored, ornate robes. The din of conversation abruptly hushed. The samraat climbed a small set of stairs onto a raised golden dais, then he took a seat on a bed of cushions and addressed the gathered crowd in Rachanan. Yaday stood off to the side and translated for Milena and her friends.

"Welcome, warriors, nobles, and honored guests," Yaday said. "Tonight we come together in celebration to honor the Great

Ten. We call on their strength and wisdom to guide us on the dangerous mission ahead."

With a wooden mallet, Ajeet struck the side of a large bronze bowl, and a loud *gong* reverberated around the room. He then ran the head of the mallet around the lip of the bowl in a circular motion, and the single note grew louder and more resonant, washing over the hall. Milena's breathing slowed, and the tension in her body melted.

Once the note faded, the dinner commenced. Servants emerged from side doors carrying bowls and plates filled with a variety of fragrant foods. Ajeet must have had an army of chefs to make so many unique dishes. Milena was dipping a ladle into a steaming bowl of yellow stew when Yaday walked over.

"Would you like to eat with us?" Giacomo offered.

Yaday glanced over at Milena, who met him with an icy stare.

"It's all right, I'll give you some time with your friends," Yaday said, turning to slink away.

Giacomo grabbed Yaday's sleeve. "There's plenty of room. Sit." Giacomo nudged Milena over, knocking her arm holding the ladle. Yellow liquid splashed onto her dress. Milena glared at Giacomo, but he was too busy fussing over Yaday to realize what he had done.

"So, Yaday, Giacomo told me you've been teaching him to meditate," Milena said, her voice barely hiding her contempt.

"That's correct," Yaday said. "Giacomo will need a calm mind to face Vrama."

Milena shook her head with disbelief and elbowed Savino. "Are you hearing this? Yaday has Giacomo convinced he can go up against a dangerous Preta as long as his mind is calm."

"What does that even mean?" Savino said.

"The most dangerous threat to Giacomo will come not from without, but within," Yaday answered.

"Yeah, that didn't make things any clearer," Savino said flatly.

Milena huffed. "Savino, Aaminah, and I have been killing ourselves to get ready for this mission. What have you two been doing? Just relaxing?"

"Meditation is a lot harder than you think," Giacomo shot back. "I was skeptical of Yaday's methods at first, but it's the only way to defeat Vrama."

"Then you two have a plan?" Milena pressed. "Care to share it?"

But before Giacomo could elaborate on what he and Yaday had discussed, another bell rang out. Once again, Samraat Ajeet stood and addressed the gathering while Yaday translated.

"Before dessert is served, the samraat would like to acknowledge the brave warriors who will join him tomorrow on this most important of missions." Ajeet gestured at Lavanthi. "First, his fearless daughter will lead a team of Rachana's finest—Govind, Azad, Devika, and Kavita." Two male and two female warriors stood and bowed as everyone around the room applauded. Milena recognized Azad and Kavita from her training sessions.

Lavanthi rose and declared that she was honored to add Ozo Mori to the team as well, and when Ozo raised a cup to Lavanthi and smiled, saying, "The honor is mine," it became clear that Ozo's motivation wasn't money. Aaminah's hunch about them being in love had been right. Samraat Ajeet seemed to take notice of their connection too. He smiled warmly at his daughter, and Milena guessed he was glad that Lavanthi had found happiness again.

Next, Ajeet recognized Yaday and Giacomo, holding them up

as a shining example of what could be accomplished when two powerful empires worked together. He finished by thanking Giacomo for his selfless offering and said that Rachana and its Geniuses owed him an enormous debt.

Giacomo waved, looking self-conscious, and Milena wondered what kind of offering he was intending to make.

Through Yaday's translation, Ajeet continued. "And by Giacomo's side will be his loyal friends Milena Solari and Savino Poletti." The samraat gestured for them to rise.

Milena stayed put, waiting for Ajeet to call out Aaminah's name. He didn't.

"Don't make me stand up here all alone," Savino whispered, looking down at her.

Begrudgingly, Milena got to her feet and acknowledged the applause with a polite curtsy. As she sat back down, she glanced over to Aaminah, whose usually bright demeanor had been consumed by a gloomy scowl.

"This is so unfair," she fumed.

"I know . . . The samraat's making a mistake." Milena got back up.

"What are you doing?" Aaminah asked.

"I'm going to have a word with Ajeet."

"No, don't," Aaminah protested.

But Milena was already marching toward the dais. As she got closer, two guards stepped into her path.

She looked past them and got Ajeet's attention. "Could we speak, Your Excellency?"

Ajeet nodded and waved off his protection. Milena approached, trying to keep calm, but her heart pounded in her chest.

"I hope you found the meal enjoyable?" Ajeet said merrily.

"It was delicious, thank you," Milena said, briefly disarmed by Ajeet's small talk. "But I'm not here to speak with you about the food."

Ajeet's expression lost all trace of cheer. "You're here about your friend."

"Aaminah helped us find the Compass. All four of us work together. She has to come."

"Lavanthi's evaluation determined that she would be a burden on a mission of this importance. I need warriors who are focused, who follow orders, and who are determined to succeed at all costs."

"Then you need Aaminah," Milena insisted.

"Not according to Lavanthi."

"Aaminah will be the first to admit that she's not the strongest physically, but she has abilities that Lavanthi overlooked. She's a powerful healer. She would be enormously valuable if any of your warriors were injured. She saved Giacomo's life."

For a moment, Ajeet looked intrigued, but then he waved her off. "No, Guru Yaday is quite knowledgeable when it comes to healing poultices and medicines."

Milena's hands balled into fists, and heat flushed through her. "Are you joking? There's no way Yaday is a better healer than Aaminah!"

Ajeet glanced over Milena's shoulder, and she turned around to find Yaday standing right behind her, grimacing like she had kneed him in the gut.

"I . . . I didn't mean . . ." Milena shrank back, realizing she'd gone too far.

Aaminah, who had followed Milena to the dais, tugged at Milena's sleeve. "What are you doing? Let's go."

"I think that would be best," Ajeet said firmly.

Aaminah had begun to drag Milena away when Yaday told them to wait. While he and Ajeet conferred in Rachanan, Milena began to sweat. What if Yaday was trying to get her kicked off the mission for what she had said? She regretted ever opening her mouth.

After what felt like an eternity, Ajeet called Aaminah over to him. "Yaday has persuaded me to reconsider my decision. Be ready to head out first thing in the morning."

Brimming with excitement, Aaminah thanked the samraat and his guru and then ran off to tell Savino and Giacomo the good news.

Milena turned to Yaday, flushed with embarrassment. "Thank you. Whatever you said, thank you. And I'm sorry . . . I'm sure you're a wonderful healer."

"Have a good night," Yaday said coolly, and walked away.

JOURNEY TO THE CALDERA

The palace bell chimed early in the morning.

Way too early.

Giacomo groaned and peeled his eyes open, cursing the dawn. He had barely slept all night. He pulled himself out of bed and got dressed, then shuffled over to the basin. He splashed cool water on his face, dried himself with a towel, and gazed into the mirror.

Vrama stared back at him.

Giacomo sat up and screamed, finding himself back in bed, sweating, short of breath. Mico darted around him, chirping frantically.

"Another nightmare . . ." Giacomo said, shaking off the vision. Mico only settled down once his breathing had returned to normal.

Outside his door, Giacomo found a pack of supplies. He slung it onto his back, and he and Mico headed into the courtyard, where Milena, Savino, and Aaminah were waiting for him, carrying their own packs. Giacomo was glad that Aaminah was joining them, but he wondered what Yaday had said to change Ajeet's mind.

"Good morning," Giacomo said.

Savino and Aaminah replied cheerily, but Milena nodded silently, a suspicious look in her eyes. Giacomo looked away, knowing sooner or later he'd have to tell her the risky plan to vanquish Vrama. Better to wait until after they set out, he reasoned. *By then it will be too late for her to try to stop me.*

"All of you side by side, as it should be," Pietro announced, shuffling toward the group, still in his nightclothes. "Remember, the tetrad symbolizes strength and stability. You four are stronger together than you are apart. Take care of one another."

"We will," Aaminah said.

They hugged their teacher goodbye, Milena lingering a little longer than the rest.

When Giacomo and his friends arrived at the palace, they came upon Lavanthi and the four warriors mounting horses that were laden with bags full of supplies.

A stable boy led over four more horses. He gave the gray one to Ozo, then passed the reins of the others to Savino, Milena, and Aaminah.

"Where's my horse?" Giacomo asked.

Ozo and the stable boy spoke for a moment, then Ozo translated. "He says you're not riding on horseback."

"Then how am I getting there?"

BOOM. BOOM. The ground shook. Giacomo thought an earthquake had struck, but then he saw the source of the tremor: an enormous black elephant with tusks as thick as tree trunks

205

lumbered out from behind the palace. The animal carried Yaday on its head and a golden carriage with a domed roof on its back. Samraat Ajeet was seated on some pillows inside the carriage.

Yaday hollered a command, and the elephant came to a stop, towering over Giacomo. The elephant snorted and gently placed its heavy trunk on Giacomo's shoulder. He stared up in awe. "Uh, hello to you too."

"I think Padma likes you," Yaday called down.

"Good thing," Samraat Ajeet said, "since you'll be riding up here with me in the howdah." He gestured around him to the domed carriage.

Using a rope ladder, Giacomo climbed up into the howdah to sit next to the samraat, who had the Compass slung across his back. The Sacred Tool gave off a faint, energetic hum that Giacomo could feel in his bones. Since seizing it upon their arrival, Ajeet had kept the Compass locked away somewhere in the palace, as if it rightly belonged to him. But until they returned and the horse-Geniuses were restored to full power, Ajeet couldn't even use it. It was the whole reason they had to travel to the caldera on horseback and not through a portal.

As the sun crept over the dunes, Lavanthi led the caravan out of the fortress. Giacomo settled into the cushions, Mico in his lap, grateful for a comfortable place to meditate during the long journey.

A few hours later the world was ablaze. Hot, dusty air whipped Giacomo's face. Though the howdah's roof blocked the sun, any relief Giacomo felt was negated by the guilt eating away at him. He glanced down at his friends, who were out in the open, slick with sweat, and sagging miserably. Their Geniuses were perched on the backs of their horses' saddles, their feathers drooping.

Thankfully, once night swept over the land, the temperature dropped rapidly. The Rachanans set up camp. The warriors raised three apricot-colored tents—a small one for Giacomo and his friends, a larger one for themselves and Ozo, and an even grander one for the samraat. Afterward, the warriors built a fire over which they cooked a meal of meat and rice while Lavanthi passed around skins of water to share.

In Giacomo's tent, the food was consumed in tense silence. He was grateful his friends had been allowed to come on the journey, but now that they were here, he couldn't even talk to them honestly about what was going on.

Every so often, Savino cast a suspicious glance toward the

warriors' tent, where Lavanthi and the others ate their meal amid enthusiastic chatter. "What do you bet they're all talking about how to steal the Straightedge from us once Giacomo gets it?"

"Oh, come on, Savino." Giacomo sighed.

"Sounds to me like they're just having a good time," Aaminah said.

"So you're not even a little worried that Ajeet will leave us stranded in the desert once he gets what he wants?" Savino said.

"I wasn't until you brought it up," Aaminah replied, suddenly looking troubled.

With his belly full, Giacomo rolled out his sleeping mat and was reaching for his sketchbook when Milena pointedly asked, "So what's the plan, Giacomo?"

"I'm going to do some drawing, then go to bed," he said, playing dumb.

"I'm talking about Vrama," she said. "You and Yaday seem to have devised some secret strategy to defeat him. Care to share it with us?"

"Yeah, if we're going to help you, we need to know what to expect," Savino said.

His friends waited expectantly for a response, but something within Giacomo held him back from telling the truth. He got up and headed out of the tent. "I . . . I'm going to take a walk," he said.

"You just said you were going to bed," Savino complained.

As Giacomo walked away, he heard Milena call out after him, "Why won't you just tell us?"

Giacomo wandered past the second tent, where the warriors were still sharing food and stories. Yaday must have noticed the

troubled look in Giacomo's eyes, because he immediately came over to him.

"Is everything all right?"

"I think I'm ready to learn about that final meditation," Giacomo said.

Yaday led Giacomo away from all the noise and took him to the howdah, which had been taken off Padma's back and placed in the sand. The guru sat cross-legged facing Giacomo, who figeted on his cushion.

"Now that you've acknowledged your fears and sat with them for a while, it's time to visit their roots," Yaday explained. "I want you to think back to when you were younger. Where did your fears of losing control and ending up alone first begin?"

"With my mother and father, I guess," Giacomo said. "When I was five, my parents became Lost Souls after their Geniuses were killed. Eventually, they passed away."

"I'm sorry," Yaday said, then paused before continuing with the lesson. "Inside you, there is still that wounded child who experienced so much pain and sorrow from their deaths. For this meditation, I want you to find that child and show him compassion. Lead him out of the darkness."

"Okay . . ." Giacomo said, unsure what Yaday meant. "Does that mean opening my heart to him or something?"

"That's right. You've probably been trying to avoid that part of yourself for a long time, but that little boy needs you to return. Once you're able to treat him with kindness, fear will have a much harder time gripping you."

"And this is going to help me face Vrama?"

"If you can heal your scared inner child, you will not only set yourself free, you can help release others who are also suffering," Yaday said.

Giacomo still wasn't sure about Yaday's methods, but with time running out, he had no choice but to try the meditation. He relaxed and closed his eyes.

After Giacomo sat in silence for a while, his thoughts drifted, and he found himself in a dark stairwell. He heard someone sobbing and made his way toward the voice. When he reached the top of the stairs, he came to a door and opened it, stepping into a familiar room. Though it was hard to see in the dark, Giacomo could tell the place was in shambles—broken furniture littered the floor, and paintings had been ripped from the walls, the canvases sliced to shreds. This had been his home.

Panic swept through him, and Giacomo retreated into the hallway. He was about to escape down the stairwell when the sobbing returned, growing louder.

Giacomo stepped back inside the room, where he soon found the source of the crying—a boy of about five years old, his eyes swollen with tears, who was curled up under the table, rocking himself back and forth.

That's me, Giacomo thought.

Not sure what else to do, Giacomo held out his hand. The boy looked up at him, also unsure.

"I'm so sorry I left you here all alone," Giacomo said. "I know how horrible this all feels. But I've come back for you."

The little boy cautiously crawled out from under the table and took Giacomo's hand. Giacomo found the lantern his father had kept hanging by the door and lit it. The room filled with light, and the little boy rubbed away his tears.

When Giacomo opened his eyes again, he found them damp and quickly wiped them dry with his sleeve. He looked over at Yaday. "Thank you for helping me find him," Giacomo said.

"Keep visiting him," Yaday urged. "He'll need you."

The journey moved out of the desert and into wide, grassy plains. As they traveled, Giacomo spent hour after hour in the howdah meditating, strengthening his bond with his inner child. At night, he took his meals with Yaday and slept in the howdah.

But Giacomo could sense his friends' silent resentment growing stronger with each passing mile. And he realized that by avoiding them, he had only succeeded in pushing them further away. If he told them about the plan to deal with Vrama, they still might not want to have anything to do with him, but at least they would know the truth. So one evening after dinner, he returned to their tent and laid out the plan.

He reminded them that weapons and sacred geometry attacks would be useless against Vrama. As he had expected, his friends were skeptical when he told them that Yaday would perform a ritual to subdue Vrama. They turned hostile when Giacomo explained that he was to be the bait.

"What are you thinking? It's too dangerous," Milena objected.

"Ajeet and Yaday are playing you," Savino said. "They don't care if you make it out alive or not."

"There has to be another way," Aaminah protested.

"I had all the same reservations at first, but you don't know Yaday like I do. I trust him, and I really think this plan will work."

"And what if it doesn't?" Milena said. "What if Vrama takes control of you, and you turn around and attack us?"

"That won't happen," Giacomo insisted.

"If I had known this was the plan, I never would have agreed to come," Milena said.

"What else am I supposed to do?" Giacomo glanced over at Ajeet's tent. "I promised to help the samraat and his people. I can't give up on them now."

"We're not asking you to," Aaminah said, offering some reassurance. "But aren't you scared?"

"Terrified. That's why I could really use your support." Giacomo looked over his friends' faces. "It's like Yaday said, I need a calm mind to face Vrama. And if I know you're all behind me, my mind will be a whole lot calmer."

"Of course we're behind you," Aaminah said, then looked at the others. "Right?"

"It's not like we can turn back now," Savino grumbled. "Just be careful, okay?"

"We're stronger together than we are apart, isn't that what Pietro told us?" Milena said, though she didn't sound entirely convinced.

It wasn't the huge show of encouragement Giacomo longed for, but it was better than nothing.

PRISONERS

Upon returning to Virenzia, Nerezza had put Enzio in the care of her Minister of Security, Rudolfo DeFabbrini. A gaunt man with a thin mustache, DeFabbrini was such a cunning interrogator he could persuade even the most rebellious prisoner to give up their own mother to the gallows, knowing she was innocent. If he couldn't get Enzio to reveal Giacomo's location, no one could.

Each evening, Minister DeFabbrini updated Nerezza on Enzio's mental state, but his report was always the same. "The boy still hasn't talked."

Nerezza was surprised to learn Enzio's will was so strong. He had lived a life of luxury with his mother and father in their villa, never wanting for anything. According to Minister Barrolo, Enzio was a sullen boy who had only become more so when Barrolo began taking in the other children and their Geniuses. Was Enzio's hatred of his father so deep-seated that he was willing to die to protect Giacomo, a boy he barely knew?

"You've kept him isolated this whole time?" Nerezza had asked DeFabbrini during his most recent visit, doing little to hide her impatience.

"Of course, Your Eminence. His cell is completely dark. His only human contact has been with me and his guards."

Barrolo had pleaded with Nerezza to allow him to visit his son. It was a request she took great pleasure in refusing.

"And his food and water intake has been limited?"

A hint of annoyance crossed DeFabbrini's face. "Yes, I'm following procedure." Anticipating Nerezza's next question, the minister added, "The sleep deprivation hasn't broken him yet, but give it another few days. It will."

Nerezza didn't have a few days. It had already been over two weeks since Giacomo fled into the portal to places unknown. He could be well on his way to finding the Straightedge by now. Assuming he didn't already have it.

"I'm going to pay our prisoner a visit," Nerezza said.

With DeFabbrini by her side, Nerezza made her way to the bowels of the palace, a place she hated visiting because of the stifling air and putrid odors. She ignored the moans and mad howling that echoed through the stony passageway.

The guard unlocked the metal door to Enzio's cell and opened it. Torchlight from the hall spilled into the room, where Nerezza found the boy much as she expected—in a grim state. He dangled in the center of the room, arms overhead, wrists shackled to the ceiling by two long chains. The way DeFabbrini had strung him up allowed Enzio's feet to touch the floor, but it had made it impossible for him to sit or lie down. He was shirtless and covered in sweat. His pants drooped around his skinny waist.

"Unchain him immediately," Nerezza ordered, feigning outrage. Hopefully the act would be enough to convince Enzio she was his best chance at survival.

The guards unlocked Enzio's cuffs, and he collapsed with a pained groan.

"Get him some food and water!" Nerezza howled, and the guards rushed off. She wheeled around on DeFabbrini. "This is how you've been treating our prisoner? Worse than you'd treat a sow? It's disgraceful!"

DeFabbrini stared back, putting on his best confused face. He muttered a weak protest, which Nerezza forcefully rejected. They'd performed this little act so many times over the years it had become second nature. DeFabbrini, the heartless tormentor, and Nerezza, the compassionate savior.

The guards returned with a bowl of cold gruel and a goblet of water. Enzio devoured both instantly.

"Leave us," Nerezza ordered.

"Are you sure, Your Eminence?" DeFabbrini said, according to script.

"Now!" Nerezza bellowed. The minister and his guards hustled out the door.

Nerezza leaned down and tipped Enzio's haggard face to meet her gaze. "My sincerest apologies. This is no way for the son of a minister to be treated."

Enzio stared back with a glazed expression, like he wasn't certain where he was. Dark circles hung under his half-lidded eyes. His skin was pale, his cheeks hollow.

"I can get you out of here and into a comfortable room with some real, warm food," Nerezza said in her gentlest voice. "All you need to do is tell me where Giacomo went."

Enzio let out a heavy exhale, and his head dropped. His shoulders shuddered as he let out stifled sobs. "Please . . ."

"Yes, Enzio. I'm listening." *Finally*, she thought.

"Please . . ." Enzio looked up, and his blank expression became charged with emotion. "Get . . . out!"

Nerezza jerked away, stunned by the boy's defiance. "You're a fool!" she spat back, then stormed out, slamming the door behind her with a clang.

"Did he confess?" Minister DeFabbrini asked.

Nerezza strode past him, her gown whooshing around her. "He will."

She found Minister Xiomar in his study, a decrepit vault far away from the other ministers' offices. It was overstuffed with ancient tomes, models of the heavens, and countless glass containers full of colored liquids, some bubbling over small flames.

Xiomar looked up from his worktable, where he was placing one of the Ghiberti gems on a scale. Next to him, the other gem was clamped into a bizarre metal contraption.

"Your Eminence, I wasn't expecting you." Xiomar shuffled out from behind the table. "The experiments are going well, but I'm afraid I'll need more time."

"I'm not here about the gems," Nerezza said. "I need some of the sacred brimstone you spoke of. Barrolo's son is proving more strong-willed than I had expected."

"I see . . ." Xiomar opened a cabinet where he had stored racks of vials. He pulled one out, then siphoned its contents into a syringe with a long metal needle.

Xiomar followed Nerezza back to the dungeon, and while the guards held Enzio still, Xiomar plunged the needle into Enzio's arm. The boy gritted his teeth, then began thrashing against his chains.

Nerezza offered Enzio her unspoken respect. He had resisted her longer than most. Even now, he was waging a valiant fight against the poison coursing through his veins. But defiance was no antidote. Before long, Enzio succumbed, and his body fell limp.

"Now tell me, where is Giacomo?" Nerezza asked.

"He . . . went to . . ." Enzio's voice was ragged, breathless. He looked stunned that the words were coming out of him, as if his own mouth had betrayed him.

When he uttered Giacomo's location—"Rachana's palace"—Nerezza wasn't sure she had heard him correctly.

"The samraat's palace? Are you sure?"

Enzio nodded weakly.

No doubt Pietro was the one who had taken the children to Rachana, but why? He had no allies there. And what did this mean for the Sacred Tools? Had Giacomo abandoned his search for them? Or had he located one of them in enemy lands?

Just as she called Minister Strozzi to her chambers to begin preparations for an assault on Rachana, a guard barged in bearing surprising and fortunate news: Zanobius had been captured.

In the pirate ship's dank hold, Zanobius crouched in a cage, his shackles digging into his wrists and ankles. Outside, the sky flashed and thunder roared. Waves and rain battered the hull. The ship groaned as it fought against the heaving sea. With each swell, Zanobius's stomach lurched, and his metal prison clanged.

To distract himself, Zanobius stayed mentally focused on the task ahead. He kept envisioning his arrival at Nerezza's palace, being brought before her, her eyes bulging with fear as he broke from his prison . . .

However, each time he tried to picture ending Nerezza, his imagination refused to cooperate, as if something deep inside was warning him not to go through with it.

But so many have died at the Supreme Creator's hands, Zanobius told himself. *She deserves it.*

After several days, the churning sea finally calmed, and the sun returned. Through the porthole, Zanobius spied a sliver of green land. Soon, the red bricks of Virenzia's outer wall came into view, and the pirate ship slipped into the bay, lurching to a stop at the dock.

With a metallic scrape, the hatch opened, and sunlight spilled in. Zanobius craned his neck to find Captain Wolff staring down at him from the deck. "Hope you had a nice trip," he said sardonically, then he turned and called out, "Bring up the prisoner!"

One of the pirates cast down a thick rope with an iron hook and hitched it to the top of the cage. The crew used a rope-and-pulley system to hoist the cage onto the deck. It landed with a *thunk*, and Zanobius teetered inside.

Wolff covered the cage with a piece of tattered sailcloth. Through rips in the canvas, Zanobius glimpsed the busy port, where two black-armored soldiers—one holding a sword, the other a spear—marched up the gangplank and confronted Captain Wolff.

"What kind of cargo are you transporting?" the sword-wielding soldier demanded.

"The dangerous kind," Wolff said, then lowered his voice. "I've captured the Tulpa that the Supreme Creator's lookin' for. I've come to collect my reward."

The pirates transferred Zanobius's cage to a horse-drawn cart, then a convoy of soldiers escorted Wolff and his men through the city's back alleys.

When they reached the palace, the cart jerked to a stop. With a collective grunt, the pirates lifted the cage and began carrying it. Behind the sailcloth, Zanobius listened as the buzzing sounds of city life gave way to the hollow *clomp* of boots on stone.

"Put him there," someone ordered. The cage dropped with a *clang.*

Zanobius spotted slivers of his surroundings: onyx marble columns, paintings of soldiers locked in battle, a black-robed figure hunched on the throne. He heard the heavy breathing of Nerezza's Genius, Victoria.

Zanobius readied himself.

"Let me see him!" Nerezza's shrill voice filled the chamber.

With a *whoosh*, the canvas was pulled away. Zanobius squinted as his eyes adjusted to the bright light streaming in through the high windows. A face came into focus—wrinkled and worn. Two beady black eyes. Lips painted a harsh red.

"It's really you," Nerezza said with a satisfied smile. "Welcome back to Virenzia, Zanobius."

Zanobius glanced around the room, looking for an opening to launch his attack, but all he found were obstacles. Dozens of soldiers filled the hall; in front of the dais loomed the robed figures of Nerezza's Council, Baldassare Barrolo among them; Victoria lurked behind Nerezza's throne.

This was a reckless idea, he thought. Breaking free of his cage would be easy enough, but Zanobius hadn't anticipated the number of people he'd have to contend with to get to Nerezza—people he didn't want to harm.

"We delivered the Tulpa," Captain Wolff said, flanked by his crew. "Where's our reward?"

Nerezza turned to Captain Wolff. "It appears he's missing an arm."

Wolff scowled. "Not our fault. It was already gone when we found him."

Zanobius was beginning to grow nervous. Nerezza knew full well that the pirates weren't responsible for his injury.

"Nevertheless, you can't expect me to pay for damaged goods."

"You greedy, double-dealin' scoundrel!" Wolff shouted.

Nerezza nodded to her soldiers. "Show these ruffians out."

Wolff's hand went to his sword's hilt. "We're not going anywhere until we get our—"

Before Wolff could finish, Nerezza pulled a brush from her black robe and swiped. From the shadows, a streak of violet shot from Victoria's crown, crashing into Wolff and propelling him down the length of the hall. His body slammed into the far wall and crumpled in a smoking heap.

Wolff's men raised their blades and charged; Nerezza's soldiers leaped to her defense. With both sides clashing, Zanobius knew he wouldn't get a better shot at Nerezza, so he snapped his shackles, bent an opening in the metal bars, and squeezed through. The Council members clambered behind the dais. "Your Eminence, follow us!" Baldassare shouted.

But Nerezza didn't flee. She locked her gaze on Zanobius, her eyes widening with a familiar expression, and Ugalino's voice echoed in his mind.

She knows she will never be able to create anything as magnificent as you.

Zanobius charged through the throng of pirates and soldiers. Nerezza shuffled backward, brushing sharp strokes in his direction. He dodged Victoria's first beam, then leaped over the second. But the third blasted Zanobius off his feet and launched him through the air. With a deafening *crack*, he crashed into a column and dropped to the floor. Shards of marble rained down around him.

Zanobius groaned and staggered to his feet. Victoria crawled over the dais, her giant claws clacking on the floor. Nerezza waved her brush again, and Victoria roared.

The light was blinding. Zanobius jumped out of the way and somersaulted, tumbling into another column. He ducked behind it, and an instant later, a blaze of violet exploded against the marble.

Dust and smoke clogged the room, making it difficult to see more than a few feet in any direction. Zanobius spotted Nerezza's silhouette through the haze and ran headlong at it. He reached out, grasping handfuls of velvet. Nerezza's robe cinched around her bony frame as Zanobius lifted her off her feet. He batted her brush away and latched a hand around her throat.

"Release me!" The air went out of Nerezza with a wheeze. She writhed in his grip. Somewhere in the hall, Victoria shrieked in pain.

"You're done terrorizing the world," Zanobius said.

But something inside him stayed his hand. He realized he had been waiting for Ugalino to give him the order to end Nerezza. But with his master gone, the choice to kill would have to come from Zanobius himself. As much as it pained him to admit it, he knew he couldn't go through with it.

Now, he had to get out of there. With a roar, Zanobius threw Nerezza to the floor and looked for the nearest door, but the way out was hidden by the haze. He picked a direction and headed that way. He didn't get far.

A stabbing pain shot through his upper back, and Zanobius was stopped in his tracks. He looked down, horrified to find the tip of one of Victoria's talons poking from his chest. Gray fluid spilled everywhere.

Victoria wrapped the rest of her claws around Zanobius and brought him close, studying him with her creepy yellow eyes, as if she was deciding whether to eat him whole or tear him into bits first. Not wanting to find out, Zanobius wrested one of his arms free and punched Victoria's eye, which squelched on impact. In concert with Nerezza's scream, the Genius screeched and reeled back, but her grip held. Victoria pinned Zanobius to the floor and bore down with all her weight. Her maw snapped open, ready for the kill.

Zanobius had been at the mercy of Nerezza and her Genius

before. But this time when they blasted him into oblivion, there would be no one waiting to rebuild him, no waking up from this fight.

This is truly the end.

"Victoria, to me!" Nerezza climbed back to her feet. One of her own eyes was swelling from the injury Zanobius had inflicted on her Genius, but Nerezza retrieved her brush and held it.

The Genius tilted her head toward her, unsure what to make of the command.

"Release him!" Nerezza shouted. With a viscous sucking sound, Victoria pulled her claw out of Zanobius.

Zanobius stumbled to his feet, but a spiral of light tangled around him, pinning his arms to his sides. With a wave of her brush, Nerezza suspended him above the floor.

Baldassare and another Council member emerged from behind the dais. "What are you waiting for?" Baldassare shouted. "Destroy him!"

Zanobius awaited his fate. With another stroke, Nerezza could obliterate him. But something had stayed her hand as well— though Zanobius doubted it was her conscience.

"No, he's more valuable to me in one piece," Nerezza said, then turned to the second Council member. The ancient, hunchbacked man crept forward. "Are you still confident our plan will work, Minister Xiomar?"

What plan? Zanobius began to panic. All this time, Zanobius had assumed Nerezza had wanted him captured alive so she could destroy him personally. Clearly, he had made a grave miscalculation.

The hunchback edged closer, studying Zanobius with a look of curiosity and disgust. It reminded Zanobius of the way a human regards an insect before squashing it. Xiomar's gaze pondered the space where Zanobius's arm was missing.

"Yes. I'll take some measurements and you can begin at once," the hunchback said. His breath smelled of death.

THE PRETA

Late one afternoon, Ajeet and his caravan left behind the grasslands and crossed into a vast, rocky expanse. The sky turned gloomy, and the thickening haze choked the afternoon sun. The group forged through the volcanic wasteland until they arrived at the rim of an enormous crater. The journey to Vrama's lair was finally nearing its end.

Giacomo climbed down from the howdah and gazed into the caldera. It looked as if a giant hole had been dug in the earth. Off to his left, he noticed the tattered remains of a few tents and some scattered supplies, half buried in ash. "Maybe we should set up camp and head in at first light?" Giacomo suggested.

"No, we're going in now," Ajeet insisted.

"Vrama may have already sensed our arrival," Yaday said. "The longer we wait out here, the more vulnerable your Geniuses will be."

Giacomo glanced at Mico and his friends' Geniuses, realizing

that once Vrama saw them, he might use the Straightedge to drain their power too. *I'm not going to give him that chance.*

Ozo scanned the caldera. "I don't see any passageways. What's our best path in?"

Samraat Ajeet hollered an order at his warriors and they all dismounted. Yaday informed Giacomo and his friends that they should all wait while Lavanthi and the others scouted for an entry point.

Before they could leave, Savino stepped forward. "That will take too long. Give Giacomo the Compass. He'll find us a way in."

Giacomo caught on to Savino's plan. "That's right, I was able to use the Compass to home in on the Straightedge. It'll be the quickest way to find Vrama."

Ajeet looked to Yaday, and the two men conferred privately. Whatever Yaday said must have been convincing, because the samraat took the Compass off his back and held it out to Giacomo.

Giacomo grabbed it, but Ajeet's grip held firm. "I'm giving this to you because I trust you. Do not make me regret this decision."

"I won't," Giacomo said. Ajeet released the Compass, and Giacomo ran his hand over its smooth handle, relieved to have it in his possession again.

With the Compass pointed in front of him, Giacomo immediately sensed a faint thrumming from somewhere deep in the earth. Mico gave a wary trill, and Giacomo descended a narrow path that hugged the caldera's inner wall. The group's footfalls crunched behind him.

Halfway down the slope, the Compass vibrated and jerked left, pointing at a crevice hidden behind a jutting stone.

"I think I found our way in," Giacomo called out. "But it's going to be a tight squeeze."

Ajeet peered into the slit of darkness, his katar at the ready. "We'll manage."

With Mico lighting the way, Giacomo entered first, followed by Yaday. Milena, Savino, and Aaminah were spread out among the warriors, with instructions from Ajeet to project sacred geometry supports should the walls start caving in.

The rocks pressed close. Giacomo's heartbeat quickened. He checked behind him, where the sliver of daylight grew smaller and smaller until it vanished altogether. They advanced steadily, boring deeper into the earth. A sharp odor stung Giacomo's nostrils, and he covered his nose. "Ugh. What's that smell?"

Yaday coughed. "The gases from the magma."

The crevice broadened into a long tunnel that eventually emptied into a wide underground chamber, and Giacomo's nerves calmed a bit. The group spread out, and the bird-Geniuses illuminated the space, adding their casts of blue, green, and yellow to Mico's red beam. Several more passageways became visible along one side of the cavern wall. Along the other, a deep fissure cut into the earth. Standing near its edge, Giacomo could see a river of glowing magma bubbling far below. A wave of stinking, scalding air slapped Giacomo, and he stepped back.

Ajeet turned to Giacomo. "Which way now?"

Giacomo steadied his breathing and focused again on the Compass. It tugged his arms, more forcefully this time, and dragged him toward one of the middle tunnels.

Giacomo heard the others fall into line behind him, but then they all stopped short. Out of the tunnel's blackness stepped the ghostly form of a man with sallow skin, a scraggly white beard, and tattered robes. His neck was extremely thin, his stomach distended. He held a katar in one hand, its blade jagged and worn as if it had seen many battles.

"Vrama . . . ?" Giacomo said, his heart pounding.

"No," Ajeet said, stepping to Giacomo's side. "That's . . . That's Samraat Jagesh."

In Giacomo's growing panic, it took a moment for the name to sink in. "Your father . . . ?"

Out of the black stone walls, six more wraithlike figures emerged, all with the same pale yellow skin, impossibly thin neck, and swollen belly. They wore remnants of armor and carried broken daggers.

Lavanthi moved toward one of the men. "Mahesh?"

Ozo grabbed her arm to pull her back, but she broke away, muttering something in Rachanan. Ozo's face filled with shock, and he looked at Giacomo. "She says that thing is . . . *was* . . . her husband."

A final Preta emerged, and despite his grim appearance, Giacomo connected his face to the portrait of the man he'd seen in Yaday's chambers—Guru Pankaj. Yaday's eyes widened, and his jaw went slack. To Giacomo's ears, it sounded like Yaday asked his teacher a question, but there wasn't time for a translation.

Guru Pankaj didn't reply, at least not with anything that sounded like words. Instead, he and the other Pretas emitted droning groans as they closed in.

"Steady . . ." Ajeet said, backing away. The group followed his lead.

Aaminah's hand latched onto Giacomo's arm. "I can feel their suffering . . . They're in so much pain."

"I know . . ." Giacomo replied. "Try to stay calm. Pretas feed off your fears."

The Pretas converged on the living, forcing them closer to the fissure and the long drop to the river of magma. With conflicted looks, the Rachanans stared at what remained of their friends and family.

"What are you all waiting for?" Savino shouted. He gestured at the warriors. "Shouldn't we attack them?"

"No!" Ajeet snapped. "I don't believe they mean to harm us." Giacomo sensed the tenderness in Ajeet's heart battling the terror in his eyes. It was precisely how Giacomo would have felt had his parents' ghosts suddenly appeared.

"Fighting will only anger them more," Yaday cautioned.

"Then how do we get rid of them?" Milena said, her voice rising.

Growing frantic, Giacomo tried to figure out a way he could help, but Yaday had prepared him to deal with only one Preta, not a whole group.

With a long, rattly exhale, Samraat Jagesh uttered a command and pointed his shaky hand at the tunnel they had come through. Giacomo didn't need anyone to translate—the Pretas wanted them gone.

"Giacomo, maybe you should make a portal out of here," Aaminah suggested.

"Not without the Straightedge," Giacomo said.

"And not without vanquishing Vrama," Ajeet added. "My father just said that as long as Vrama haunts the caldera, they can never be at peace."

Yaday looked to Aaminah, desperation on his face. "Can you play something for them?"

With a troubled look in her eyes, Aaminah plucked out a sorrowful tune on her tambur as Luna washed the cavern in waves of yellow light. Yaday joined her with his drum, chanting in Rachanan. The Pretas slowed their advance, as if the air had suddenly become thick. Yaday looked relieved.

But the music's effect was only temporary. The Pretas pushed through Luna's light and continued their advance.

"May the gods help us all . . ." Ajeet said gravely, and raised his katar.

Jagesh lifted his dagger in reply.

"Giacomo, make a portal to the surface," Ajeet commanded. "Before it's too late!"

"But we're so close—"

"Do it!" the samraat roared.

Giacomo snapped open the Compass, and the Pretas charged. The Rachanan warriors surged past Giacomo, their blades colliding with the phantoms' weapons in a shower of sparks. Giacomo fumbled with the Compass and tried to envision the caldera's outer surface, but the sounds of battle kept pulling his attention back underground.

Ozo and Lavanthi's husband traded blows. The Preta knocked Ozo onto his back and was moments away from ending the mercenary's life when Lavanthi jumped between them and slashed her katar. Mahesh let out an ear-piercing screech and blew away like sand in a windstorm.

Lavanthi had barely helped Ozo to his feet when Mahesh reappeared, clawing his way out of the wall, writhing and hissing.

Aaminah continued to play, slowing down a few of the Pretas while Milena and Savino huddled around her and sent off streaks of light from their Geniuses. But every time someone eliminated a Preta, with either a blade or a burst of light, he would materialize in another part of the cavern and resume his attack.

Giacomo looked away from the fight and shut his eyes, dampening the clatter. Finally, he glimpsed a shimmering image of the outside world and started to spin the Compass, but something stopped him.

His eyes snapped open to find one of the Pretas grabbing the Compass's legs. The Preta ripped the Tool from Giacomo's grip and flung it toward the edge of the drop-off. Giacomo tried to dive after it, but the Preta's bony arm wrapped around his throat. Giacomo thrust his head back and slammed it into the Preta's chin, to no effect. Choking, Giacomo fished for his pencil. He pulled it from his pocket and swiped. Mico's gem lit up and fired off a swirl of red, knocking the Preta away.

Mico screeched a warning, and Giacomo looked to his right, where another Preta was closing in. Giacomo stumbled away from him, toward the wall of tunnels.

There's still one way to save everyone, Giacomo thought.

He frantically jabbed his pencil, and Mico sent out a barrage of light that kept the Pretas momentarily at bay. Giacomo's gaze swept the cavern, searching for assistance, but Yaday was busy grappling with Guru Pankaj, and his friends were similarly occupied. Giacomo knew that if he didn't make a go at getting the Straightedge now, he might not have another chance. He realized he'd have to trust that one of them would be able to get the Compass back for him.

He bolted down the tunnel that had been calling to him earlier. Two Pretas gave chase, but something about this tunnel prevented them from going farther, and they vanished into the walls. A moment later, there was a deep rumbling. Giacomo looked back as the passageway collapsed and the fallen rocks cut him off from the group.

With Mico lighting the way, Giacomo steeled himself and forged on. Before long, the passageway became unbearably hot and stuffy. Giacomo soon discovered why—rivulets of lava trickled down the rocky walls.

I've been here before, Giacomo realized. He slowed his pace and took a few deep breaths in anticipation of facing Vrama.

Mico's beam glinted off something shiny up ahead. Giacomo made straight for it.

Like in his vision, the tunnel opened up into a triangular-shaped cavern that resembled the inside of a pyramid. *Or a tetrahedron*, Giacomo realized. He recognized the sharp black rocks jutting from the floor and ceiling.

In a shadowy corner, Giacomo made out the L shape of the Straightedge. But it appeared to be moving. Vrama's skeletal form emerged from the dark, clutching the Sacred Tool in his right hand.

Giacomo's fear flared up. With a few calming breaths, he tamped it down before it could spread.

Vrama inched closer and studied Giacomo for a long, tense moment. The Preta tilted his head, and his bulging eyes sparked with recognition. Vrama whispered something in a raspy voice, but without Yaday to translate, Giacomo couldn't figure out what he was saying.

"I . . . I don't speak your language," Giacomo said.

Vrama lowered his head and closed his eyes, as if he were praying. A circle in the center of his chest lit up with an emerald glow.

Giacomo couldn't believe what he was seeing. It looked like a piece of glass had been partially absorbed into Vrama's skin. Then it hit him—the green light wasn't coming from glass. It was coming from a Genius's gem!

When Vrama spoke again, Giacomo was astounded to discover he could understand the Preta.

"I recognize you . . . You're the boy who appeared to me once before. But you vanished before I could strike you down. This time, you won't get away!" Vrama raised the Straightedge and came at Giacomo. Mico erupted with a frightened trill.

"No! Wait!" Giacomo shouted. "I'm a Tulpa!"

The Preta stopped and lowered his weapon. "I sensed there was something different about you. You're so young and innocent, the perfect vessel to house my tortured soul."

"You must be tired of endlessly suffering, trapped in this cave," Giacomo said, letting his heartbeat settle. "If you promise to return power to all the horse-Geniuses, I'll set you free." As Yaday had predicted, Vrama was tempted by the offering.

"Agreed," the Preta hissed, and stepped toward Giacomo.

Giacomo had no intention of letting Vrama's soul inside him, but the Preta didn't need to know that. He gripped his pencil tightly and waited for Vrama to get closer. All Giacomo had to do was land one clean strike and knock the Straightedge out of his bony hands.

Vrama came to a stop in front of Giacomo. "When this is all over, you won't remember a thing." A menacing smile stretched across his face . . . and kept going. His mouth widened and his jaw unhinged, like a snake about to devour its prey. An inky-black strand wound its way out of Vrama's narrow throat.

Giacomo's breath caught, his eyes fixed on the sinewy darkness twisting toward him.

Is that . . . Vrama's soul . . . ?

Mico squawked, snapping Giacomo out of his trance.

He swiped his pencil, and a red blaze lit up the cavern. Vrama went flying toward one corner, the Straightedge to another.

Before Giacomo could reach his prize, Vrama sucked up his soul like it was a long black noodle, then was on him, clawing and biting at Giacomo's flesh. He dragged Giacomo away from the Straightedge and hurled him against the rocks.

As Giacomo lay sprawled on the cave floor gasping for air, he regretted his decision to face Vrama alone.

Vrama stalked toward him, the Straightedge back in his possession. He raised it like a scythe, and the web of patterns across its surface lit up. Vrama brought the glimmering weapon down fast, and Giacomo rolled, lashing out with his pencil.

Mico fired off strands of light, but Vrama cut through the attack. The next time he swung the Straightedge, Mico's gem was extinguished. Giacomo jabbed his pencil again in a panic, but Mico's gem stayed dark and powerless. Mico flew back and forth, chirping frantically, then plummeted to the cave floor. The hummingbird lay still.

When Vrama sapped Mico's power, Giacomo felt as if all his strength, all his hope, drained away too. What remained was his fear, which crashed through him in a wave.

Vrama loomed over him, the Straightedge's glow casting a shadow onto his shriveled face. His jaw hinged open again, and the same oily tendril slithered out.

Giacomo crawled backward until he met the wall and couldn't go any farther. The tendril slipped closer. Giacomo turned his head away, but the blackness twined around his neck, forcing its way into his mouth.

An iciness raked down Giacomo's throat. He tried to scream and found his voice had been taken from him. For a moment, an inky cord hung between Preta and Tulpa like a tether, then Vrama's soul wound the rest of the way into Giacomo. He felt it spiraling deeper inside his body, coiling around his lungs and heart, laying claim to him.

First the gem embedded in Vrama's chest dimmed, and then his body faded away completely. The Straightedge dropped into the dirt.

Giacomo tried to inhale . . . and no breath came.

He attempted to still his mind . . . but it swarmed with fear.

He tried to reach for the Straightedge . . . yet his arms were paralyzed.

And as his vision turned blurry and dark at the edges . . . his mind began slipping away.

Giacomo cast his thoughts back to his old home. He ran up the stairway, calling out to his five-year-old self, assuring him everything would be all right and that together, they could stop Vrama from taking control. He burst through the door, but instead of connecting to his own past, Giacomo was plunged into someone else's.

He saw a boy about his own age with dark-brown skin running alongside a rushing river. He was laughing, glancing behind him at a younger girl with a long black braid who was giving chase.

"You're too slow, sister!" the boy shouted.

"Wait for me, Vrama!" the girl hollered back.

She tried to catch up to her brother, but her foot stepped too close to the riverbank. The loose dirt gave way, and she plunged into the rapids.

When Vrama looked behind him again, he saw that his sister was missing. "Anuja? Where are you? Are you hiding on me again?"

He heard a high-pitched scream and spun toward the river, where the rushing water was pulling Anuja away.

Vrama raced along the riverbank, keeping pace with his sister. She fought the current, but the river overpowered her and dragged her under. Vrama watched, panic in his eyes, waiting for her to surface again.

She never did.

Giacomo experienced the sadness and anger that had coursed through Vrama as if he had lived through the tragedy himself. Feeling helpless, Vrama blamed the gods for taking his sister from him, and he made a silent vow to one day become the most powerful warrior in the empire. He would protect and defend all the people in Rachana so no one would have to experience the suffering he had endured.

The memory faded, and Giacomo was back in the cavern. Vrama's soul writhed and twisted within him.

I'm sorry for what happened to your sister, Giacomo said voicelessly. *That must have been so horrible.*

Anuja was a part of me, Vrama replied. *She was my life. Do you know what it's like to have a part of you ripped away like that?*

I do, Giacomo said. *My parents were taken from me.*

A high-pitched twang startled Giacomo, bringing his awareness back to the physical world. The note echoed through the cavern, accompanied by a pulse of light. More notes followed until the cave—and Giacomo—were awash in yellow. Mico stirred next to him. Giacomo's eyesight cleared enough to see a shadowy figure approaching, strumming a tambur.

Aaminah . . .

But the tunnel had caved in. How had she reached him?

With the music humming through Giacomo, Vrama's thrashing soul began to relent. Giacomo felt control returning to his own body, but he feared the music's paralyzing effects on Vrama would be only temporary. It would take both him and Aaminah to eliminate the Preta for good.

First, he had to restore Mico's power, but to do that, he needed the Straightedge.

With his remaining strength, Giacomo extended his arm toward the Sacred Tool, but it was out of reach. Aaminah, whose hands were busy playing the tambur, kicked it into range. Giacomo's fingers wrapped around the warm metal. He brought it closer, gripping it with both hands. The patterns burned brightly. At the same moment, the gem in Mico's crown glowed, and the Genius fluttered back to life.

Next, Giacomo needed to find a way to force Vrama out of his body.

You have so much power inside you . . .

Milena's words came back to him in a flash of inspiration. Vrama couldn't be destroyed by an outside force, but maybe by summoning the energy within himself, Giacomo could drive him out.

Focusing on Aaminah's music, Giacomo closed his eyes and steadied his mind, visualizing the Creator's Pattern. He pictured the glowing outline of the cube coming out of the pattern and boxing in Vrama's soul.

Giacomo opened his eyes to find Mico's red beam was trained on his chest, projecting the outline of a cube. To Giacomo's surprise, the Creator's Pattern briefly flashed across his body. Mico created a three-dimensional cube from the pattern, and as he pulled the shape out, Giacomo felt as if his skin were going to burst open.

The cube hovered in the air between Giacomo and Mico now, and Giacomo could see Vrama's soul trapped inside. The black tendril surged against the glowing square walls, trying to break free.

The Straightedge's energy coursed through Giacomo, giving him a newfound strength. He rose to his feet and raised the Tool over his head.

"Leave this realm," Giacomo said, relieved to find his voice had returned. "Be with Anuja."

He swung down hard at the cube, shattering the light and tearing Vrama's soul into a thousand pieces. As the Preta met his end, a high-pitched screech ripped through the cavern and drowned out the music.

Giacomo let out a giant exhale. "Aaminah . . . thank you . . ."

But Aaminah didn't respond. Giacomo turned to discover that she was sprawled on the ground, knocked out by the force of the blast. Luna lay on her chest, her wings quivering.

Giacomo rushed to Aaminah and propped her up, checking for

a heartbeat. She was still alive, and Giacomo saw her eyes flutter weakly. He looked around and noticed a second tunnel in the back of the cavern, opposite the one he had come through—that must've been how Aaminah had gotten to him. Giacomo dragged her over to the passageway, hoping it would lead back to their friends.

Then the world began to shake. Lava seeped through the cracks in the walls. Within moments the cavern became a furnace. The noxious fumes stung Giacomo's nostrils and made him dizzy.

Jagged rocks broke from the ceiling and crashed around them. If Giacomo didn't figure a way out quickly, he and Aaminah would be buried alive.

RETURN

A warrior Preta rushed at Milena. She swiped her brush and drove a rectangular light shield at him, knocking her attacker backward. The Preta scrambled to his feet and came at her again.

The Pretas' onslaught had been relentless. The Rachanans were trapped in an endless battle with their lifeless counterparts, while Milena and Savino fought their way toward the Compass lying on the cavern floor.

There was still no sign of Giacomo. Or Aaminah, either. After Giacomo had bolted down one of the tunnels and it caved in, Aaminah had become more and more worried until finally she'd left Milena's side, shouting, "Luna can track down Mico!" Milena had called after her to stop, but Aaminah had already vanished into another passage.

"Got it!" Savino shouted, and Milena whirled around to find him holding the Compass. But before he could make a portal, a Preta leaped from the fracas and charged.

"Behind you!" Milena warned.

Savino spun around, swinging the Compass like a sword. The warrior Preta caught it in mid-arc, and they grappled over it. Nero squawked and scratched at the Preta's face to no effect.

Though claws and weapons didn't make a mark on the Pretas, sacred geometry could do a little damage. With a precise brushstroke, Milena triggered Gaia to launch a sliver of green that sliced the Preta's hands, causing him to release the Compass.

But he was only momentarily injured; in the next instant, the Preta overpowered Savino and hurled him through the air. Savino slammed into the ground and rolled toward the edge of the fissure. With Savino still hugging the Compass, Milena watched as her friend vanished over the cliff, his Genius swooping down after him with an urgent *caw*.

"Savino!" Milena yelled, and furiously barraged the warrior Preta with light. He uttered a screech, then exploded into dust.

Knowing he would soon return, Milena raced to the fissure and found Savino clinging to a rocky ledge with one hand and holding the Compass with the other. Below, lava bubbled. Nero squawked frantically and tugged on Savino's collar.

"Help!" Savino hollered.

"You need both of your hands," Milena called back. "Pass me the Compass!"

Savino swung his arm, hoisting the Sacred Tool over his head. Milena leaned over the edge, grasped the Compass's legs, and reeled it in.

With both hands free, Savino grabbed the ledge and began to climb up, but he soon ran out of holds to grip. "I can't make it any farther," he cried.

Milena went to help, but two bony hands seized her by the leg and dragged her away. Milena clung to the Compass but dropped her brush, which disappeared into the fissure. She looked behind her and groaned in frustration. The Preta she'd just vanquished had already re-formed and resumed his attack. She struggled against the warrior while Gaia stabbed him with her beak. The Preta batted Gaia away, and Milena felt her own head sting from the blow. Gaia screeched and crashed. The Preta pinned Milena to the ground with the Compass and pressed it to her throat, cutting off her air.

Milena thrashed and gasped for breath, her mind turning foggy. In that moment, she thought of Pietro and all the times in her lessons when she'd made a mistake and he had been there to guide her. She imagined his weathered hand taking hers and leading her out of this nightmare. But suddenly, his image was replaced by another: Savino, dangling helplessly over the lava. If Milena died, he would die too. And she refused to let that happen.

Summoning all her strength, Milena rolled, jostling the Preta off her just enough to drive a knee up into his swollen belly. The Preta groaned and reeled back.

Milena knew he would come at her again. And again. She just had to get to Savino before his next assault. She glanced over her shoulder to see that the Preta was about to move in for the kill, but to her surprise, he turned away and staggered off, as if being led by an unseen force.

All around the cave, the other Pretas were doing the same. Milena could see their leader, Samraat Jagesh, who had still been fighting his son. She watched as Jagesh's tortured expression became still and he gave up his battle against Ajeet. Then his body broke apart into tiny specks of light. One by one, the Pretas' forms separated into luminous swirls that wound together and drifted upward, then flickered away.

Milena looked around the cavern, waiting for the Pretas to reappear. None returned. The Rachanans cheered, exhausted by their efforts.

"Still down here!" a voice called.

Savino!

Milena called Ozo and Lavanthi over to help, and the three of them hoisted Savino out of the steaming fissure. "You're all right!" She hugged him tightly, and the emotion she felt when holding him in her arms was intense, unlike anything she could remember. She told herself it was because he had been in serious danger. But was that really the only reason?

"Yeah . . . I'm fine," Savino said, pulling away. He looked around the cavern. "What happened? Where did all the Pretas go?"

"They disappeared," Milena said with relief. "Giacomo must have vanquished Vrama."

"I heard Samraat Jagesh say they would all finally be at peace," Yaday said.

But before they had a chance to catch their breath, the caldera rumbled. Chunks of rock crashed around them, and the tunnels started caving in.

Ajeet pointed to Milena. "Get us to the surface! Now!"

Milena glanced back at the tunnels where Giacomo and Aaminah had vanished. "What about our friends?"

"If Giacomo defeated Vrama, they're probably already on their way out," Ajeet assured her.

Milena wasn't so confident, but there wasn't time to argue. With the world shaking and booming, she brought to mind the caldera's rocky rim, then she raised the Compass and spun open a portal. Ajeet ushered his warriors, Ozo, and Yaday, through, then disappeared into the light. Looking around for Giacomo and Aaminah one final time, Milena, Savino, and their Geniuses dove in after the Rachanans.

Milena spilled out of the portal, ran to the edge of the caldera, and looked down into it. The earth had cracked, and lava was bubbling out of it. Steaming molten rock began filling the caldera's bowl. She shook her head, refusing to believe the sight before her.

Please . . . help them find a way out, she prayed.

Her thoughts were interrupted by an explosion on the far side of the caldera. Milena turned toward the sound, assuming more of the caldera had collapsed. Instead, a red beam cut through the sky, dust and smoke billowing around its base.

"Mico's light! That has to be Giacomo!" Milena shouted.

Yaday and Ajeet climbed onto the elephant and lumbered away down the slope. Savino, Milena, and the warriors all mounted their horses and galloped toward the distant light.

By the time they reached the site of the explosion, the sun had set and the dust was beginning to clear. Giacomo staggered through the haze with Aaminah propped against him, her arm slung over his shoulders. The Straightedge hung in the crook of his arm.

Milena gasped. "He found it! They're all right!"

As her horse slowed to a trot, Milena jumped from its saddle and raced to Giacomo. Upon her arrival, Giacomo fell to his knees, letting Aaminah spill into Milena's arms.

"Aaminah . . . ?"

Aaminah let out a faint, wheezing exhale, and Milena realized her relief had been premature.

Milena looked at Giacomo. "What happened to her?"

"I'm not sure . . ." Giacomo coughed and gasped for air. "She helped me stop Vrama. Then I used the Straightedge to destroy him. Maybe she got hit with the blast."

Milena felt a hand on her shoulder. Savino leaned in and touched Aaminah's cheek. "Where's Luna?"

Giacomo held out a ball of purple and orange feathers in his cupped hand. Luna stirred and let out a faint chirp. "She can't fly."

The other warriors gathered around. "How were you able to escape?" Ajeet asked.

"I had to use the Straightedge to blast our way out," Giacomo explained.

With a panicked look on his face, Yaday hurried over. Aaminah was unresponsive, her head lolling against Milena's chest. He peeled back the collar of Aaminah's torn tunic, revealing a dark bruise near her shoulder. The bruise moved. It looked like a worm had burrowed into Aaminah and was squirming underneath her skin. Milena shuddered. "What is that?"

"I fear that when Giacomo destroyed Vrama, part of his soul entered her," Yaday said.

"What?" Giacomo said. "No . . . I didn't mean—"

"It's not your fault," Yaday said. "Vrama is trying to cling to this world with every last shred of his being."

"Get it out!" Milena pleaded.

"Not here. It's too dangerous. We need to get her back to the palace, where the healers and I can tend to her." Yaday whistled, and Padma's trunk wound toward Aaminah.

Milena held tight to her friend, refusing to let her go.

"I'm sorry," Yaday said. "It should have been me helping Giacomo put an end to Vrama, not Aaminah."

Milena loosened her grip as Padma's trunk wrapped around Aaminah and hoisted her gently into the howdah.

"She's going to be all right," Savino said, putting an arm around Milena. "Aaminah's tougher than both of us combined."

"I know." She gulped in air and squeezed Savino's hand in thanks, trying to hide her tears.

Savino pulled his hand back, like he'd realized he had lingered too long. Or regretted it. Milena found herself wishing he had hung on a little longer.

Savino opened a portal, and Giacomo followed him into the light.

They emerged at the palace steps, where the stars sparkled in the cloudless night. Giacomo took in lungfuls of the fresh air, cleansing himself of the caldera's poisonous fumes and Vrama's polluted soul.

As soon as the elephant squeezed through, Yaday was already calling for guards to hurry to take Aaminah from the howdah and straight to the healers. Milena climbed down after them, cheeks damp with tears. She met Giacomo with a dark look. It could have been because of how upset she was, though Giacomo suspected she blamed him for what had happened to their friend.

Aaminah will be all right, Giacomo told himself. *She has to be*.

Once Aaminah was in the palace, Ajeet pulled Giacomo aside. "Now that you have the Straightedge, I need to take you to Kavi."

A short time later, Giacomo arrived at the stables, where the samraat's horse-Genius, along with dozens of others, tiredly trotted out onto the grassy field.

Gazing into Kavi's large, glassy eyes, Giacomo saw his own reflection staring back, looking unsure.

"Are you ready?" Ajeet asked.

Giacomo ran his fingers over the Straightedge's intricate, embossed patterns. "I . . . I don't know if I should do this. What if Vrama corrupted the Tool somehow?" It had been one thing to restore Mico to power, since they shared a connection. He didn't have the same bond with Rachana's Geniuses. They weren't even birds. "What if something goes wrong and I make things worse?"

"You won't." Milena came over, and to Giacomo's surprise, she gave him a hug. "You can do this."

"But after what happened to Aaminah . . ."

"That wasn't your fault. She wanted to help you," Milena said. "She believes in you so much. I do too."

Giacomo hugged her back, heartened by her support.

Yaday approached. "Your intention influences how the Straightedge's power manifests. If you keep your mind clear and your thoughts positive, you'll be able to heal Kavi and the other Geniuses. Come, I'll lead you in a meditation."

Giacomo sat on the grass with Yaday and concentrated on removing any self-doubt or hesitation. Then, once Giacomo's mind felt light and calm, he rose to his feet and arced his pencil in Kavi's direction. As Mico cast a brilliant beam that connected to Kavi's gem, Ajeet and the warriors waited with anticipation.

Slowly but surely, the Genius's stone lit up with a silver glow. Soon Kavi's wings sprouted a coat of white feathers, and his body filled out. He stamped the dirt and whinnied. With his newfound strength, Kavi cast out his own glowing tendrils, which connected to the gems of the other horse-Geniuses, creating a sparkling web of light. One by one, the Geniuses returned to health and stretched their wings.

Ajeet smiled and patted Kavi's sturdy frame. Lavanthi hugged her Genius's neck. The warriors whooped with joy and mounted their Geniuses. They all took to the skies, soaring over the palace with a chorus of joyful neighs.

From every corner of the fortress, guards, servants, workers, and artisans emerged, cheering the revival of the Rachanan Geniuses. Kavi swooped down and landed with a triumphant *whoosh*. With a flourish of his wings, he trotted before the supportive crowd, Ajeet waving from atop his back.

Giacomo caught sight of Lavanthi and Ozo hurtling through the sky on her black-winged Genius. Lavanthi turned to the mercenary and leaned in for a kiss. Giacomo smiled to himself, hoping this meant the mercenary had finally found some happiness.

Savino clapped Giacomo on the back. "Nicely done."

Milena came to Giacomo's side, her Genius on her shoulder. "It's beautiful, isn't it, Gaia?"

Giacomo glanced at Mico darting excitedly around him and imagined a day in the future when he would be able to soar across the sky on his Genius.

Yaday turned to Giacomo. "I should have been there to help you face Vrama. I'm sorry. I feel like I let you down."

"You didn't," Giacomo replied. "Without your guidance, I wouldn't have been able to silence Vrama and cast him out of me."

Then he turned to Milena, who looked a little forlorn. "What you taught me saved me too."

"It did?" Milena said, perking up.

"I'm realizing that sacred geometry is physical and mental," Giacomo said. "I had to use both methods to survive."

"We should go check on Aaminah," Milena said. Savino slung the Compass over his shoulder, and they started off for the palace, but Kavi trotted in front of them, blocking their path.

"I'm going to need the Sacred Tools now," Ajeet said, rearing over them.

"What?" Giacomo said. "No, I kept up my end of the deal."

"I knew we couldn't trust you!" Savino shouted. "We all almost died to save your Geniuses!"

"You misunderstand," Ajeet said. "The Tools are yours, but I need them for a little while longer. I must travel to the other cities in Rachana and restore power to the rest of the horse-Geniuses."

Giacomo felt foolish for mistrusting the samraat. Naturally, other horse-Geniuses would still be in need. He handed the Straightedge to Ajeet.

"Thank you," Ajeet said, then turned to Savino, who reluctantly passed over the Compass.

Ajeet asked Giacomo, Milena, and Savino to join him. "I'm sure my people would love to meet the children who helped save their Geniuses."

Giacomo looked at his friends. The offer was tempting, but in the end, he decided he'd rather stay at the palace.

"I want to be here when Aaminah wakes up," Giacomo said.

"I understand," Ajeet said. "I'll be back as soon as I can." Kavi trotted away.

Pietro swooped down on Tito. "I heard all the commotion. It sounds like the mission was a success! I knew you four would come through." Then he paused and tilted his head, sensing something was amiss. "Wait . . . where's Aaminah?"

Giacomo and his friends set to telling him the whole awful tale.

THE FOUNDRY

Cries and screams echoed through the dungeon. Zanobius listened to his fellow prisoners' anguish day and night, unable to help them from inside his iron coffin.

Nerezza had sealed the metal box with her Genius's beam. Hundreds of metal spikes protruded from the walls, so if Zanobius shifted in any direction, the barbs pierced his skin. This was one cage he wasn't going to be able to break free of.

Through a narrow slit, Zanobius saw his cell door swing open and four soldiers march in. Grunting, they rolled Zanobius's coffin out of the dungeon and through a labyrinth of dimly lit tunnels. The wheels clunked over uneven stones, and the air turned hotter and smokier. With a clatter, the soldiers heaved Zanobius up a ramp and into a huge underground foundry, where workers clad in sooty aprons stoked blazing fires and poured glowing liquid metal into giant blocks of plaster.

Is that Nerezza's plan? Zanobius wondered. *To cast me in bronze and display me in her throne room like some kind of trophy?*

If that was the case, Zanobius had only himself to blame for his predicament. He was still berating himself for showing Nerezza mercy, knowing she was incapable of showing him any.

The soldiers wheeled Zanobius onto a platform that was so large even Victoria could stand on it, though how Nerezza's Genius had gotten into the underground foundry was a mystery.

Nerezza flicked her brush, and Victoria struck the coffin with a violet beam, breaking the seal on the door. It fell open and hit the platform with a heavy *clang*. Zanobius made a break for it but took only two steps before a spiral of light wound around him, freezing him in place.

"Stay put," Nerezza said, disdain engraved in her wrinkles. "Minister Xiomar?"

An old man dragged himself up the platform steps, out of breath. He was followed by a burly worker with a soot-marked face who set a large block of plaster on a table next to the Supreme Creator.

"Open it," Nerezza ordered.

With a hammer and chisel, the worker split the plaster in two. The pieces fell away, revealing an exact replica of Zanobius's arm. It was like the arm Savino had sculpted, except this one had been cast in dark bronze, its hand clenched in a fist.

"Beautiful work, Your Excellency." Xiomar turned to the worker. "Put it in place."

The worker slipped the hollow end of the bronze sculpture over Zanobius's stump.

Xiomar smiled. "A perfect fit."

That was when it hit Zanobius. There was only one explanation for Nerezza wanting to repair him. *She wants to control me*.

Zanobius thrashed against his sacred geometry restraints.

Nerezza watched Zanobius struggle, the foundry's flames reflecting in her eyes. "I wish Ugalino were here to see this."

She gestured sharply with her brush, and Zanobius felt his chest ache. When he looked down, his pattern was ablaze with the outline of a cube.

"Bound to me through the Creator's Pattern and the energy of the five Universal Solids—" Nerezza intoned.

Those words . . . I've heard them before . . .

With another swish of her brush, Nerezza changed the shape to the triangular-faced icosahedron. "You are a Tulpa—"

The ache became a burning.

Ugalino recited the same incantation to me, many times . . .

The tetrahedron appeared. "My creation—"

The burning became hotter. His insides were on fire.

I'll forget everything again . . .

The octahedron flashed. "Mine to order—"

The last shape—the dodecahedron—flared. "Mine to control!"

With Nerezza's final flourish, the end of Zanobius's sculpted arm liquefied. Tendrils of bronze twisted up his biceps and across his shoulder and chest. They seared his skin, burrowing into him. He pictured the metal snaking through his insides, wrapping around his mind, strangling every last memory from it.

Zanobius shut his eyes and fought with all his strength to rip the impostor arm from his body. But he couldn't move a muscle.

Once the burning in his chest faded, Zanobius opened his eyes again. He found that he could still recall everything, including, most important, the reason he had come to Virenzia. He locked onto Nerezza's smug face and obliterated any thoughts of mercy. Victoria's gem dimmed, and as soon as his sacred geometry restraint had vanished completely, Zanobius lunged.

"Stop!" Nerezza commanded.

Zanobius froze in motion, his outstretched hand inches from Nerezza's throat. The corners of her mouth twisted into a satisfied grin.

"The Tulpa is yours now," Xiomar said.

"I need to be absolutely certain," Nerezza said, then shouted to one of her guards, "Bring him in!"

Two armored soldiers escorted a prisoner in tattered clothing onto the platform. At first, Zanobius thought Nerezza's influence was muddling his mind, but as the prisoner stepped closer, there was no question whom Zanobius was looking at.

"Enzio?" he said weakly.

The boy's cheeks were sunken, his face bruised. Enzio stared back blankly, as if he didn't recognize Zanobius.

"What did you do to him?!" Zanobius spat.

"Silence!" Nerezza shouted, and with a muffled grunt, Zanobius's jaw locked.

"Now, throw Enzio into the molten metal." Nerezza commanded him, pointing down at the foundry floor, where giant crucibles filled with white-hot liquid bubbled.

I won't! Zanobius wanted to shout, but he was still unable to speak. To his horror, he watched himself lumber over to Enzio, lift him off his feet, and hold him over the railing.

The wave of heat seemed to snap Enzio out of his stupor, and he started to struggle. "Please, Zanobius, don't do this!" he begged.

Zanobius looked into Enzio's fear-filled eyes. *This shouldn't be happening*, he wanted to reply. The whole reason he had left Giacomo and fled hundreds of miles was to prevent something like this from ever occurring again. He cursed Ugalino for turning him violent, he cursed Nerezza for making him into a monster, and if he had believed in the Creator, he would have cursed him too.

Zanobius hoisted Enzio over his head. Sweat dripped down the boy's face. He screamed.

"That's enough," Nerezza interrupted. "You can put him down."

Zanobius lowered Enzio back onto the platform. The boy collapsed against the rail, breathing heavily and wiping his face.

Nerezza nodded to the armored soldiers. "Take him back to his cell." The soldiers pulled Enzio to his feet and dragged him away.

With the handle of her brush, Nerezza tapped the bronze plating that covered half of Zanobius's torso.

"Tell me, Zanobius. Have you ever visited Rachana?"

The morning sun sparkled on the Bay of Callisto. Nerezza took Victoria up higher, then banked away from the water and toward a rocky outcrop beyond the city's walls. They arced over the top of the cliff, then glided down into a cavernous space inside the earth. Three winged ships were docked within the hollow mountain.

Teams of Marinai filed belowdecks, where they would soon take their seats in the galleys. Each vessel required nearly a hundred wing-rowers to fly. Nerezza had requested double that so teams could rotate. The journey to Rachana would be much longer than the one to Niccolo's villa.

Companies of soldiers were milling about, but as soon as they saw Nerezza, the troops scrambled into orderly columns and stood at attention in front of the ships.

Victoria landed on the deck of the largest ship, the wood

groaning under her weight. Zanobius dismounted, then helped Nerezza down.

Minister Strozzi, clad in a golden suit of armor, marched over to Nerezza and bowed. He scowled at Zanobius, but if he disapproved of the Tulpa joining them, he didn't bring it up. "We're almost ready to depart, Your Eminence." In the crook of his arm, he cradled a helmet with carved wings and a brim that stuck out like a bird's beak. "But may I speak honestly?"

"If you must."

"Rachana is a formidable enemy. I've gathered our best, but I fear that three ships alone won't be sufficient to achieve a decisive victory. If we send more forces by sea—"

"No, that will take far too long," Nerezza said, cutting him off. "Giacomo and the Tools might be gone by then. We leave today."

Heavy footfalls thudded across the deck, and Nerezza turned to find a red-faced Barrolo heading her way. "You had assured me Enzio was being treated well!" he sputtered. "I just saw his injuries. What did you do to him?"

Nerezza looked past him at Enzio, who was standing with a group of young recruits, all of whom wore brown uniforms. His contusions had begun to heal but were still apparent. "Don't act so surprised," Nerezza said. "He underwent the same interrogation methods we've always used. They never bothered you before."

"He's my son!"

"That doesn't mean he should receive special treatment," Nerezza said coldly.

"But he's certainly in no condition to take part in a battle."

"Don't worry," Minister Strozzi interjected. "He'll be with the archers on deck. As it turns out, he's an excellent bowman, and we need as many able-bodied fighters as possible for this mission."

Barrolo began to protest again, and Nerezza silenced him with a stern glare. "Your son is coming. But one more outburst and I'll leave you behind."

Barrolo shrank back without another word.

Nerezza called Zanobius to her side, and they approached the ship's bow. She raised her arms, greeting the rows of soldiers gathered below her.

"My loyal sons and daughters," she began, her voice amplified and carried by the cavern's walls. "Today marks Zizzola's return to glory! For too long our empire has languished, forced into inaction by an outdated and ill-conceived peace accord.

"Though most of you were too young to remember Zizzola's last conflict with Rachana, you have all heard accounts of its savage, bloodthirsty warriors. And now, I have learned that the fugitive Giacomo Ghiberti and his companions have sought refuge with Rachana's samraat. Giacomo has already acquired one of the Sacred Tools—the Compass—and if he is not stopped, he may soon find the others."

Nerezza paused as gasps and surprised murmurs filtered through the army.

"An alliance between Giacomo and the samraat would be disastrous. With the Sacred Tools at the empire's disposal, Rachana could transport its warriors into the heart of Virenzia and use its Geniuses to raze the city to the ground. We cannot let that happen!"

The soldiers roared their agreement.

"So before the Rachanans can strike at us, we will take the fight to them. We will reclaim the Compass and bring the samraat and his warriors to their knees!"

Again, the soldiers responded with approval, their voices booming like thunder.

As soon as her army had marched aboard the ships, Nerezza ordered Minister Strozzi to take her fleet up. He blew a long, low note from a large animal horn. From the decks of all three ships, soldiers began to beat drums.

Pulleys squealed and ropes pulled taut. The ship's wings slowly rose, then lowered. The flapping gradually got faster, then the ship lurched. While some of the crew stumbled around her, Nerezza held her balance as her ship ascended through the opening in the cavern's roof. Her other two ships followed.

Once they cleared the mountain, the three ships sailed forth into the sunlit sky.

The war drums beat a steady rhythm. It was music to Nerezza's ears.

IN TIMES GONE BY

After returning from the stables, Milena had refused to leave Aaminah's bedside in the palace. For days Yaday and his healers buzzed around Aaminah, administering various poultices, prayers, and offerings. But Aaminah didn't respond to any of the treatments. She and Luna lay next to each other in the bed, their breathing soft.

During the daytime, Pietro, Savino, and Giacomo joined Milena's vigil, but the nights were long and lonely. While her friends slumbered in their quarters, Milena wandered up and down the palace halls, hoping to tire herself out. Patrolling guards eyed her suspiciously, but they understood that she was one of the girls who had helped save the horse-Geniuses, so they left her alone.

Over the course of several nights, she must have passed the painting of the Rachana-Zizzola peace accord a hundred times. She imagined Pietro standing at his easel all those years ago, mixing his paints, Tito by his side. The entire painting was a wonder to behold, yet even though the main subject was Emperor Callisto signing the treaty, the shafts of light coming through the windows directed the viewer's eye toward Nerezza's black-robed figure, and cast her in a warm, ethereal glow. Surely, Pietro hadn't done that by accident.

One morning, after such a night of staring at the painting, Milena decided to ask Pietro again about his first visit to Rachana.

"As I already said, there's not much to tell." Pietro took a seat on a long bench in the palace's hallway. Savino and Giacomo joined him. "I didn't do much except paint."

"What was Nerezza doing?"

"I . . . I'm not sure. She was with her father a lot." Pietro leaned on his cane and pushed himself up. "I should probably go check on Tito."

Milena read Pietro's hesitation as proof that he was holding something back. She grabbed his sleeve and shoved some tea in his direction. "You just got here. I'm sure Tito's fine, but obviously you're not. Why don't you want to talk about that time in your life?"

"Because there's no use dredging up the past," Pietro snapped.

"There's no use keeping it to yourself," Milena argued. "What happened?"

Pietro snatched his sleeve back. "Nerezza and I were more than simply acquaintances. Is that what you'd like to know?"

"Aha!" Giacomo pointed at Pietro, as if he had caught him in a lie. "I knew you'd told me you and Nerezza were friends."

Milena gave Giacomo a knowing look. "I think he means they were *more* than friends." She turned back to her teacher. "Is that right?"

"It was . . . complicated," Pietro muttered.

Milena guided her teacher back to the bench. "Then explain. Please. We want to know the truth."

Pietro took a sip of tea, let out a sigh, and began his story.

"Nerezza and I were seventeen. We had known each other since we were children, but only as classmates. We had studied under the same artist."

Pietro explained that Emperor Callisto didn't usually involve Nerezza in political matters, but she had persuaded her father to let her join the delegation to Rachana, insisting that she needed more experience.

"This was the first time Nerezza and I had spent long stretches together. Aboard the ship, there wasn't much to do except draw and talk, and it was a long journey across the sea. By the time we arrived here at the Rachanan palace, we had become inseparable."

And while Emperor Callisto and the Council members negotiated the armistice with Ajeet's father, Nerezza and Pietro explored the palace grounds, their Geniuses by their sides.

"Back then, Tito was still able to sit on my shoulder," Pietro said wistfully. "Anyway, I was taken by the palace's beautiful architecture and its gardens, and soon, I became taken with Nerezza, as well."

But Pietro didn't believe the emperor's daughter would ever think of him in a romantic way. "She was royalty. I was just a poor artist from the countryside. So I kept my feelings to myself."

Then one afternoon, as they strolled through the gardens, Pietro had gotten the shock of his life when Nerezza kissed him.

"Are we talking about the same Nerezza?" Savino said. "How could you have fallen for a woman who made it her mission to kill Geniuses?"

"She wasn't always like that," Pietro said. "At least not early on in our relationship. But I began to notice a change in her around the time her father died."

Five years after their visit to Rachana, Emperor Callisto was assassinated in a plot to overthrow the government and replace the Council of Ten. That was the official story, anyway. In studios and taverns around Virenzia, rumors began to spread that Nerezza might have been involved in her father's demise. Some suggested that she had hired the assassin personally. Others insisted there was no assassin at all.

"You think Nerezza killed her own father?" Giacomo asked.

"I never learned the truth," Pietro said. "The Nerezza I cared for seemed incapable of such an evil act, but looking back, I'm not so sure. In the months leading up to her father's death, I had noticed Nerezza acting withdrawn and secretive."

Pietro explained that shortly after she took power, Nerezza became more ruthless, imprisoning anyone who spoke out against her. She believed that Zizzola had grown weak under her father's rule and that it was up to her to reestablish order and strength.

"Nerezza demanded absolute loyalty from her subjects. That was something I could no longer give her myself, so I finally put an end to our relationship."

"I'm guessing she didn't take it well?" Milena said.

"She cursed me, called me a spineless coward, and from that day forward did everything in her power to ruin me."

Pietro's career had been built on commissioned portraits for the city's wealthiest citizens. But after their breakup, Nerezza forbade anyone to hire him, threatening people's livelihoods and families if they hung his paintings on their walls. Baldassare Barrolo was the only one who continued to pay Pietro for his art, but his patronage remained a secret.

Forced to start over, Pietro opened a small studio that he

operated in secret. For years Nerezza seemed to have forgotten about him, and he was able to teach undisturbed. Then one day a young sculptor named Ugalino became one of his students.

After Ugalino created Zanobius, Nerezza took notice of Pietro again. She was convinced that Pietro had encouraged Ugalino's rebelliousness, and from then on, she viewed all artists and their Geniuses as threats to her power.

"I tried to escape the city," Pietro said. "But before I could, she found me. Victoria clawed Tito's eyes out, and then my own world went dark . . ."

"But she let you go," Milena said. "Why?"

"That's a question that's haunted me for years," Pietro said.

"It sounds like she took pity on you," Giacomo said. "Part of her still had feelings for you."

"Maybe," Pietro said. "Perhaps there was a shred of kindness left somewhere in her cold heart."

"If someone cares about you, they don't make you go blind," Savino said.

Milena fumed. She hadn't thought it was possible to despise Nerezza any more than she already did, but after hearing how horribly she had treated Pietro, Milena discovered new, deeper depths to her hate.

"It's my greatest regret in life that I didn't do more to stop her in those early years," Pietro said. "I saw the warning signs, but I was too afraid to confront her. Instead, I walked away like a coward and told myself she wasn't my problem anymore. By the time she became everyone's problem, it was too late to stop her."

Milena finally understood why it had been so difficult for Pietro to open up about his past. "You're not a coward." She leaned over and put her head on her teacher's shoulder. "And I'm so sorry you had to go through all that."

Pietro squeezed her hand in silent thanks.

"Excuse me, may I interrupt?" Yaday approached.

Milena snapped upright. "Is it good news?" she asked.

A slight smile formed on Yaday's lips. "Yes, Aaminah is awake now. You can all go see her."

Milena barreled into Aaminah's room, relieved to find her sitting up in bed with Luna nestled in her hair. Milena wrapped her arms around Aaminah, careful to avoid her bandaged shoulder, and held her tight.

Aaminah didn't return the hug.

Milena pulled away and looked into her friend's eyes. She was met with a vacant stare. "Aaminah?"

Aaminah didn't reply. She didn't so much as blink.

"What's wrong with her?" Giacomo asked as he, Savino, and Pietro came into the room.

"I don't know," Milena said, fighting back her sadness. She turned to Yaday. "I thought you said she was all right."

"I said she was *awake*," Yaday corrected. "We were able to extract the bit of Vrama's soul that had lodged in her, so she's out of immediate danger."

"But she won't even look at me," Milena protested.

"To hold that kind of darkness in your body . . . It's more than most can withstand. Aaminah is quite a spiritual warrior, but it will take some time for her to return to her normal self."

CHANGE OF PLANS

Giacomo was relieved that Aaminah had regained consciousness, but it took a couple of days before she was up on her feet again and talking. Even then, it was clear she still had a long way to go to make a full recovery.

Once Aaminah was well enough to leave the palace, Giacomo, his friends, and Pietro gathered around the table in the gazebo for a celebration dinner. But Aaminah wasn't enjoying herself. She sat in her chair, head hanging, petting Luna in her lap. Milena tried to get them both to eat, but neither Aaminah nor her Genius would take a bite.

Because Vrama's soul had invaded his own body, Giacomo understood how painful it felt to have that kind of darkness weighing you down. He felt guilty that, as a Tulpa, he had easily shaken off any lasting effects from the encounter while his friend had paid so dearly. He leaned over to Aaminah and put his hand on hers. "I want you to know, if you hadn't been there to save me, Vrama would be controlling me now. I owe you my life."

"You would have done the same for me," Aaminah said quietly, staring at her food.

"Come on," Milena said, helping her out of her chair. "Let's all take a walk in the gardens."

"Sure," Aaminah said, shuffling out of the gazebo.

Giacomo turned back. "Pietro, aren't you coming?"

"Go ahead without me," Pietro said. "The four of you should spend some time together. Besides, someone needs to eat all this food!" He slurped up a spoonful of soup.

Milena held Aaminah's arm as they ambled through the gardens. Birds sang and flitted through the sky, the frogs croaked with life, and the wind smelled like lavender. Normally, any of those things would have delighted Aaminah, but not today. Instead, she stared at the ground.

Milena picked a bright yellow flower and handed it to Aaminah. "It's your favorite color."

Aaminah glanced at the flower, then looked away without a word.

Giacomo stopped and pulled a flute from his belt. "What about playing some music? That always cheers you up." Gently, he took Luna from Aaminah's cupped hands and passed her the instrument.

"I'm not sure I ever want to play again," Aaminah said softly.

Milena and Savino stared at her, incredulous. Giacomo was so shocked by Aaminah's words, he didn't quite know how to respond at first. She still wasn't feeling like herself, Giacomo reasoned. "You don't really mean that. Music is who you are. It would be like one of us giving up art."

Aaminah opened her fingers and let the flute roll out of her hand. It clattered onto the stones.

Giacomo's heart sank. He retrieved the flute and put it back in his belt. "Maybe later . . ."

Milena guided them to a secluded area ringed by manicured bushes, where she found a bench beneath a tree with white bark. The four of them sat peacefully for a while, until finally Aaminah spoke. "Do you ever think the Creator is up there having a big laugh at our expense?"

"What do you mean?" Milena asked.

"We've been running around the world chasing after the Sacred Tools, and for what?"

"We have to defeat Nerezza," Savino said.

"And if we do? The world keeps going on, people keep suffering, wars keep breaking out . . ." Aaminah let out a heavy sigh.

"But with Nerezza gone, there will be hope again," Giacomo said, as much for his own benefit as for Aaminah's. "Hope for a better future."

"The future doesn't feel too hopeful right now," Aaminah said, stroking Luna's feathers.

"Speaking of what lies ahead," Savino said, "once Ajeet gets back with the Compass and the Straightedge, Giacomo can use them to track down the Creator's Pencil."

Giacomo had been so worried about Aaminah's condition, he hadn't given much thought to the final Sacred Tool. But Savino was right, they had to start preparing for the last part of their mission. "My hunch is we'll find the Creator's Pencil somewhere in Katunga next."

"I still have Garrulous's journals," Milena said. "I'll start reading about his travels there and see if I can find any clues about where to start looking."

Aaminah perked up. "Katunga? Are you sure?" For the first time, her voice sparked with life.

Giacomo smiled at Aaminah. "Don't worry, we won't go anywhere until you're feeling better."

"I wonder if . . ." Aaminah stopped herself.

"What is it?" Milena asked.

Aaminah shook her head. "It's stupid. Never mind."

"Tell us," Milena insisted.

"I just thought . . . If we're going to Katunga, maybe I could try to find my father."

Giacomo recalled that Aaminah's Katungan father had left for his homeland when she was only a baby, shortly after Luna arrived. He had promised Aaminah's mother he would return once he found a safe place to take Aaminah and her new Genius. But he was never heard from again.

"I have a feeling he's still out there," Aaminah said. "During our training, when Lavanthi had us picture the one person who could get us through anything, I thought of him—or what I imagine he might look like."

"We'll do whatever it takes to help you find him, I promise," Giacomo said.

Luna stirred. Aaminah pushed herself off the bench, standing tall, some of her old strength returning. "So when do we leave?"

They were interrupted by the blare of horns. The palace bells tolled. Horses brayed.

"What's that all about?" Savino said.

Giacomo peered through the trees and saw a portal glowing in front of the palace. "Samraat Ajeet's back!"

Everyone gathered on the palace steps to welcome the samraat and his warriors home. Ajeet was happy to report that the Geniuses throughout Rachana had all made a complete recovery, and true to his word, he returned the Sacred Tools to Giacomo.

"The Compass and Straightedge are now yours to wield," Ajeet said. "Don't let them corrupt you the way they did Vrama."

"I won't," Giacomo said.

But everyone's good mood was short-lived. Shortly after Ajeet's arrival, a horse-Genius flew over the battlement and glided to a landing in front of the palace. Its rider jumped from the saddle and rushed up the stairs, calling to Samraat Ajeet with an urgent tone.

Giacomo turned to Yaday. "What's going on?"

Yaday's eyes were wide with shock. "This warrior flew in from the east. He says that a few days after Ajeet visited their city, Zizzolan ships were spotted heading this way."

Giacomo's heart thumped. "Flying ships?"

Yaday listened in, translating bits and pieces of Ajeet's conversation with the warrior. "Yes. Three of them. Along with an enormous bird-Genius."

"Nerezza," Giacomo said, dread creeping over him.

Yaday also looked unsettled. "He says he flew here to warn us as quickly as he could, but the ships were moving at a steady clip. He thinks they'll be here by dawn."

"I bet she finally got Enzio to talk," Savino said. "I knew he would break."

"Don't blame him," Giacomo shot back. "I'm sure he did everything he could to protect us." He prayed for Enzio's well-being.

It didn't matter how she had found him, Giacomo thought. Deep down, he'd known it would only be a matter of time before she tracked him down again. Giacomo had foolishly believed that Rachana was out of Nerezza's reach, but the truth was, there was nowhere in the world he could escape her grasp.

War was coming to Rachana. And it was all Giacomo's fault.

FIRST STRIKE

Before first light, Giacomo and his friends headed to the palace, anxious about the impending battle. Pietro glided overhead on Tito.

"Does this feel wrong to anyone else?" Savino said, keeping his voice low.

"Does what feel wrong?" Giacomo asked.

"We're Zizzolan. We're not supposed to fight *with* Rachanans, we're supposed to fight *against* them."

Giacomo stopped and glared at Savino. "After everything we've been through in Rachana, you still see Ajeet and his people as your enemy?"

"No," Savino said, growing defensive. "I'm just saying . . . historically, that's been the case."

"Then today, we change history," Giacomo said, and marched off.

On the palace steps, he found Ajeet conferring with Yaday,

Lavanthi, Ozo, and several other warriors. Soraya stood with her mother, crying and stomping her foot.

When Ajeet noticed the children approaching, he waved them over. "Join us. We're going over our strategy. We think Nerezza's ships will come from the east, so we're going to concentrate our forces along that battlement." He pointed to the wall in the distance, where archers and other warriors were already lining up. "Giacomo, you and the Sacred Tools will be with me. Savino and Milena, you're with Lavanthi and Ozo."

Pietro and Tito landed with a heavy *whoosh*. "We'll patrol the skies," Pietro said. "Tito will alert everyone the moment he senses Nerezza and her Genius getting close."

"Excellent," Ajeet said.

"What about me?" Aaminah asked.

Milena put an arm around her shoulder. "Maybe it's better if you sit out this fight?"

"I can handle it," Aaminah insisted.

Giacomo wasn't so sure. Her energy had perked up a lot since yesterday, but he worried she might get hurt again.

"I'd feel a lot better if you stayed somewhere safe," Milena said, echoing Giacomo's thoughts.

Yaday stepped forward. "The healers and I set up a recovery area inside the palace. We could really use your help tending to any injured."

"That's perfect," Milena said. "What do you say, Aaminah?"

Aaminah grumbled her disappointment and reluctantly agreed to the assignment.

"And take my granddaughter inside with you," Ajeet said. "She thinks she's ready to see battle today, despite what her mother tells her."

Lavanthi ushered a pouty-faced Soraya over to Aaminah and gave her a nod of thanks. Aaminah took the girl's hand, and they followed Yaday into the palace.

Giacomo flew to the battlement with Ajeet on his horse-Genius, Kavi. Bronze-armored archers and silver-armored swordspeople lined the walls. A horse-Genius and its warrior stood at

attention every twenty feet. Down in the palace grounds, more warriors wielding swords and spears were at the ready in case Nerezza's ships sailed over the fortress and Zizzolan soldiers dropped in.

Ajeet guided Kavi back and forth in front of his troops, spurring them on. Giacomo didn't understand a word of what he was saying, but Ajeet's passion and motivation came through in his booming voice. The warriors called back to him with a resounding roar, and their Geniuses whinnied.

Kavi glided down, and Ajeet joined his troops on the battlement. Giacomo dismounted, then looked back up at Ajeet. "Any words of encouragement for me?"

"I'll tell you what I told my warriors," Ajeet said. "Zizzola has tried to invade our lands countless times in the past, with one aim: to force the Rachanan people into servitude. But time and again, we fought back, refusing to give up our freedoms to a foreign empire. And as long as we don't cower today, no one will be able to control us." Ajeet pointed at Giacomo. "And no one will control you."

Ajeet's words quieted Giacomo's anxiety like a cooling salve on a burn. "Thank you," Giacomo said.

As the sun peeked over the faraway mountains, silence fell over the fortress. Everyone stood motionless, waiting for the fleet's arrival. Giacomo became aware of the wind rushing in his ears and the chirping of birds in the gardens, knowing that in only a few minutes such a moment of peace would be impossible to find.

Farther down the battlement, Milena and Savino stood with Lavanthi. Gaia and Nero were perched on the triangular merlons in front of them. Giacomo caught Milena's eye and gave her a nod. She smiled back, but the rest of her face was etched with worry. He wished he could relay some of Ajeet's confidence and convince her they'd be victorious.

Then, out of the quiet came a low, ominous hoot, followed by the heavy *whoosh*ing of wings. Tito glided over the fortress with Pietro on his back. Two warrior scouts and their horse-Geniuses flanked them. "Nerezza is close!" Pietro shouted.

It wasn't long before a warning bell began clanging from one of the towers.

Giacomo focused his eyes on the distant part of the sky where the silhouette of a bird appeared, wings flapping. At first he thought it was Victoria, but its movements were too even and mechanical to be a Genius.

It had to be Nerezza's ship.

But Giacomo had been expecting three of them. *Where are the others?* he wondered.

He gripped the crook of the Straightedge tightly—one side ran the length of his arm, the other angled toward the ground. The ship sailed closer. From Giacomo's shoulder, Mico trilled warily.

Kavi trotted up to Giacomo. "Wait until the ship is in range, then fire a warning shot," Ajeet said. "Once Nerezza witnesses the Straightedge's power, she'll have second thoughts about continuing the assault."

Giacomo readied himself to strike, though he suspected that once Nerezza realized he had the Straightedge, her hostility would only intensify.

One of the warriors, Azad, ran up to Ajeet, speaking in a rushed and worried voice. Ajeet called out to his army, and in an instant, the orderly group turned chaotic as warriors, archers, and soldiers scattered and sprinted to opposite ends of the fortress. A modest force remained with the samraat on the eastern battlement.

"What's going on?" Milena said as she and Savino rejoined Giacomo.

"I think Nerezza might have outsmarted Ajeet." Giacomo turned southward and pointed into the distance, where a second flying vessel emerged from the morning haze. A similar vision appeared to the north.

"I hate to give Nerezza credit, but a three-pronged attack is pretty good strategy," Savino said.

The wind gusted, carrying a terrifying screech with it. Giacomo looked to the west, where Victoria dove out of the sky. "Make that a four-pronged attack!" he shouted.

Nerezza fired off a violet whorl from Victoria's gem, cutting a swath of destruction through the center of the gardens and taking out several warriors in the process. Bushes and trees burst into flame.

Victoria swooped low, strafing the ground. A cadre of warriors charged, futilely hacking with their swords at the creature as she sped past. The archers to either side of Giacomo fired a volley of arrows, but Victoria batted them away with her giant wing.

"Take out that beast!" Ajeet commanded.

Giacomo raised the Straightedge and aimed at Victoria. The patterns on the handle glowed. Mico flew out in front of him, his gem blazing red. Nerezza closed in.

But Giacomo's arm froze when he noticed what looked like a soldier in bronze armor seated behind Nerezza.

"What are you waiting for?" Ajeet said, growing agitated. "Fire!"

Giacomo realized it wasn't a soldier with Nerezza—*it was Zanobius.*

Giacomo's arm dropped, and the patterns on the Straightedge dimmed.

Victoria arced upward and *whoosh*ed right past Giacomo, slapping him with a wake of air. His body and mind reeling, Giacomo stumbled back and caught himself against the stone parapet.

As Nerezza and her Genius curved through the sky, Giacomo homed in on Zanobius. What he had mistaken for armor appeared to be metal that covered part of his torso; in place of his missing arm was a bronze one.

"How in the world did Zanobius end up with Nerezza?" Savino shouted in a panic. Milena stood next to him, mouth agape.

"I . . . I don't know," Giacomo muttered. But Zanobius's new bronze arm seemed to suggest only one possibility—that Nerezza had somehow become Zanobius's new master.

Giacomo felt the Straightedge pulled from his grip. "If you won't take her down, then I will," Ajeet said, claiming the weapon. He flicked the reins, and Kavi took off, galloping through the air toward Victoria. Once he was away from the battlement, Ajeet swung the Straightedge in a downward arc, and Kavi fired off a spiraling helix of light, bucking from the force.

A blinding blaze lit up the sky. Victoria dropped, avoiding the crackling energy, but the beam didn't dissipate immediately. It continued, eventually hitting the bow of the approaching ship, splintering its hull and pitching the vessel forward. Small figures plummeted from the deck.

Giacomo gasped—all those lives, gone in an instant. "No . . ."

From Victoria's back, Zanobius locked eyes with Giacomo. Savino and Milena ran to their friend's side, and they all gaped up at him, no doubt realizing that he had become Nerezza's slave.

"The samraat has the Straightedge!" Nerezza shouted. "Take it from him before he brings down the other ships!"

As Victoria arced back toward the fortress, Zanobius watched the damaged vessel list to one side and slowly descend. The blast from the Straightedge had sheared off the front of the ship's hull, causing cargo and bodies to spill out. The great, groaning beast crashed into the dunes in an explosion of dust and snapping wood.

Nerezza waved her brush, and Victoria launched a beam. The white-winged horse-Genius dodged, then looped around. The samraat slashed again with the Straightedge, sending a flume of silvery light directly at them.

Victoria shot upward, cresting over the helix, which kept on its trajectory. This time, it harmlessly broke apart into sparkling trails across the sky. Nerezza guided Victoria high above the fortress until they were flying directly above the samraat's Genius.

"Go!" Nerezza ordered. "Get the Straightedge!"

Zanobius looked down, found his mark, and jumped.

For a moment, all he heard was the wind rushing in his ears. He spanned his arms wide and imagined sprouting wings and flying away. For the first time since Nerezza had captured him, Zanobius felt free.

The experience was fleeting.

The samraat craned his neck, and his eyes went wide as he saw Zanobius hurtling toward him. He pulled his Genius's reins, and the horse whinnied and reared back, but it was too late.

Zanobius slammed into the creature's hindquarters and grabbed his armor, dragging him down. The Genius bucked and thrashed, trying to fly higher. Zanobius held on tightly and pulled himself up to sit behind the samraat.

The samraat twisted, stabbing behind him with his dagger, but the blade just glanced off Zanobius's metal skin. He pinned the samraat's arms to his sides and wrested the Straightedge away. Then he picked the man out of his saddle and hurled him off his Genius. The samraat plummeted and crashed into a tree below.

The Genius bucked again, jerking wildly now that his warrior had been overthrown. Zanobius grabbed the reins and yanked, forcing the flying horse into a nosedive. Moments before they plunged into a long pool, Zanobius leaped away and rolled across the grass. Behind him, Kavi splashed into the water, then pulled himself out and galloped away toward where the samraat had fallen.

Straightedge in hand, Zanobius scanned his surroundings and saw that Nerezza's two other ships had reached the fortress's outer wall. From the decks, Zizzolan archers launched arrows, keeping the horse-Geniuses at a distance. Meanwhile, hand-gunners rained down bullets. The Rachanan archers on the wall scattered as the volley blasted away chunks of stone. More soldiers stormed off the ships and onto the battlements. The clanging of swords echoed across the gardens.

Nerezza was already directing Victoria back in his direction, so Zanobius ran toward the great bird, but before they could meet, a blast of orange light struck Victoria from behind. She screeched and pulled up. Tito and Pietro swooped past, flanked by three horse-Geniuses. Their warriors cut shapes with their daggers, barraging Victoria with streams of color from their Geniuses' gems.

Though his new master was in danger, Zanobius was compelled to follow her original orders: *Find Giacomo and the Compass and bring them to me.*

Before their arrival, Nerezza had made it clear that this was to be Zanobius's primary objective. It took precedence over anything else.

Zanobius looked toward the battlement where he'd last seen Giacomo, Milena, and Savino, but he saw only warriors and soldiers in the throes of battle.

He stalked through the gardens, dreading his inevitable encounter with Giacomo, but before Zanobius could locate his fellow Tulpa, a horse-Genius swooped past. Her rider cut a mark with her dagger, and the Genius's gem spun a helix of amber light around Zanobius. He leaped away seconds before the light could completely trap him, and fled. But a dozen warriors ran into his path and came at him with their swords and spears.

"Stay away!" Zanobius warned. "I don't want to hurt you!"

But it was too late. The warriors were already upon him, slashing and stabbing.

Zanobius felt his fist hit flesh and heard the *crunch*ing of bones.

TULPA'S TERROR

Giacomo sprinted down a stairwell inside the battlement, Milena and Savino at his heels. He stopped at the bottom and peered out from the archway. Nerezza's remaining two ships had docked at the outer wall, and soldiers swarmed the fortress, quickly turning the palace grounds into a battlefield. Swords clanged and sacred geometry attacks hummed. Nerezza's army might have easily overrun the fortress had it not been for Rachana's horse-Geniuses.

Giacomo spotted Zanobius with the Straightedge by the reflecting pool, where a group of warriors had him surrounded. Zanobius tried to wave them off, and Giacomo wondered if maybe he had been wrong about Nerezza controlling his friend. But then the warriors moved in, and Zanobius grabbed one man and threw him against a tree trunk, where he fell, unconscious. Giacomo looked away, his worst fears confirmed.

"Nerezza definitely controls Zanobius, which means he's going to come after me." Giacomo held up the Creator's Compass. "And this."

"You should stay out of sight," Milena said.

"We can hide you somewhere in the palace," Savino suggested.

Giacomo shook his head. "If Zanobius hands over the Straightedge to Nerezza, this battle is over. She'll wipe out every Rachanan warrior and any Genius in sight—including ours."

"But we'll never be able to overpower Zanobius," Milena reminded him. "So how do we steal the Straightedge from him?"

Giacomo snapped open the Compass, an idea taking form. "We take him by surprise."

Giacomo careened out of a portal, coming to a stop inches from the reflecting pool. Zanobius stood across the water with his back turned, shoulders heaving with each breath. The warriors who were still standing abandoned the fight, dragging their injured counterparts out of harm's way.

"Zanobius!" Giacomo screamed, his voice a mix of anger and desperation. He spun open a second portal and waited.

Zanobius turned, his eyes filled with regret. But upon seeing Giacomo, Zanobius's gaze hardened, and he charged through the reflecting pool, kicking up waves.

Giacomo held his position. Mico zipped past his shoulder and hovered high overhead.

As Zanobius closed in, Giacomo dove out of the way. With a flick of Giacomo's pencil, Mico fired off a shot that landed squarely on Zanobius's back and knocked him into the light.

Zanobius appeared out of the other end of the portal, which was off in the gardens. While Zanobius stumbled around, trying to regain his bearings, Milena and Savino leaped out from behind a tree, and their Geniuses barraged him with streams of green and blue, but their attacks failed to knock the Straightedge out of the Tulpa's hand.

With a roar, Zanobius jumped straight up, grabbed a branch, and swung himself over Milena's and Savino's heads. He dropped down directly behind them.

Giacomo screamed, "Look out!" but they were too far away to hear. He raced into the portal, willing himself over to his friends.

As he scrambled out of the light, Giacomo found Zanobius

holding Milena and Savino by their collars, their feet dangling above the ground. Giacomo fired off a shot from Mico's gem and hit Zanobius in the back, but he didn't release his grip. He slammed Milena and Savino together, and their heads collided with a *crack*. Giacomo froze in horror as Zanobius dropped their unconscious bodies on the grass and turned to face him.

With a swipe of his pencil, Giacomo targeted the bronze appendage. Back at Niccolo's, Zanobius had escaped his trance when Milena shattered his stone arm. Maybe destroying this new one would have the same effect. But no matter how many times Mico's beam struck it, the arm wouldn't break.

Out of the corner of his eye, Giacomo caught a glint of sun off steel. He stumbled back as Ozo sped past, sword raised. The mercenary's eyes were wide with rage, his scream full of vengeance. He leaped at Zanobius.

Giacomo felt like he was reliving a nightmare.

Zanobius backed away from Giacomo and turned to face the onrushing mercenary. It was like they were back at the piazza all over again.

Ozo's sword cleaved the air. Zanobius raised the Straightedge and deflected the steel with a *clang*. The mercenary staggered, raised his weapon again, and met Zanobius's gaze with eyes burning with hate.

"You're not getting away this time!" Ozo shouted.

To his right, Zanobius glimpsed Giacomo creeping up on him, pencil raised, his Genius hovering next to him. But the moment Zanobius turned to go after him, Ozo swung once more.

Zanobius spun back around. With a *clang*, he batted away Ozo's sword with his metal hand, then took a swing with his other fist.

The mercenary sidestepped the punch and parried, cutting a sizable gash up Zanobius's fleshy forearm.

A flash of red filled Zanobius's periphery, and he was hit from behind. He lurched forward, trying to regain his balance. Ozo sliced low, this time lancing Zanobius's thigh.

"Thanks for the assist!" Ozo called to Giacomo.

"Just don't kill him!" Giacomo pleaded.

"And here I thought we were fighting on the same side!" Ozo resumed his assault.

While his two opponents traded words, Zanobius picked a stone off the ground, and using a technique Enzio had taught him, he flung the rock like he was going to skip it across the water. The rock clipped Mico's wing, and the Genius let out a pained squeal and darted away. Giacomo went down to one knee, clutching his side. Zanobius offered a silent apology.

With Giacomo temporarily incapacitated, Zanobius focused back on Ozo, who was charging fast. Zanobius lifted his bronze arm in time to catch the sword's thrust, and they met in a shower of sparks. The mercenary had withdrawn his sword and readied himself for another strike when a high-pitched scream startled them both. For the first time, Ozo's attention turned away from Zanobius.

Across the gardens, a little girl, no more than six years old, looked around in terror as she ran through the middle of the battlefield, soldiers and warriors clashing around her.

"Soraya!" Giacomo shouted, climbing back to his feet.

The moment the mercenary saw the girl was in danger, his vengeful scowl melted into an expression Zanobius had never seen in Ozo before—true fear. The girl wasn't a random lost child, she meant something to Ozo.

"Get out of there!" Ozo bellowed. He glanced back at Zanobius like he was trying to decide whether to attack again, then he turned and raced toward the girl.

With Ozo out of the picture, Zanobius turned back to Giacomo. Mico flew in staggered bursts and landed on the boy's shoulder.

"Turn over the Straightedge!" Giacomo demanded. "Please! If Nerezza gets her hands on it, more people are going to die. I know you don't want that."

More people dead, because of me . . . The thought was like a dagger in his heart.

Zanobius searched his mind for any trace of self-control he might have left. A single thread was all he needed, something he could pull to unravel Nerezza's hold over him. He found nothing.

Zanobius gripped the Straightedge tighter. "I can't."

"Then I have to take it from you." Giacomo arced his pencil, and Mico fired a blazing beam that hit the end of the Straightedge, causing it to fly out of Zanobius's grip and splash into the reflecting pool. Another swath of light hit Zanobius with enough force to send him sprawling.

By the time Zanobius was standing again, Giacomo was already in the water and recovering the Straightedge.

Find Giacomo and the Compass and bring them to me, Nerezza's voice whispered once more.

As much as Zanobius wished for this fight to be over, he knew it had only just begun.

Giacomo climbed out of the pool, his lower half soaked. He tucked the Straightedge under his arm and readied the Compass, scanning his mind for a place that would put him out of Zanobius's reach.

But as his fellow Tulpa prowled closer, a new plan began to emerge. Giacomo was tired of Zanobius trying to capture him. Maybe it was time to turn the tables. If Giacomo could trap Zanobius, he could focus on taking out Nerezza. Once she perished, her hold over Zanobius would die too.

Just like when you killed Ugalino, Giacomo's conscience reminded him. *Do you really want another death on your hands?*

Giacomo took no pleasure in the thought, but considering all the terror Nerezza had inflicted on others—*Niccolo, Pietro, my parents*—she deserved her fate.

With Zanobius closing in, Giacomo pictured the one place in the fortress where he had the best chance of confining Zanobius. He spun the Compass and dove into the light.

He spilled out into the cellar beneath the palace, slamming against the wall. With a ruffle of feathers, Mico chittered and picked himself up off the floor. Giacomo looked up at the relief sculpture, where Vrama's image loomed over him. Giacomo shuddered, scooped up Mico, and scrambled behind a pillar at the far end of the room.

Once the portal jettisoned Zanobius, it began to contract, and its light began to wane. Giacomo waited patiently for the chamber to turn pitch-black. That was when he would strike.

Zanobius stalked from pillar to pillar, moving closer to Giacomo's position. The room dimmed, turning Zanobius into a charcoal silhouette.

As the last of the portal glimmered away, Zanobius spotted Giacomo and lunged. Giacomo leaped out of the way and fired off a red blaze from Mico's gem. A chunk of stone near Zanobius's head burst into dust.

The room plunged into total darkness.

"Why did you bring us down here?" Zanobius shouted, his voice echoing through the chamber. His heavy footfalls stomped louder, then softer as he moved away.

Giacomo tiptoed from pillar to pillar, picturing the staircase at the far end of the room. Once he found it, he would bolt to the surface and cave in the stairway behind him, trapping Zanobius underground.

At least that was the plan. But Giacomo hadn't counted on getting lost. He had passed through this room several times on his way to Yaday's chambers, but torchlights had guided him. He blindly groped his way through the darkness until his hands finally met the wall.

He slid his hand across the rough stones until he found the passageway, but as he entered, he hit something hard. Something metal.

"I'm sorry, Giacomo," Zanobius whispered.

Mico screeched. Giacomo fumbled to open the Compass, but Zanobius shoved him, jarring the Tool from Giacomo's hand. It clattered onto the floor.

There was no sense in staying in the dark now. Giacomo flicked his pencil, and the room lit up red from Mico's gem. But Giacomo hadn't been able to see where he was aiming, so the light skirted over Zanobius's head and exploded above the passage. The stones crumbled and clogged the stairway. Now they were both trapped.

Mico's gem pulsed dimly. Zanobius picked up the Compass with one hand, Giacomo with another. Using his two free arms, he dug through the rubble. "I have to take you to Nerezza now."

"Don't," Giacomo pleaded as he struggled against the metal arm. "Resist her!"

"I've tried!" Zanobius snapped. "I can't release myself from Nerezza's control. But there is one way you could set me free."

"How?"

Zanobius shoved aside more stones, easily opening the passage. So much for Giacomo's plan. "Use the Straightedge to destroy me. I watched it take down that ship, surely it has enough power to put an end to me."

Giacomo couldn't believe what Zanobius was asking of him. "End you . . . ? No!"

With the rubble now cleared, Zanobius carried Giacomo up the stairs. "I've suffered enough. I'm a scourge on this world. It's the only way I'll ever be at peace."

Even in the dim red light, Giacomo could see that Zanobius's eyes had been turned from blue to black. They looked soulless, like Vrama's eyes had. Or the eyes of a Lost Soul.

Giacomo's fingers grazed the Straightedge's surface. It called to him, begging to be used.

"Please," Zanobius said, his dark eyes softening for a moment. "Have mercy on me."

But Giacomo couldn't give Zanobius the kind of mercy he wanted. He truly believed in his friend's goodness and knew that his actions weren't his own. So instead of wielding the Straight-edge, Giacomo surrendered it.

PIETRO'S PLEA

Soft, soothing notes drifted in the breeze, finding purchase in Milena's ears. The music seeped through her muscles and deep into her bones. Sensation began to return. She tasted dirt in her mouth and felt the cool grass brushing against her cheek. Her head throbbed like it was being repeatedly hit with a hammer.

What happened . . . ?

In a flash, it all came back: Zanobius's grabbing her, hoisting her up . . . Then, nothing.

Milena's eyes fluttered open, taking in the daylight. She rolled onto her side, and Savino groaned next to her. Aaminah knelt between them, playing her flute. Yellow circles pulsed from Luna's gem and slowly passed over Milena's and Savino's bodies. Yaday stood behind her, looking on.

Gaia shook her feathers and stretched her neck, cawing.

Aaminah lowered her flute, and the yellow light dissipated. "Are you all right?" she asked, her voice trembling.

Milena rubbed her temples. "I think so . . ." She got to her feet, and her legs gave way. Yaday reached out and steadied her. Once she regained her balance, Milena looked around at the warriors and soldiers still engaged in fierce battle. "Where are Giacomo and Zanobius?"

"We're not sure," Yaday said.

Savino stood up, and Nero flew to him, landing on his arm. "How did you know we were out here?"

"We were in the palace when we heard all the fighting," Aaminah replied. "The next thing I knew, Soraya was running off. We followed her outside and found her caught in the middle of the battlefield. I was about to try to get her when Ozo rushed in." Seeing the alarm on Milena's face, Aaminah quickly added, "Soraya's safe now. Ozo carried her out of harm's way."

"That's when I saw Giacomo disappear into a portal with Zanobius," Yaday explained. "We rushed over here and found you both knocked out."

"We need to figure out where they went," Milena said, her heart racing.

"Found them!" Savino announced suddenly, gesturing to the palace. Zanobius lumbered down the steps, pulling Giacomo with two hands; in his other two, he carried the Compass and the Straightedge.

"Oh no," Aaminah muttered.

"Let's go!" Milena waved for everyone to follow her.

They were too late. In the sky, Nerezza had been fending off attacks from Lavanthi and Pietro, but seeing Zanobius loft the Straightedge skyward, she guided Victoria down and grabbed the Tool as she flew by. Victoria swooped back up and circled the dome. Nerezza lifted the Straightedge, and its patterns began to glow, along with her Genius's gem.

"Take cover!" Milena shouted as Nerezza sliced the Sacred Tool through the air. The group dove behind a row of hedges.

A blinding beam cut through the sky. Milena winced as a wave of heat washed over her. The rest of the warriors and soldiers must have felt it too, because they all ceased fighting for a moment and crouched down. When the light receded, the gardens were smoldering, with trees lying strewn about, and the main path had been obliterated.

With a heavy *thump*, Victoria landed at the bottom of the palace steps, about a hundred feet from where Milena was hunkered down with her friends. Giacomo squirmed in Zanobius's grip as the Tulpa dragged him toward Nerezza. Milena looked around for Mico but didn't see him. She hoped he had escaped.

A loud hoot rang out, and Tito sailed overhead, then landed across from Victoria. Nerezza's Genius screeched her displeasure. Pietro slid off his Genius's back and leaned heavily on his cane.

With Savino and Aaminah by her side, Milena raced over to her teacher. "What are you doing?"

Pietro waved them away. "Stay back. I'll deal with Nerezza."

Milena found Savino's and Aaminah's hands and squeezed, praying for Pietro's safety.

Nerezza smirked. "You think a few wise words will persuade me to stand down? Not a chance."

"Remember the last time we stood in front of this palace?" Pietro said, his voice growing calmer. "Our first kiss was right over there." Pietro gestured out toward the gardens. "You were different then. We both were."

"You must have lost your mind as well as your sight, *traitor*," Nerezza said. "You never meant anything to me."

Pietro tensed. "That's a lie!" he shouted. "We were in love once, but maybe all the horrors you've committed over the past sixty years have clouded your memory."

"What I remember is how you betrayed me," Nerezza fired back. "And apparently, nothing has changed. You and your students will face the harshest punishment for fighting alongside Rachana."

Milena traded worried looks with her friends. The likelihood that Pietro was going to talk their way out of this was growing slimmer by the moment, but he pressed on.

"When we were young, you were so optimistic. So full of hope . . ."

Nerezza scowled. "My youth is gone, my optimism left when you walked away, and as for hope? It's nothing but a myth used by the weak to soothe their fragile minds."

"You deceive yourself. You once had hope," Pietro insisted. "Why else would you have taken pity on me all those years ago? You could've killed me, but instead you let me live. There's still a sliver of your heart that's capable of goodness. I know it."

Nerezza cackled with disbelief. "You think I showed you mercy? No, I wanted you to suffer. Art was everything to you; it was your life. I knew that living as a blind painter would be a far worse punishment than death."

Too stunned to form a response, Pietro fell silent.

Milena tensed, listening to Nerezza's callous words. Whatever remorse Nerezza might have had buried within her was nowhere to be found. All Pietro had been able to unearth was the woman's evil core.

"But perhaps you've suffered long enough," Nerezza continued. "You want me to take pity on you? Fine." She raised the Straightedge. Its patterns gleamed. Victoria's gem erupted with a powerful blaze.

"No!" Milena screamed.

Pietro's reaction was swift. He swung his brush, and Tito countered with an orange beam that collided against the violet, the energy pouring out like molten light.

Victoria let out an earsplitting roar and thrust her head forward. Boosted by the Straightedge's force, her ray easily overpowered Tito's beam, driving it back toward his crown. In an instant, Nerezza's attack had devoured Pietro's, turning the world violet.

Milena had to shield her eyes from the brightness, and when the light dimmed, Pietro lay sprawled on the ground. Tito had collapsed next to him, a lifeless mass of feathers. His gem had been dislodged from his crown and now lay dull and fractured in the grass.

Nerezza wound a sacred geometry spiral around the gem and brought it to her. She dropped it into her lap and ran her spindly fingers over its surface. A satisfied smile crept across her face.

"Give that back!" Milena screamed.

Giacomo tried to break free, but Zanobius threw Giacomo onto Victoria's back and climbed on after him.

Nerezza called to her soldiers to retreat, then soared away, but she wasn't done wreaking havoc yet. She cut an arc with the Straightedge, and Milena and the others ran for cover as Victoria's deadly ray focused on the palace itself. It obliterated the dome and most of the top floors. Shards of stone rained down, and melted gold dripped from the remains of the white marble walls. By the time Nerezza had returned to her ship, Victoria's beam had cut down any Rachanan warrior in her path and the earth was torn apart by fissures.

As Nerezza and her Genius flew away, Milena rushed back to her fallen teacher. She dropped to her knees and gently laid Pietro's head in her lap. His form blurred through her tears. Aaminah and Savino gathered next to her.

Aaminah leaned in close to Pietro's face. "He's still breathing . . ." On instinct, she brought her flute to her lips and began to play.

But Tito was beyond saving. With mournful squawks, Gaia and Nero circled the fallen Genius as he broke apart into specks of light that floated away.

"Keep Pietro stable," Milena said, wiping away her tears. Aaminah nodded as Luna wove strands of light around their teacher.

Savino put a hand on Milena's shoulder. "She can't play forever," he said sadly.

"She won't have to," Milena said, her resolve slowly returning. "Not if we save him."

"How?"

Milena gazed up at Nerezza's remaining two ships, which had become dark smudges against the dusky sky. Giacomo was up there with them, along with the Sacred Tools. He could be rescued, the Tools recovered. And along with them, Milena sought another prize. "We need to get Tito's gem back."

REBEL SOLDIER

Giacomo sat on Victoria's back, caught between Nerezza and Zanobius. The wind whipped his face, and dizziness overcame him, but not because he was flying hundreds of feet above the ground.

Pietro is dead . . .

Or at least he would be soon. As they sailed away from the fortress, Giacomo looked back to see Tito break apart into light. The faint whisper of Aaminah's flute traveled up to his ears, but not even her music would be powerful enough to save Pietro now.

If only Giacomo had been more courageous—*more cruel*, he thought—he would have destroyed Zanobius. Then maybe Giacomo would have been able to help save Pietro and his Genius. Maybe Nerezza wouldn't have gotten away with the Sacred Tools. *Maybe I wouldn't be Nerezza's prisoner right now . . .*

Victoria neared one of the winged ships and glided toward its stern. Archers and soldiers with handguns cleared the rearmost deck as Victoria came in for a landing. Giacomo noticed Baldassare's sullen face among the crowd, and he wondered why the man wasn't basking in Nerezza's victory.

Giacomo looked off into the distance as the samraat's fortress disappeared behind the dunes. He was on his own now. Zanobius grabbed Giacomo and jumped off Victoria's back, landing with a *thud*.

"Where's his Genius?" a deep voice demanded. Giacomo turned to find a man in golden armor and an opulent bird-shaped helmet crossing the deck to meet Zanobius. "Did you capture it?"

"It flew away before I could grab it," Zanobius replied.

That was the one bright spot in all the darkness—back beneath the palace, Mico had darted away before Zanobius could get his hands on him. Giacomo had no idea where his Genius had taken off to, but at least Mico was out of harm's way.

"Don't worry, Minister Strozzi," Nerezza said. "It won't be a problem. Soon, Giacomo's Genius will be compelled to return to him."

"Is that what Minister Xiomar told you?" Strozzi asked, looking skeptical.

Who is Xiomar? Giacomo wondered, dread creeping through his bones. *And why is Nerezza so sure that Mico will come back?*

Nerezza snatched the Compass from Zanobius and ordered him to take Giacomo inside. Zanobius ushered Giacomo down a set of stairs that led from the quarterdeck to the main deck. As they passed by Baldassare, Giacomo locked eyes with him.

"I'm sorry it had to come to this," Baldassare said, sounding like a man defeated.

"What happened to Enzio? Is he all right?" Giacomo asked. Baldassare shook his head and looked away.

Before Giacomo could ask any more questions, Zanobius hauled him off.

"What's Nerezza planning to do to me, Zanobius?" Giacomo said.

Zanobius stopped short of a cabin door directly below the quarterdeck. "My orders forbid me to tell you," he said. "But you'll find out soon enough."

"What are you waiting for?" Nerezza snapped as she and Baldassare came up behind them. "I told you to take him inside."

Zanobius pushed on the door, but it didn't open. "It's locked."

Nerezza's face flashed concern. She tried the door herself, then banged on it. "Minister Xiomar! Are you in there?"

No one answered.

Nerezza scowled and turned to Zanobius. "Break it down!"

Zanobius kicked with his two left legs, splintering the wood. He kicked again, and the door fell away. Nerezza marched into the cabin, then halted abruptly, emitting a sharp gasp.

Giacomo quickly took in the space. In the center of the room was a metal table equipped with restraints. At the rear of the cabin, a uniformed soldier stood behind a hunchbacked old man, holding a knife to his throat.

"Stay back!" the soldier shouted desperately.

"Enzio?" Even through the bruises and dark circles under his eyes, there was no mistaking him. Enzio's ragged appearance seemed to explain why Baldassare had looked so upset. Perhaps he cared more for his son than Giacomo had realized.

Nerezza fumed and paced toward Enzio.

"Not another step!" Enzio shouted. "Or Xiomar is a dead man."

Nerezza froze. Giacomo found a pleasant satisfaction in watching her follow someone else's orders for once.

Baldassare cowered in the doorway. "Enzio, don't do this. Please, let Minister Xiomar go."

"Not unless Nerezza releases Giacomo first," Enzio said, then mustered up the strength to give a smile. "Hi, Giacomo."

Aaminah continued to play as Luna's light wafted over Pietro. Normally, Milena would have enjoyed her friend's music, but today it was tinged with death.

Now that the fighting was over, Ozo emerged from the warriors' quarters and carried a frightened-looking Soraya over to her mother. Lavanthi grabbed her daughter and hugged her tightly. Then she leaned in to Ozo with a warm smile. Ozo touched her cheek gently, and they kissed.

At least one good thing came out of this horrible day, Milena thought.

She looked at the smoldering wreckage of the fortress. Part of the outer wall had crumbled, the once-beautiful gardens were in ruins, and many warriors had been wounded, some killed. Those who had survived began to collect the fallen, and the healers took the injured to the warriors' quarters for treatment. Many horse-Geniuses had been wounded as well.

"We're going to need some horse-Geniuses if we want to catch up to Nerezza's ships," Savino said.

Milena nodded. "I was thinking the same thing."

She spotted Kavi in the garden swishing his tail. The Genius's mane was still dripping from when Zanobius had plunged him into the pool. Nearby, two warriors were loading the injured Ajeet onto a stretcher. Milena and Savino rushed over to speak with him.

Ajeet was bloodied, and half his armor had fallen off. He was in no condition to lead a charge against Nerezza, but other warriors could.

"Your Excellency, we need your help," Milena said. "Savino and I need to borrow some of your warriors to get on board Nerezza's ship."

"Look around—we lost this battle." Ajeet winced in pain. "I'm not about to risk any more lives."

"But we have to get Giacomo and the Sacred Tools back," Milena said, growing desperate. "If you really want to protect your empire, you can't let Nerezza keep her hands on the Compass and the Straightedge."

Milena's words seemed to hit a nerve. Weakly, Ajeet waved his daughter over, and they conferred in Rachanan.

"So . . . ?" Milena said, looking to Ozo. "Is it good news or bad news?"

Ozo summed up the conversation. "Lavanthi thinks a few warriors could drop you off on the ship and keep the army distracted while you rescue Giacomo. But getting you off is another story . . ."

A spark of inspiration hit Milena. "Once we recover the Compass—" Milena started.

Savino seemed to have had the idea at the same instant. "We can make a portal back here!" he finished.

Overhearing their suggestion, Ajeet turned to Milena. "I won't order any warriors to go, but if anyone wishes to volunteer, surely the gods would look favorably upon them."

Milena wanted to hug the samraat but thought that might not be appropriate, so she hugged Savino instead.

"All right, all right, don't get too excited," Savino said, pulling away. "We still have to actually go through with this crazy plan."

Lavanthi called to the warriors nearby. They gathered around as she explained the situation. While Milena waited to hear if anyone would be willing to join them, Yaday approached, carrying bellows.

"I'd like to come too," he said.

"No offense," Milena said. "But you're not exactly a fighter."

"I know, but I failed Giacomo back at the caldera. I want to make it up to him. And I can help you deal with the other Tulpa." Yaday held up the bellows. "I think this will subdue him."

Savino grabbed the bellows out of Yaday's hand. "You're not going to overcome Zanobius by blowing a little air in his face, trust me."

"Be careful!" Yaday said, snatching back his device. "There's a very potent sleeping powder inside." Yaday pointed to the bag between the two handles on the bellows. "I use a small amount in my tea for relaxation. But in large amounts, it can calm Padma when she's anxious."

"It'll take an elephant's worth of powder to knock out Zanobius, that's for sure," Savino said, then turned to Milena. "I say we bring him."

"Fine," Milena said, nodding to Yaday. "You're in."

Yaday bowed his head. "Thank you."

Lavanthi mounted her Genius. The four warriors who had accompanied them to the caldera had volunteered to join her. The team was smaller than Milena had hoped, but she was grateful to every one of them.

Milena worried that Ozo might try to join the mission so he could continue his pursuit of Zanobius, but to her surprise, he picked up Soraya and kissed Lavanthi again.

"I'm going to sit this one out and keep an eye on Soraya," Ozo told Milena. "Good luck."

Milena went to Aaminah and told her to keep playing until they returned. Aaminah responded with a nod, then Milena leaned down to Pietro, who was still unresponsive, and kissed his forehead. His skin had taken on a sickly yellowish tint. "Stay with us. We'll be back soon."

Lavanthi pulled Milena up into the saddle behind her while Savino got on with Govind and Yaday joined Azad. With a chorus of neighing and the heaving of wings, the horse-Geniuses galloped into the sky.

Nero and Gaia flew alongside the horse-Geniuses as they ascended higher and higher, gaining speed. Milena prayed to the Creator to watch over Pietro while they were gone. *Please . . . don't take him yet. I'm not ready to let him go.*

She had no idea if her prayer would be answered, but the request gave her comfort.

"Release him immediately, soldier!" Nerezza demanded.

"I'm not your soldier anymore!" Enzio snapped, pressing the tip of the knife against Xiomar's wrinkled neck. "I'm through playing the obedient dog."

Giacomo wasn't sure what Enzio's ultimate plan was, so he began to formulate one of his own. He eyed the Compass slung across Nerezza's back. If he could somehow get free of Zanobius, he might be able to make a portal back to the palace.

Nerezza glared at Xiomar. "You assured me the elixir would keep him under control."

Xiomar strained against the blade at his throat. "With time . . . the effects wear off . . ."

"And you didn't think to administer another dose?" Nerezza screeched. "I should let him cut you open right now."

"Strozzi forbade it . . . Said he wouldn't give it to any soldier under his command . . ."

"My Council is full of incompetents!" Nerezza complained, then turned to Baldassare. "Care to prove me wrong? Do something about your son!"

Baldassare moved slowly toward Enzio, hands in front of him like he was begging for alms. "Listen to the Supreme Creator, son. Walk away from this."

"And turn my back on Giacomo, like you did?" Enzio spat back.

"You're in over your head."

"So now you're trying to save me? Where were you when I was locked up in Nerezza's dungeon being tortured? Where were you when Xiomar was injecting me with poison?"

Hearing what Enzio had endured made Giacomo shudder.

"I tried to get them to stop," Baldassare insisted.

"Or were you secretly hoping I'd turn into the obedient son you always wanted?" Enzio said.

"Of course not!" Giacomo had never heard Baldassare sound so distressed.

"This is going nowhere," Nerezza said, forcing Baldassare aside. She looked at Enzio and with a dismissive wave of her hand said, "Fine, go ahead and kill Minister Xiomar."

"No, I've always been loyal to you!" Xiomar pleaded.

Enzio's hand trembled, his face etched with confusion. "But . . . I thought you needed him to help you take control of Giacomo."

Giacomo's blood ran cold. So that was Nerezza's plan? To control him as she did Zanobius?

"Is that what Xiomar told you?" Nerezza said with a smirk. "He likes to believe he's indispensable, as do all the ministers." She glanced at Baldassare. "But the truth is, I don't need any of them. No one is irreplaceable."

Baldassare stared back icily.

Nerezza turned to Zanobius. "Secure Giacomo, then restrain Enzio."

Giacomo thrashed as Zanobius slammed him on top of the table and locked the wrist and ankle restraints. The metal table felt cold against his back. Unyielding.

Zanobius turned his focus to Enzio, who pressed the knife closer to Xiomar's skin, drawing blood. "Stay back!" he shouted, his voice betraying his panic.

Zanobius closed in. With a grunt, Enzio shoved Xiomar at Zanobius and skirted around the edge of the cabin. Zanobius caught the old man, dropped him to the side, and continued his pursuit.

Backed against the wall, Enzio proceeded to slash wildly with his knife. Zanobius barely registered the cuts appearing on his forearms and hands. Zanobius lunged, and Enzio snaked through the Tulpa's legs. He ran to Giacomo and lodged the knife's blade into one of the shackles, trying to pry it open.

"I'm sorry we left you behind at Niccolo's" was all Giacomo could think to say.

"It's okay," Enzio said. The blade snapped in the lock.

"Behind you!" Giacomo shouted, and Enzio spun around, throwing the broken knife at Zanobius. It pinged off his metal shoulder and clattered across the floor.

Enzio dove under the table and bolted for the door, where Baldassare stood.

"Stop him!" Nerezza ordered. Baldassare didn't move.

Enzio had almost made it out when Zanobius leaped clear across the room and tackled him, pinning him to the floor.

"Finally," Nerezza muttered. "Bring him here."

Zanobius picked Enzio up by his collar and dangled him in front of Nerezza.

"You certainly are a defiant one," Nerezza said, lifting Enzio's chin with a skeletal finger so she could look him in the eyes. "I'd normally send a soldier like you in for reconditioning, but I think I'll cut my losses." She looked at Zanobius and flatly said, "Throw him overboard."

"No!" Giacomo thrashed against his bonds.

"You will not take my son from me!" Baldassare bellowed. Enzio's broken knife reappeared, now in Baldassare's trembling hand.

Giacomo was surprised by Baldassare's disobedience, and Enzio's incredulous expression suggested he was too.

"You wouldn't dare," Nerezza challenged, seeming not the least bit threatened.

Baldassare glared back, teeth gritted and breathing heavily, like he was trying to muster the will to attack her, but in the end Nerezza was right not to worry. Baldassare lowered his arm and the knife clattered to the floor.

"I'm so sorry, Enzio," Baldassare said, his face full of shame.

"I never thought you cared at all for your son, but it appears that you do, a little," Nerezza commented. "Too bad he won't be around for you to make amends."

Having heard the commotion, Minister Strozzi and four soldiers rushed into the cabin. "Are you all right, Your Eminence?" Strozzi asked.

"Yes, everything's under control, no thanks to you." Nerezza looked to the soldiers. "Escort Minister Barrolo belowdecks. And make sure he's by a window. I want him to watch his son fly."

The soldiers led Baldassare away. Zanobius followed, carrying a thrashing Enzio.

Once everyone had left, Xiomar picked himself up off the

floor and staggered to the back of the cabin. He propped his withered frame against a wooden table, upon which rested a strange contraption—a metal stand that held two glass spheres with hollow tubes running into and out of each one.

"Begin the preparations," Nerezza ordered.

"That was a foolish bluff," Xiomar said, lighting flames underneath the two glass orbs. "If the boy had killed me, you'd have had no way of turning Giacomo."

"But the bluff worked," Nerezza said. "Therefore, it wasn't foolish at all."

"Of course, Your Eminence," Xiomar muttered. He leaned over the glass spheres to inspect their contents. From Giacomo's vantage, each appeared to hold a stone. But when the light glimmered off their surfaces, he could see they weren't ordinary stones after all; they were Genius gems.

Giacomo looked again, and the air was sucked out of his lungs. He recognized those gems. They had belonged to his parents' Geniuses.

"Those aren't yours!" he yelled. He wanted badly to throttle Nerezza, but his shackles held him back.

Nerezza approached the metal table and leaned over Giacomo. "Now you and I finally have a chance to talk."

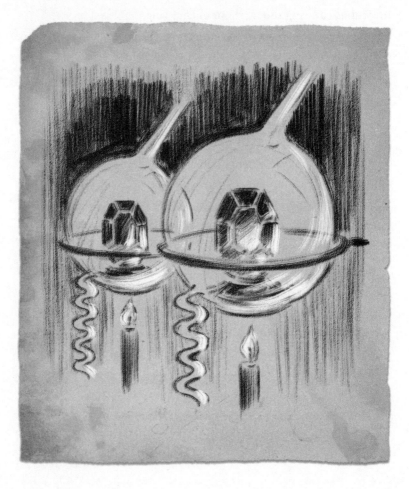

THE GHIBERTI GEMS

Nerezza studied Giacomo's face closely, as if she were scrutinizing the brushstrokes of a painting.

"Your parents did a remarkable job creating you," she said, running her bony finger down his cheek, her pointed black nail scratching into him. "Much more impressive than that monster Ugalino cobbled together. You can grow, adapt, learn . . ." She exhaled, and Giacomo wrinkled his nose. Her breath stank like a musty old room. "It's a shame they wasted their talents fighting against me."

"Go ahead, torture me like you did Enzio. I'll never serve you!" *I resisted Vrama*, Giacomo thought. *I can resist you too.*

Nerezza narrowed her eyes, her gaze boring into him. "Torture won't be necessary. But your rebellious ways will end today." She glanced in Xiomar's direction.

The hunchback uncorked a long tube on his strange contraption and poured in a vial of green fluid. The liquid coiled down to where the tube split, funneled into the glass spheres, and dripped onto his parents' gems, causing sparks to erupt.

Giacomo felt a burning pain between his eyes, as if the greenish solution were dripping on him. To his shock, the gems lit up, filling the glass spheres with a bright pink glow. The light began to snake through two more glass tubes that extended from the bottoms of the spheres. Xiomar seemed to have devised a way to extract whatever energy remained in the gems.

What kind of dark sacred geometry is this? Giacomo wondered.

He didn't want to find out. His mind hunted for a means of escape, searching the room for anything he'd overlooked. Out the window, a streak of orange and blue caught his attention. A moment later, it returned and hovered, peering through the glass.

Mico . . .

Nerezza noticed Giacomo looking at something and turned toward the window just as Mico zipped away.

If his Genius had found him, that meant there was a chance Giacomo's friends weren't far behind. Clinging to his last shred of hope, Giacomo tried to buy himself more time.

"Tell me one thing," he said, hiding his fear behind a veil of defiance. "What did you gain by killing all those Geniuses and turning artists into Lost Souls? Do you really think Zizzola is better off now?"

"Do you have any idea what the empire used to be like?" Nerezza said. But she didn't wait for Giacomo's answer. "Of course you don't; you hadn't been created yet. Under my father's rule, there was no order. People did as they liked. It was chaos. Emperor Callisto even let ordinary citizens into the throne room to seek an audience with him. 'The people should always have a voice,' he taught me. But I learned there was no end to people's complaints or opinions."

Giacomo's eyes followed Nerezza as she paced around the table and continued her diatribe. "By allowing everyone to share their vision of what the empire should be, my father ended up having no vision at all," she said with disdain. "Can you imagine a hundred artists all working on one painting at the same time? It would be bedlam. Any great work of art must be created from a singular vision. The same is true in governing an empire, a fact my father failed to understand."

"From everything I've heard, Emperor Callisto treated the people with respect," Giacomo countered. "He was beloved."

"My father was weak!" Nerezza snapped, raising her voice. "You know what his response was to every single person who came before him seeking aid? 'The Creator provides for all.' He had no real solutions to problems, only a blind faith in some invisible being. And he used it as an excuse to take responsibility off his shoulders."

Nerezza had a point. Though Giacomo had always believed in the Creator, it was clear he didn't provide for all, at least not when it truly mattered. Because if there really was a Creator guiding everything, why had he let Giacomo's parents die? Or Aaminah's mother? How could he have allowed Pietro to go blind or Niccolo to become a Lost Soul or Zizzola's Geniuses to almost die out? So many tragedies had occurred under Nerezza's rule, while she went unpunished.

"He tried to use that hollow line on me once," Nerezza continued, her voice softening. "When I was a girl, after my mother died, he told me not to worry . . . that the Creator would provide for me. When I asked him if the Creator could give me back my mother, he told me to stop being such a foolish child. 'The Creator can't bring people back from the dead,' he declared."

Nerezza gazed out the window, lost in her memories. "That was the day I realized my father was nothing but a cruel liar. That was the day I stopped believing in the Creator's power and started relying on my own."

To his surprise, Giacomo found himself feeling sorry for her—*almost*. "We've all lost people important to us," Giacomo said. "It doesn't excuse all the terrible things you've done."

Nerezza watched the clouds pass by. "To achieve order, sometimes sacrifices have to be made."

"Like assassinating your own father?" Giacomo accused.

Nerezza whirled around, scowling. "Has Pietro been spreading rumors about me?"

"Is it true?"

"My father was an aging emperor, out of touch with what the people truly needed."

"You didn't answer my question."

"He would have died eventually . . ." The corners of her frown edged up, forming a smirk. "I simply sped up the process a little."

Giacomo's breath caught, and he lost all sympathy for her. While he had lost both parents, she had destroyed the one she had had left. Evil had consumed so much of Nerezza's soul, he imagined it must look like a shriveled, blackened lump.

"You don't have any creative vision," Giacomo said. "You just steal other people's ideas and pretend they're your own. You're not a Supreme Creator, you're a fraud."

Giacomo's words had struck a nerve. He could see Nerezza's veins pulsing through her parchment-thin skin, and her lips pursed into a small red oval. "Enough!" She whipped around to Xiomar, who was collecting the glowing fluid dripping from the gems into a vial. "Is it ready?"

"Yes," Xiomar said, swirling the luminous liquid. Giacomo's parents' gems, which had glimmered pink, now looked dull and gray, as if all their remaining energy had been drained.

Xiomar brought the glass cylinder to Giacomo's lips. "Drink."

Giacomo shut his mouth tightly and jerked his head from side to side, trying to knock the vial away, but Xiomar held it steady.

"If you won't drink, I have other methods," Xiomar said ominously, hurrying back to his makeshift laboratory.

When he returned, he held a long, thick needle. Xiomar plunged it into the vial, siphoned up the glowing liquid, and then brought the needle to Giacomo's wrist. Giacomo felt a prick, and his fingers locked into claws. The needle plunged in deep. Faint red lines illuminated Giacomo's veins, and a hot pain shot up his arm.

It felt like Xiomar had injected him with some kind of creature that was now snaking through his body, strangling him from the inside. *Like when Vrama's soul took hold of me*, Giacomo thought as he gasped for air. His heart thudded. Stopped. Thudded again. Then his thoughts were drowned out by his own screaming.

Finally, a jolt of energy shot through him, and he fell silent, along with the rest of the world. The rushing wind from outside disappeared. He could see Nerezza's mouth moving but couldn't hear what she was saying.

A bright light filled the lower half of his vision. Giacomo couldn't find its source until he lifted his head and saw that the front of his tunic had burned away, exposing his skin. His torso blazed with the lines and circles of the Creator's Pattern.

FLIGHT OF THE GENIUSES

Milena and Lavanthi hurtled upward, gaining on the flying ships. From a distance, Milena scanned them, trying to determine where Nerezza might be keeping her friend. Soldiers lined the decks of both vessels, bows drawn and guns steadied on shoulders. But there was a crucial difference between the ships—Victoria was perched on the lead one's stern.

Giacomo must be there, Milena thought.

She tapped Lavanthi on the shoulder and pointed to their target. Lavanthi nodded her understanding and snapped the reins, urging her Genius to speed up. The horse-Geniuses arced toward the ship's starboard side, and the Zizzolan troops concentrated their forces to meet the oncoming threat.

BOOM! BOOM! BOOM!

Puffs of smoke erupted from the handgunners' barrels; archers released their arrows. Milena swiped her brush while Lavanthi swung her katar. In unison, their Geniuses projected square shields—one emerald, one gold—and deflected the projectiles. She and Lavanthi made a better team than she'd anticipated. She wondered how everyone else was faring. Milena glanced behind her to where Savino and the other warriors deftly repelled more attacks.

Without warning, Milena pitched forward, and her stomach dropped. Lavanthi had taken them into a dive underneath Nerezza's ship. Milena flinched as the hull whizzed past, inches from her head. When they climbed back up, Milena saw that the deck's port side was nearly empty—ideal for a clear landing. The other warriors followed Lavanthi's lead.

On the starboard side, soldiers were still busy reloading their guns while the archers peered over the deck, looking for Lavanthi and Milena. A man in golden armor shouted at his troops to wake up and look behind them, directing their attention to where the Rachanan warriors were landing on the deck.

Govind and Azad slowed their Geniuses to a trot to allow Savino and Yaday to dismount, then galloped back into the sky. They circled the ship, firing off streams of light that knocked several soldiers to the deck.

Lavanthi swooped down and Milena poised himself to jump, but then she spotted Zanobius near the front of the ship, pushing a soldier onto a plank. Even from this distance, she could see that the boy in uniform was clearly Enzio.

"Zanobius, don't!" Milena shouted. He looked her way, but her plea didn't seem to register, and he shoved Enzio overboard.

Enzio's screams mixed with the howling winds.

Milena grabbed Lavanthi's shoulder, and when she turned, Milena pointed at Enzio's plummeting figure. "We have to save him!" she shouted, hoping Lavanthi would understand the urgency in her voice if not the words themselves.

Lavanthi pulled the reins, and they steered clear of the ship, diving after Enzio. Milena clasped her arms around Lavanthi's waist, holding on for her life. Enzio's cries for help grew louder as they closed in. Lavanthi's Genius raced past Enzio, then swooped under him, halting abruptly. Milena's head slammed into the back of Lavanthi's armor, and then she heard a heavy *thump* behind her. Enzio grabbed her shoulders, yanking her back.

"Calm down or we're both going to fall!" Milena shouted. "We got you!"

"Th-thanks . . ." Enzio said, trembling.

Milena craned her head back and took in his frightened face, which was a mess of bruises and welts. His skin was sweaty and pale. What must he have gone through? She would have to get the story later.

"Where's Giacomo?" she said.

Enzio looked back up at the ship. "She has him in a cabin. She's trying to take control of him!"

Lavanthi flicked the reins, and her horse-Genius ascended. When they reached the ship, Govind, Azad, Devika, and Kavita were trading volleys with the Zizzolan soldiers, keeping them away from Savino and Yaday.

Lavanthi's horse-Genius landed on the deck, just long enough for Milena and Enzio to dismount. Then Lavanthi returned to the air, joining her warriors in fending off Nerezza's troops. Milena looked around for her own Genius, and right on cue, Gaia swooped onto Milena's shoulder. They hurried over to Savino and Yaday.

"You're alive!" Savino's eyes widened at the sight of Enzio. But they didn't have time to catch up right now.

"Enzio says Giacomo's back there!" Milena told them, pointing to a cabin below the quarterdeck. The door had been broken open, and Milena caught a glimpse of Giacomo restrained on a table, Nerezza looming over him. She found it odd that Victoria held her perch on the deck above the cabin, ignoring the threat of the horse-Geniuses.

Unless Nerezza needs her Genius to take control of Giacomo, Milena realized. "Come on, we have to hurry!"

As they raced toward the back of the ship, two mountainous men—identical in appearance—came at them with their swords drawn. Milena and Savino fired off strands of green and blue from their Geniuses, blasting the soldiers back and disarming them. As the soldiers climbed to their hands and knees, Enzio ran over and kicked each one in the gut, making them groan.

"That's for turning me over to Nerezza!" Enzio shouted, then he grabbed one of their swords and kept running.

Their path looked clear until Zanobius dropped down from one of the masts, blocking them. His hands were formed into four fists—*one for each of us,* Milena thought darkly.

Yaday jumped between Milena and Savino, pointing his bellows at Zanobius. He pumped the handles, expelling a powdery cloud from the nozzle that enveloped his target. The Tulpa coughed, slowing his pace, then staggered. Finally, he dropped to his knees.

"Nice work, Yaday!" Savino shouted.

But then Zanobius rose back up, holding his head like he was dizzy. He shook off the effects of Yaday's sleeping powder and went at him. Yaday frantically pumped the bellows again and to his horror found it empty. Savino fired off a blast from Nero, but Zanobius ducked, and the light sped past him.

Zanobius grabbed Yaday and threw him overboard. Milena rushed to the edge in time to see Yaday hit the ship's huge canvas wing and bounce across its surface. He yelped and flailed, yet somehow had the wherewithal to take hold of one of the wing's wooden struts.

"Hang on!" Milena shouted.

Yaday was splayed out on top of the slowly flapping wing. "I'm trying!"

Milena heard a roar and the hum of energy. She turned from Yaday long enough to glimpse Zanobius tackling Savino to the deck. Trails of blue dissipated into the sky. Savino's Genius screeched and clawed at Zanobius until the Tulpa reached behind and grabbed Nero by the neck, then flung him into some crates. Savino went limp as well.

Milena's legs felt weak, but she pushed away the fear and raised her brush. Above her, Gaia let out a panicked squawk.

"Go help Giacomo!" Enzio called out. "I'll deal with Zanobius!" He swiped his sword, but Zanobius grabbed it out of his hand and bent it in half. "Never mind!"

Milena swiped her brush in long, forceful strokes, and a viridescent wave spread out from Gaia's crown, smacking into Zanobius and sending him sprawling. Enzio scrambled to Milena's side.

"See that guy on the wing?" Milena said. "Yaday's with us. Pull him in while I cover you."

Enzio grabbed a coil of rope and tossed one end over the rail. As soon as Yaday had a grip on the rope, Enzio began to reel him in.

A growl caught Milena's attention, and she turned back to Zanobius, who was on his feet again. But as he came toward her, she noticed he was staggering. He blinked repeatedly and held his head, apparently still fighting off the residual effects of the sleeping powder. Milena lifted her brush straight overhead, then arced it down. Gaia projected a glimmering emerald shield in front of her. As Zanobius lunged at Milena, he came up hard against the field of energy and was repelled. On his next advance, he hammered the shield with his fists. The impacts rippled through the light, but the barrier held. *For now . . .*

A flurry of movement caused Milena to glance toward the back of the ship, where Victoria had splayed her wings and was peering down into the cabin through an opening that had appeared in the quarterdeck.

The giant bird-Genius's gem glowed brightly, searing a spot in Milena's vision. Then Victoria directed a beam into the cabin and drowned Giacomo in light.

UNBOUND

After the initial shock of the poison in his system, Giacomo had regained his senses. From outside came the muffled sound of gun blasts. The humming of sacred geometry attacks. The whinnies of horses. The screeching of a falcon. The noises mixed and were amplified into a sonic rush, filling Giacomo's ears with the clamor of battle.

His friends had come to rescue him.

Now Giacomo became aware of a cranking, mechanical noise, and the roof parted, sending a howling wind through the cabin. He stared through the opening at the passing clouds and found Victoria's bulbous yellow eyes gazing back at him. She unfurled her wings, blocking out most of the waning daylight, then bared her fangs and growled.

Nerezza swiped her brush, and Victoria's gem lit up, forcing Giacomo to look away. Squinting, he gazed beyond the broken door and found a sight that nearly stopped his heart: Zanobius beating his fists against a green shield that Milena and Gaia struggled to maintain; behind her, Enzio leaning over the rail, pulling hard on a rope; and Savino lying sprawled on the deck, knocked unconscious.

"Your friends are too late," Nerezza said. "No one can save you now!" She made a series of sharp strokes with her brush, and the violet light in the cabin intensified. When the glow finally died down, Giacomo saw an octahedron hovering over him.

"Bound to me through the Creator's Pattern and the energy of the five Universal Solids . . ." As Nerezza chanted, she lowered the octahedron's shimmering point closer to Giacomo's chest. "You are a Tulpa. My creation. Mine to order. Mine to control!"

She drove the Solid into Giacomo like a sword. Agony seared through him.

One after another, Nerezza brought each of the Universal Solids to light and plunged them into Giacomo, their bladed edges carving through every muscle, every bone.

When the tetrahedron disappeared into Giacomo's flesh, it was like a thousand of Xiomar's needles being driven into him at once. The pain eventually became so intense he turned numb to it. And as the final Solid—the cube—shimmered over him, Giacomo's eyes rolled into the back of his head.

His mind began to drift far, far away . . .

When Giacomo came to, the ship, Victoria, and Nerezza had all vanished, replaced by the vast cosmos. He floated in place, stars in every direction. Bands of light formed a barrier around him, and it took him a moment to recognize the shape of his luminous cage—an octahedron.

Giacomo tried to punch through the Solid, but its shimmering face sent a shock through his fist and up his arm. He kicked at one translucent triangular wall, but the energy shoved back.

Sensing someone else's presence, Giacomo turned to find an enormous, glimmering cube suspended across from him. Within it was a tetrahedron, and inside that was a dodecahedron, followed by an icosahedron, the shapes all nested inside one another;

at its center hovered Zanobius, limbs slack, eyes closed, like he was floating unconscious in a tank of water.

Outside the walls of Giacomo's octahedron, shimmering triangles appeared, taking the form of the icosahedron. He frantically tried to figure out a way to break free before he was encased in his own sacred geometry fortress, compelled to obey Nerezza's every command.

I'm not strong enough to escape on my own, he thought.

You're not alone, a woman answered, her voice soft and serene.

We're here for you, a man's deep, calm voice followed.

He might not have been strong enough to escape Nerezza's mind-prison by himself, but Giacomo's parents were with him.

He closed his eyes, focusing on the sounds of his parents' voices, and all his training with Yaday came back to him.

His breathing calmed . . .

His heartbeat slowed . . .

His muscles relaxed . . .

A sense of peace swelled through him . . .

And his fear floated away like clouds in a cool autumn wind.

When Giacomo opened his eyes, the Solid rippled, and an image of his old home gleamed on its surface. His mother sat in a chair, smiling down at a baby she rocked in her arms. His father leaned over her and stroked the baby's head with his finger.

You're not alone, his mother reassured him.

We're here for you, his father said.

And you have all the strength you need inside you, his mother said. *We created you in the spirit of love and hope.*

And to withstand any challenge, his father said resolutely. *Resistance flows through your blood, my son.*

Giacomo couldn't believe what he was seeing. He had glimpsed his parents before in dreams, but nothing like this. He seemed to be witnessing a memory, but it couldn't be his own. He had only been a baby.

It must be their gems, Giacomo realized.

The energy from Amera's and Orsino's gems was coursing through Giacomo. It had made him vulnerable to Nerezza's will, but maybe it also was allowing him to reconnect with his parents' past. He thought of all he could learn about how they had created him, and why. He longed to see more, to know more. But if he didn't break free now, he wouldn't get another chance.

He let the memory go, and the image on the Solid's surface faded.

Giacomo thrust his fist forward again, and this time, the octahedron shattered into shards of light. It had worked!

As the final pieces of the icosahedron locked into place, Giacomo launched himself through the air and smashed those too. Letting his momentum carry him, Giacomo hurtled toward the next Solid that was forming—the dodecahedron. Giacomo drew his knees to his chest and kicked, driving his feet through the barrier in a flash of light. He sailed across space as a large tetrahedron crystallized around him. Giacomo readied his next strike, then glimpsed Zanobius's prison, its tetrahedron flickering and beginning to vanish.

Giacomo rammed both fists into the face of his tetrahedron, disintegrating it. He was almost free. Looking back, he noticed that Zanobius's tetrahedron had glimmered back to life.

What's going on? Giacomo thought.

Enormous squares appeared around him. Giacomo was like a seed encased within a massive, cube-shaped hull.

At the same time, the cube containing Zanobius faded.

That was when it hit Giacomo—their prisons were interlinked. What affected one affected the other, which meant . . .

Nerezza can't control both me and Zanobius at the same time.

Zanobius rammed his shoulder into the luminous green barrier Milena had created, and a section gave way. He read the terror on Milena's face as she swiped her brush again, trying to repair her shield. But before Gaia could cast her light over the area, Zanobius shoved his arm through the opening and wrapped his fist around Milena's hand, snapping her brush. Gaia squawked frantically as her gem dimmed, and the defense vanished.

He moved in, shoving Milena against the rail.

"Zanobius, stop!" she pleaded.

A loop of rope cinched around Zanobius's neck. Enzio and Yaday pulled on the other end, yanking him away from Milena. Zanobius grabbed the tether behind him, and all it took was one hard tug to propel the two off their feet. As their faces hit the deck, he placed a foot on each of their backs and pinned them down. He wrapped a hand around Milena's throat, applying pressure until her eyes bulged and her face began to turn blue.

On the outside, Zanobius had once again become a monster. But inside, his heart was breaking. He wished he'd never left the Blemmyes and their peaceful forest to seek revenge against Nerezza. What good had it accomplished? His quest for vengeance had only turned him back into a violent slave. If Zanobius could have hurled himself overboard, he would have, but Nerezza's commands forbade such an act of self-destruction.

Enzio and Yaday wriggled underfoot like dying fish. Milena grasped his wrist, trying to wrench it free as the life dimmed from her eyes. Gaia dropped onto the deck, her wings flapping desperately.

Concentrating with all his will, Zanobius made one final attempt to break free from Nerezza.

As the realization swelled within him, Giacomo wavered between relief and dread. He had been so focused on his own escape, he had forgotten about his friends, who were still at Zanobius's mercy. Even if Giacomo broke free of Nerezza's mental prison, back in the real world he remained bound to a table. At least here, he had the power to help his friends and save Zanobius. But it meant he couldn't save himself.

Giacomo righted himself, slowing his approach toward the final Solid.

His thoughts turned to those who had sacrificed themselves when he had been in danger: Niccolo, Enzio, Aaminah . . . He hoped that by offering himself up to Nerezza, it would give others a chance for freedom.

He spun around and kicked, propelling himself back toward the center of the cube.

The tetrahedron reappeared, followed by the dodecahedron. As each Universal Solid materialized inside his own prison, the corresponding shapes holding Zanobius vanished.

By the time Giacomo returned to where he had started, the icosahedron had returned, and finally the octahedron. His prison was complete.

He looked out at Zanobius, no longer bound by the Universal Solids. The pattern on his fellow Tulpa's chest flared up, and then his form vanished.

Giacomo's senses became dull, his vision hazy. He tried to clear his thoughts, but his mind became engulfed by a thick fog and began slipping away. He felt tired . . .

Yet unafraid.

To Zanobius's surprise, the Creator's Pattern was illuminated, blazing from his chest.

His mind was torn in two, like an ax had come down in the center of his head. He'd felt this kind of splitting pain before, when Ugalino had died. Zanobius wasn't sure what he had done to siphon away Nerezza's power, but it seemed to have worked.

Zanobius dropped Milena and stepped off the boys. He staggered away as the bronze melted off his torso. Sensing its bond weakening, Zanobius bashed his metal arm against the mast. Sure enough, the metal tore away and landed on the deck with a *thud*. Zanobius picked up the severed appendage and hurled it off the ship.

The throbbing in his head was finally beginning to subside. He turned back to find Milena on her knees, gasping for breath.

"Zanobius . . . ?" She met him with a worried stare.

"Nerezza's out of my head," Zanobius said, overcome with relief.

"How did you break free?" she asked.

"I'm not sure." But Zanobius began to suspect there had been more at work than mere willpower.

Enzio and Yaday picked themselves up and helped Milena to her feet. Still wary, they kept their distance.

"If you're not being controlled by Nerezza anymore, then help us save Giacomo and get the Sacred Tools back," Enzio said.

"Gladly." Zanobius was eager to put things right.

Milena went to Savino, who had regained consciousness and

was struggling to stand. "So he's on our side again?" Savino asked skeptically.

"Looks that way," Milena said.

Enzio picked up a bow and arrow that were lying on the deck, and the five of them bolted to the back of the ship, where Victoria was still looming over Giacomo, her gem pulsing dimly. The Genius saw them coming but made no move to stop them from entering.

They raced into the cabin, and Zanobius absorbed the situation. Nerezza stood against the far wall, the Straightedge in one arm, her brush in the other, the Compass slung across her back. An unconscious Giacomo lay on the table while Xiomar unlocked the restraints.

Zanobius read the confusion in Nerezza's face as she took in his bronze-free appearance. "Don't come any closer!" she shouted.

Defiant, Zanobius marched toward her.

"Stop!" Nerezza ordered.

"Your commands won't work on me anymore," Zanobius replied.

Nerezza glanced angrily at Xiomar. "Why didn't you warn me I would lose control of Zanobius?"

"I didn't know that would happen," Xiomar said. "I swear!"

Nerezza scowled at Zanobius. "No matter. You've been replaced." She looked at Giacomo. "Wake up, Giacomo."

His eyes opened.

"Rise."

Giacomo sat upright, then swung his legs off the table and got to his feet.

No, Zanobius thought. *It's not possible* . . .

Mico darted through the opening in the roof and hovered by Giacomo's shoulder. Xiomar handed Giacomo a pencil, then backed out of the cabin.

"Now, help me get rid of these intruders," Nerezza ordered.

To Zanobius's horror, Giacomo pointed his pencil at Milena and the other children.

"Yes, Your Eminence."

ELEGY

Giacomo regarded Milena with a hollow stare, as if she were a stranger.

"What happened, Giacomo?" she asked, even though she could guess—Nerezza had somehow taken control of him, but in the process lost her hold over Zanobius.

Giacomo lashed out with his pencil, and Mico fired off a beam. On instinct, Milena raised her arm, but her brush lay in pieces on the deck. Thankfully, Savino had her back. A glimmering blue square appeared in front of her, and the red light exploded against it.

"Giacomo, stop!" Milena screamed. "Pietro's going to die unless we get Tito's gem back to him."

But her plea did nothing to sway Giacomo. His expression remained hardened and fierce.

"It's no use trying to get through to him," Zanobius said. "Believe me."

What was she supposed to do? Leave Giacomo behind? What

kind of friend did that? But Zanobius was right—Giacomo was incapable of listening to reason. And without knowing how Nerezza had gained control over him, there was no saving him. At least not yet.

On a table at the back of the room, Milena spotted Pietro's gem. "Zanobius, get the Sacred Tools from Nerezza," she said, keeping her voice low. She turned to Savino. "Cover me."

Milena bolted for Pietro's gem, and the cabin erupted in a chaos of colors. Violet, blue, and red lights clashed as the Geniuses' gems fired off their beams. Everyone scattered. Victoria poked her long neck into the room, and Nerezza climbed on, Giacomo right behind her. Enzio fired an arrow that *thunk*ed into the giant bird's neck. Nerezza, feeling the connection, screamed in pain, and Victoria snapped at Enzio, who reeled back.

With Victoria distracted, Zanobius leaped after the injured Nerezza, grabbing the Compass strapped to her back. Giacomo hit him with a ray and he went flying, smashing into the wall. Yet Zanobius had managed to keep hold of the Compass.

Milena reached Tito's gem and scooped it up in her hands. She noticed two other, smaller gems held in a strange contraption. Suspecting they had something to do with Giacomo's transformation, she smashed the glass and pocketed them.

A screech startled her, and she spun around to see Victoria lifting off, soaring away with Nerezza, the Straightedge, and Giacomo on her back.

Soldiers rushed the cabin and unleashed a torrent of bullets and arrows. Wood splintered and glass shattered. Zanobius dodged the blasts and sheltered Yaday and Enzio as they made their way over to Milena. Savino followed, raising up a latticed shield that bisected the cabin, but it soon buckled under the pressure of so many bullets.

"Let's get out of here!" he hollered.

"Trade you, Zanobius," Milena said, exchanging Tito's gem for the Compass. She unsheathed the Sacred Tool and spun open a portal. Yaday dove into the swelling light, followed by Enzio and Zanobius.

"I'm right behind you!" Savino shouted, urging Milena on.

She let the light consume her.

Milena spilled out the other side, in front of the palace. Aaminah's music filled the air, and Luna had Pietro wrapped in a sacred geometry cocoon.

Milena readied the Compass, waiting for Savino to come through so she could close the portal. She counted the seconds, and when she got to five, she began to panic. Then an arrow shot out of the light, followed by bullets.

Come on, Savino, come on . . .

She refused to move until Savino appeared.

Finally, the portal jettisoned him, and Milena quickly shut it. She heard a groan behind her and turned to find Savino lying on the ground, clutching an arrow embedded in his shoulder. She dropped next to him, but before she could ask if he was all right, Savino waved her off.

"Help Pietro. I can wait."

She took Tito's gem from Zanobius and raced to Pietro's side. With a nod, she gave Aaminah permission to stop playing. The cocoon of light broke apart and faded.

Milena laid the gem on Pietro's chest. Unsure of what else to do, she prayed.

ʃ the minutes passed, Pietro's skin regained its color. He took

ʌeep breath, grimaced, and began to sit up.

Milena helped him the rest of the way. "Master Pietro, you're—"

"Still alive, apparently," Pietro grumbled, as if he was annoyed by the fact.

"You're here," Milena said, feeling a tear run down her cheek. "You're with us."

"Milena saved you," Savino said proudly.

Milena smiled up at him, then looked over at Aaminah. "I certainly didn't do it alone."

Pietro took Tito's gem in his hands and ran his fingers over its surface. "He's really gone, isn't he?"

"I'm so sorry," Milena said.

"What about the rest of you? Is everyone else all right?"

Soon, she would have to tell him what had happened to Giacomo, but right now, she didn't have the strength for it. All she could do was give her teacher a hug.

"You're with us," she repeated. "That's all that matters."

Their reunion was interrupted by Enzio's call for help. Two warriors had apprehended Enzio and were dragging him away. Milena realized they must have seen his Zizzolan uniform and assumed he had been left behind. Six more Rachanans had Zanobius surrounded, their katars leveled at him.

"Stop!" Milena rushed over and pleaded with the warriors to stand down. "Enzio's our friend. He saved Yaday's life. And Zanobius isn't being controlled by Nerezza anymore!" Her words weren't understood, but after Yaday had translated them for the warriors, they backed away from Zanobius. The two holding Enzio released him.

Milena helped Pietro back to his quarters to rest, then headed to the palace upon learning that Lavanthi and the warriors had returned. When she got there, Lavanthi was busy speaking to Yaday. He explained to Milena that the warriors had tried to save Giacomo, but with the advantage of the Straightedge, Nerezza had easily overpowered the horse-Geniuses and driven them off.

"Lavanthi says she's very sorry for what happened to your friend," Yaday said.

Milena could see the regret on the woman's face as their gazes met. "Tell her thank you for trying," Milena replied.

Later, Milena sat with Savino as Yaday carefully extracted the arrow from Savino's shoulder. While Aaminah played a healing melody, the guru packed the wound with a pungent poultice, then set Savino's arm in a sling. When Milena asked if it hurt, Savino claimed it wasn't that bad, but his grimacing and groaning told a different story. Once Aaminah and Yaday had left, Milena gripped Savino's hand tightly.

"You don't always have to act so tough, you know. I'm here for you."

"I told you, I'm fine," Savino muttered, pulling his hand back.

Milena hadn't meant to show the hurt on her face, but after everything that had happened, her emotional defenses had been shattered.

"I . . . That's not . . . That came out wrong . . ." Savino stammered, reaching for her hand again.

Milena let him take it. "Why don't you try again?" she said, a grin escaping.

"I didn't think we were going to make it off Nerezza's ship," Savino said. "But one thing kept me going: the thought of you."

Milena's heart jumped, and she pulled him close. With his free arm, Savino returned the embrace. Usually, he was the first to break away. This time, he didn't let go.

By the time dawn broke the next morning, Milena still hadn't slept. Every time she laid her head down, the sounds of battle echoed in her mind. She couldn't stop picturing Tito breaking apart into light; Zanobius's hand around her throat; Giacomo's hollow gaze.

Restless, she got up, filled the tub with water, and tried to scrub away the grime and horrors of the previous day's events. She lay back and dunked her head, letting the water surround her.

She came up for air and pulled herself from the tub. As she toweled herself dry, she glanced over at her new dark purple dress, inlaid with shiny beads. She pulled it from the back of the door where it hung and wrapped the fabric around her, tying it off at the waist. She recalled what Yaday had told her when he delivered the dress last night: *It's traditional for women to wear purple at Rachanan funerals.*

Outside, Milena found Pietro sitting alone in the gazebo, looking deep in thought. The effects of becoming a Lost Soul had already become evident. His cheeks were sunken, like he'd lost weight, and his skin was sallow.

In his right hand, he gripped a new wooden staff tipped with a bronze owl-Genius. Tito's gem sat atop the handle.

"Your staff is beautiful," Milena said, taking a seat next to her teacher.

"The gem is too big to carry around my neck, so Ajeet had his artisans craft this for me," Pietro said. "Since I need to keep a part of Tito with me to survive, at least I can do it in style, right?"

Pietro's attempt to lighten Milena's mood didn't help and they remained in silence for a while, until he finally asked her about Giacomo. "I think it's time you tell me everything that happened."

Through tears, Milena related the story of Giacomo's horrible fate.

The funeral procession began at the steps of the palace.

Samraat Ajeet, bandaged and bruised and clad in ceremonial orange robes, mounted Kavi and led the procession out through the main gate. As they neared a wide river, Milena noticed a platform in the water, the bodies of the fallen warriors lying on it side by side.

In his journals, Garrulous had described attending a Rachanan funeral during his travels.

> *Unlike Zizzola's custom, the Rachanans do not bury those they have lost. To them, death is simply another phase in our cosmic journey, and as such, it is treated as a celebration. By honoring those who have passed in this manner, they believe the soul is released from its ties to this world and free to journey to the next realm.*

And it ensures they won't become Pretas, Milena thought.

Once everyone had gathered on the shore, Ajeet offered a prayer while Yaday rang a bell and wafted incense into the air. The wisps of colored smoke eddied over the bodies.

When the crowd lowered their heads and closed their eyes, Milena clasped Aaminah's and Savino's hands in hers and offered her own blessing for the departed.

At the end of the ceremony, warriors carried torches down to the river. Milena looked away as a blaze engulfed the bodies.

The crowd thinned as people made their way back to the fortress. Since the dining hall had been destroyed in Nerezza's attack on the palace, a feast honoring the lives of the fallen would be held outdoors.

Milena was about to leave when she noticed Ozo at the shore with Lavanthi and her daughter. He held a large yellow flower with two short lit candles nestled inside. Ozo lifted the flower high, like an offering, then placed it in the water. As he watched it float down the river, he pulled Lavanthi and Soraya close.

Milena held her teacher by one arm, and Zanobius took the other. Together they helped Pietro up to the main path. He moved more slowly now, his breathing labored.

"Zanobius!" Ozo called out. Milena turned to see the mercenary marching up the slope, his hand resting on the hilt of his sword.

Zanobius stepped back, turning to Milena with a worried look. "I think I should meet you back at your quarters." He started to go.

"Wait," Ozo said.

Milena stepped in front of Ozo. "Leave him be. I don't want to see any more fighting."

"Me either." Ozo's expression looked sincere, the scowl he usually wore in Zanobius's presence nowhere to be seen. Milena glanced at Zanobius.

"It's all right," he said, waving her aside.

The mercenary stepped up to Zanobius. "My life changed that

day you and Ugalino showed up at my farm. After I wiped the blood from my eyes and saw that my wife and daughter were gone, I told myself the only reason I was still alive was so I could hunt you down and destroy you. I've never been afraid to die, as long as I took you with me.

"But seeking revenge turned my soul dark. I had become like one of those Pretas—walking this earth consumed by suffering, a shell of my former self."

Ozo looked over at Lavanthi. "Then I ended up here, and I met someone who helped me understand I had the power to live again, to have a family again." He turned back to Zanobius. "But I realized that to do that, I have to let you go."

The mercenary released the hilt of his sword, and he and the Tulpa shook hands.

"I know it probably won't mean much, but I am sorry," Zanobius said. "And I'll never forget the horror I brought to you and your family."

Ozo regarded him with a hard stare, offered a nod, and headed up the path to the palace, Lavanthi and Soraya at his side.

The Rachanans dined for hours under ceremonial canopies. When she was a little girl, Milena had attended her grandmother's funeral, and she remembered it as a somber affair, full of black clothes and sorrowful expressions. Here, the departed were honored with vibrant hues, flavorful foods, and joyous laughter. She was grateful for the glimpse of brightness during a very dark time.

The previous day's events had been so relentless that Milena hadn't had much time to eat anything. Now, she felt famished, so she devoured several helpings of food, until her stomach couldn't handle any more.

Once the feast was over, Pietro asked Milena and the group to sit with him a little while longer. "There's something I want to tell you all," he said.

Milena saw the troubled look on his face and braced herself for the worst.

"I've decided to leave," Pietro said. "I'm going to the Sacred Lands."

"What?" The news was even more terrible than she had imagined.

"Now that Tito's gone, I need to face reality. I'm a Lost Soul. Who knows how much time I have left?"

"And you want to spend it trekking across the desert?" Milena said. "How are you even going to get there?"

Pietro told her that two horse-Geniuses had perished in the battle and that their warriors would be leaving for the Sacred Lands at sundown. They had offered to take Pietro with them.

"No, you can't go," Milena insisted. "I won't let you."

"I've made my decision, Milena. You have so much life ahead of you, so much more to accomplish." Pietro tilted his head toward the rest of the group. "You all do."

"But what about the mission?" Savino asked. "What about Giacomo?"

"I'd only be holding you back," Pietro said.

"I can't believe you're doing this," Milena snapped. Pietro called after her, but she was already walking away.

She stormed off into the blackened remains of the gardens to think. All this time, Milena had feared Pietro's dying, and now that he had survived, he was still leaving her. It didn't make any sense. Didn't he want to be around people who loved and cared for him?

Milena was still puzzling over Pietro's decision when the sky faded to orange and the sound of drumming could be heard off in the distance. She made her way down the path. With their fellow warriors standing to either side of the gate, two men gave over their armor and weapons, carrying only packs of supplies and their Geniuses' gems on chains around their necks. Pietro stood between them, leaning on his staff, its gem sparkling.

Samraat Ajeet spoke first to his warriors, then to Pietro. "May the gods look upon you for the rest of your days."

Pietro leaned in and whispered something to the samraat, but Milena was too far away to hear. Then he turned and began to walk away. Aaminah, Enzio, and Zanobius watched from nearby.

Savino came over to Milena and gently touched her arm. "We all said our goodbyes already. You'll regret it if you don't too."

Milena gave a resigned nod and hurried to the gate. "Master Pietro, wait!"

He stopped and shifted his body slightly toward her. "You came . . ." he said, a delighted smile lifting his beard.

She ran to him, wrapping her arms around him. "This is only goodbye for now."

Pietro hugged her back. "Then, goodbye for now, my lovely Milena."

Milena stayed at the gate until Pietro and the warriors had disappeared over the dunes and the last light faded, sparking the heavens. A guard shouted from the wall above, and the gates groaned and began to close.

Milena felt a hand on her shoulder, and without looking, she knew it was Savino. He pulled her close, and she buried her head in his chest. With a heavy *thud*, the gates shut. Pietro was gone.

"I think it's probably time I leave too." Zanobius pointed to the Compass, which was slung across Savino's back. "You can send me back to Niccolo's villa. I can find my way from there."

"Your way to where?" Aaminah asked.

"The Sfumato Forest," Zanobius told her.

"Isn't that place supposed to be full of monsters?" Enzio said.

"It's more peaceful than you think," Zanobius replied. "And I won't be able to hurt anyone there."

"You can't leave again," Enzio implored. "Not after everything that just happened."

"Exactly," Aaminah said. "We're going to need your help to save Giacomo." She looked pleadingly at Milena. "Don't make him go like last time."

Milena met Zanobius's worried gaze, and all she could think about was how unwavering Giacomo's belief in Zanobius had been. He had understood the Tulpa's true heart, which was noble and brave and loyal. And after seeing Giacomo being controlled by Nerezza, Milena found herself more sympathetic to Zanobius's situation than she'd ever been.

She glanced over at Savino, who appeared unconvinced. "Aaminah's right. He belongs with us," Milena said.

Savino gave the idea some thought, and finally his doubtful expression softened. "All right, Zanobius, but I'm not sculpting another arm for you."

The Tulpa rubbed his stump. "I wasn't going to ask. I'm happy to leave well enough alone."

Milena offered Zanobius a warm smile. "Now it's your choice. Will you stay?"

Zanobius looked across each of their faces, and when his eyes met hers, Milena sensed a newfound tranquility radiating from him.

"There's nothing I'd like more," Zanobius said.

Acknowledgments

I had always heard authors caution that writing your second book is much harder than the first. *Warrior Genius* gave me firsthand proof that those warnings were true. I appreciate everyone who helped me find my way through the murky writing process.

To my editor, Connie Hsu, thanks for being extremely patient as I muddled through this book and for guiding its development with your insightful comments and suggestions.

Jill Yeomans provided additional editing and helped me get *Warrior Genius* across the finish line. Thanks, Jill! Also thanks to my copy editor, Tracy Koontz.

Thanks to the wonderful people at Roaring Brook and Macmillan: Jon Yaged, Simon Boughton, Morgan Dubin, Ashley Woodfolk, Nancy Elgin, and designer Andrew Arnold. It has been a pleasure working with all of you on this series.

To Nicolas Delort, who illustrated another gorgeous book cover.

Kurt Mattila and Bryan Konietzko read a draft of the novel and gave me invaluable ideas on how to improve it, along with some much-needed moral support. Thanks, fellas!

And I appreciate all the booksellers, librarians, and readers who have championed *Rebel Genius* and this series.

Also thanks to Leon Gladstone, Rich Green, and Ernest Johns.

As always, lots of love and gratitude to my wife, Shoshana, for her steadfast support, especially during the dark days when it didn't seem like I would ever finish.

During the writing of *Warrior Genius*, my wife and I also welcomed our amazing twins into this world. Hawk and Opal, you are my little geniuses who inspire me every day. I love you both!

And lastly, thank you for reading! If you want to learn more about the inspiration and writing process behind *Warrior Genius*, please visit **michaeldantedimartino.com**. There, you can also sign up for my mailing list so you'll be the first to know about all my upcoming projects, including the final book in the Rebel Geniuses series!